· T A L E S   F R O M ·

ISAAC
ASIMOV's
SCIENCE FICTION MAGAZINE

·TALES FROM·

ISAAC
ASIMOV's
SCIENCE·FICTION·MAGAZINE

Short Stories for Young Adults

Selected by Sheila Williams and Cynthia Manson

With an introduction by Isaac Asimov

Harcourt Brace Jovanovich, Publishers

Library of Congress Cataloging-in-Publication Data
Tales from Isaac Asimov's science fiction magazine.
Summary: A collection of seventeen science fiction
stories by authors including Frederik Pohl, Isaac
Asimov, Pamela Sargent, and Octavia E. Butler.
1. Science fiction, American. [1. Science fiction.
2. Short stories] I. Williams, Sheila. II. Manson,
Cynthia. III. Isaac Asimov's science fiction magazine.
PZ5.T24   1986   [Fic]   86–7591
ISBN 0–15–284209–8

DESIGNED BY FRANCESCA M. SMITH
PRINTED IN THE UNITED STATES OF AMERICA
FIRST EDITION
A B C D E

TABLE

OF

CONTENTS

INTRODUCTION

U ntil 1926, science fiction stories appeared occasionally and unpredictably in various magazines or in book form. Usually they were intended for adult readers, though young adults might well enjoy them.

But then, in 1926, the first magazine intended exclusively for science fiction appeared. At that time, pulp magazines filled the magazine racks. These were low-priced magazines, printed on cheap paper, filled with action stories of all kinds. The writers for these magazines were paid very little and, in order to make some kind of living, they had to write quickly.

The result was a certain lack of subtlety, which young readers didn't mind.

The early science fiction magazines paid even less than the other pulp magazines, and the writing was perhaps the more primitive because of that. It is not surprising then that it was among the youngsters that magazine science fiction was particularly popular in those old days.

I first picked up a science fiction magazine in 1929, when I was nine years old, and fell in love with it. So did a number of other young people, and through the 1930s, teenagers were the mainstay of the field. They wrote endless letters to the magazines (many of which were printed), founded fan clubs, and produced amateur fan magazines. Many developed a lifelong obsession with the field, and a number of them became science fiction writers.

The thing is, though, that as the years passed, those readers grew older. To be sure, new youngsters joined, but the average age rose steadily.

And as it did, the demand rose for better writing and more subtle plots. More and more writers flocked into the field, and the competition raised the level of style and content of the stories. (I sold my first science fiction story when I was eighteen and I hate to think of the kind of luck I would have had if my eighteen-year-old self, with the kind of talent I had then, were to try to break into the field today.)

As a result, in my own magazine, *Isaac Asimov's Science Fiction Magazine,* we have many stories of high literary value, taking up subjects of considerable complexity in a fashion that is not always easy for inexperienced readers to follow.

Does this mean that young adults are going to have difficulty finding science fiction suitable for them? Will they have to turn to the movies and television, where the level of science fiction is, in many cases, about that of the magazines of the 1930s?

Not at all.

Young adults who have intelligence and reading experience will indeed welcome the increased maturity of science fiction. If it is not *quite* as easy to follow such stories as it would be to read early science fiction, if the characters and situations are not as simplistically good guy and bad guy, if the endings are not as inevitably and-they-all-lived-happily-ever-after—there is the reward of penetrating and understanding something that is more complex and interesting. (Remember, crossword puzzles that are too easy are no fun at all.)

So we have chosen a handful of stories from *Isaac Asimov's Science Fiction Magazine* that, in our opinion, will be particularly interesting to young adults, and here they are.

Good reading!

Isaac Asimov
May 1986

· TALES FROM ·

ISAAC
ASIMOV's
SCIENCE FICTION MAGAZINE

THE

AMBER

FROG

Stephanie A. Smith

Alinia is shunned by her mother's family, but she has a special talent—and a special friend.

A t the edge of the farewell party, the twelve somber teach- ers of Court Elizabeth stood together in a cluster. They spoke among themselves and watched the children of their hosts begin a game of steelring. As more children joined in, the game grew fierce and loud with shouting. The humid wind tossed a few thin birch leaves across the lawn and made the tablecloths flap, as the gaggle of youngsters threw their steel- rings overhead. The metal flashed in the low light and the rings spun, whistled, and linked in midair.

One of the teachers laughed gently and then all twelve moved away from the gaming and off toward a table of sliced fruits. They did not notice the girl who had abandoned her cousins' game to follow after them. Unseen, she had been edging closer to the twelve courtsingers all afternoon. They fascinated her because they were muni, just as her mother had once been. Dressed in their stiff, unadorned black jackets and blue, pleated trousers, they appeared to the girl's eyes both serene and severe; just as she remembered her mother to have been. She wanted to talk to them and ask if she could go with them when they returned to court.

It's a risk, she thought, *but I will try asking.* She sidled past the muni and walked up to the table behind her aunt Shulane, who was busy arranging the fruit. Quietly, unnoticed by her aunt, she took a plate and filled it with peeled orange sections.

One of the muni asked Shulane a question, which the girl could not hear, and her aunt responded, "Oh, truly, yes, a shame to us." She poured a bowl of water for the muni who had spoken. "A shame. We were displeased with my sister, very much so, yes. After all, she was a Giden and a teacher. If we had known, when she left Court Eleanor carrying child, that the father was sokke, we would have done something long before that child came to being."

The girl froze, her gaze locked on her plate of fruit. Juice dripped over her fingers. She wondered whether to leave before more was said, but did not. Her face flushed. She ate a section of orange as calmly as she could and then slowly forced herself to look up. Her aunt still had not seen her, but one of the severe teachers did; staring levelly over Shulane's shoulder at the girl, the teacher said, "Your sister did bear her child?"

"Yes, yes, a girl."

"And where is the child living now—here?"

"No, of course not. She lives in the sokke quarter, where she belongs, with a friend of her father's. He died not long after he took the child on, you see. She is learning his trade, as she should." Shulane paused, adjusted the neckline of her shirt, and glanced over at the gaming children. "My daughter invited her tonight, but I don't see Alinia at the moment. . . . I thought she was playing steelring, but . . ."

"You did not present your niece at court?" asked the muni.

"Court?" Shulane plucked an apple from a basket and laughed. "A sokke at court?"

Alinia hastily put down her plate. She wiped her hands on the tablecloth.

The courtsinger said, "If this child's mother was teaching at Eleanor, then she might be entitled to a presentation. Did you not send her to Eleanor at all?"

Shulane stepped back and bit her apple twice before she answered. Staring at the exposed core, she said. "As far as the Gidens are concerned, my sister had no child. Lilasi chose to disgrace herself by taking a sokke as a lover, yes. But after her death, the family decided that she would not be allowed to continue to disgrace us."

"How is that?" asked another teacher. He tilted his head and folded his arms across his narrow chest, drumming his fingers against his sides. "There is no shame in being sokke."

"But the Gidens are muni," said Shulane. "We have always been. Sokke have their place—in their quarter and in their work. Not in ours. My sister was foolish. She could have been a fine teacher, yes. But she chose folly instead."

"Perhaps," murmured the first teacher. She took a step forward, and glanced past Shulane to smile warmly at the girl.

Shulane turned around.

For a moment, in a silence broken only by the steelring clash and jingle, aunt and niece stared at each other. Alinia tried to speak, to say something, anything, to say, "why?" She had to speak, had to, could not. The silence and her pallor spoke for her.

Shulane's face paled also. Then she blushed, put out her hand to her niece, and said, "Alinia, I—"

Alinia fled. She ran past the tables, knocking a platter to the ground, spraying juice. She ran away from the party, from the smiles changed to fish-mouth surprise at her flight, away from her aunt, calling, away from the steelring and her cousins and into the cool birch grove.

Leaves crunched under her feet as she darted past slender trunks, across a slight, bald ravine, and toward a pond. She ran until she reached the muddy bank of the pond and there, out of breath, she sat down on a buried stone, wrapped her arms around her legs, and listened for the sound of pursuit.

But no one came after her. The steelrings began to whine again and after a few minutes, she leaned back and wriggled her hand into her hip pocket. It took some tugging, but she finally pulled out a tiny, amber frog. She set the frog on the shelf of a stone that rose above the steaming pond water.

As the sun began to sink, day dusking, Alinia watched the frog as it watched the nightflies dance. Except to blink its black-flecked, golden eyes, the frog did not move.

Alinia wiped away tears and stretched herself out flat on the damp earth, rested chin on hands, and whispered, "Loren was right. They don't care about me."

The frog blinked. A thin leaf drifted down from the trees to land in the hot pool, floated, clung to the stone. The air was still. Easy laughter traveled across the grove and brought tears back to the girl's dark eyes. She listened instead to the night-flies' hum and promised herself that she would leave the party in a minute. As soon as she felt able, she would get up, march back, tell Shulane she was leaving, not cry and go. *Loren was right, after all,* she thought. *I was foolish to come here. I am not a child anymore and this is not my home.*

The frog hopped closer to Alinia. She picked it up, closed her hand over it gently, and hummed a riff of chords. The music lifted and fell. She sat up, hitched the cuff of her trousers to her knee, and dangled one leg in the hot-spring's water. She sang.

The song ended on a high, full note.

She opened her clenched hand.

Now, instead of a live, blinking frog, she held an amber ring, shaped as a frog, a hard, glittering jewel carved into a ring. Turning it over, she made the gem hold the fading sunlight. It glowed.

"I am a live-amber cutter," she said aloud. "I am sokke." She scratched her shoulder. "And I am muni, too. I don't care if I am not supposed to be both. I am." She slipped the ring onto a middle finger and then swung her long hair forward to let it drift and ripple on the surface like the tawny grasses that grew along the banks of the nearby stream. She brushed a sliver of the grass off the frog's back and caught her fingernail on the pin-sized rough spot near the frog's head, where her polishing brush had not reached. Rubbing the spot, she bit her lip, remembering how her teacher, Sheld Loren, had found the flaw instantly. Loren had glanced up at her apprentice. "Alinia, this piece caused you trouble."

"Is it such a noticeable flaw?"

"No, no." Loren rolled the amber around on her palm. "But whoever asked you to make this gave you too small a nugget for the detail you have done." She leaned back into three cushions piled against the wall of her study. "Which of your relatives commissioned this totem?"

"It isn't too small, really," said Alinia. "The jouberry amber is alive. I mean, even though the ring is tiny, the frog is alive. It moves."

"Does it?" Loren nodded. Her curly gray and blond hair fell forward. To Alinia, she seemed a formidable person, all angles in face and form. She was highly respected in the sokke quarter for her skill as master gem-cutter. All six courts—Rebecca,

Elizabeth, Eleanor, Victoria, Francine, and Marcia—had, at one time or another, commissioned amber totems from her workshop. Alinia feared Loren's censure and longed for her approval. She edged closer to her master to peer at the frog that sat quietly, ring-bound, in Loren's brown, lined palm. She knew it was a good piece. Perhaps even great.

The woman set the frog down on the lacquered table, where it remained motionless among the inlaid lilies, bathed in a pool of morning light. She sat forward, smoothed out a fold of her gray work shirt, and said, "I ask you again, child. Which of your relations commissioned this ring? The frog is the Giden family totem. Which of them wanted it made? Shulane? Or her daughter, Tulian? Tell me."

Alinia glanced at a vase of cattails, using her thick hair as a veil. "Was that man at Court Victoria pleased with the eagle I made for him?"

Loren did not answer and so Alinia kept her gaze upon the vase. A fly buzzed and landed in the cattail fluff.

Loren said, "Of course. I am a good teacher; you are a good student. You made no error. I expected none."

Alinia whispered, "Thank you."

"The truth is the truth." Loren tapped her finger on the table beside the frog. "Who moves this totem, Alinia?"

"I do."

"Y—you?" Loren caught her breath. "I—show me."

Her heart pounding, the girl knelt and then laid her hand upon the table. Her palms itched. The lacquer felt cool. She leaned over and sang a riff of chords. The strange music fell and lifted.

The frog uncoiled. It squatted on a green inlaid stem, then hopped into Alinia's palm, leaving a beaded trail of water.

Loren's eyes looked a darker shade than their usual gentle brown. The corners of her mouth tightened. She said, "How? You're sokke. You can't . . ."

"Before my mother died," said Alinia, as she let the gold frog crawl over her hands, "she taught me a few of the amber songs. Not all. But as I was making that eagle for Victoria, I wondered whether or not I knew enough songs to move a totem. So, I carved this frog for myself and tried singing and it moves, as you see. Mother told me that I was muni. She wanted me to serve Court Eleanor, as she had."

Loren moistened her lips. "All these years and all the beautiful totems I have made, never knowing how the amber song of the muni made them live. . . ." She blinked. "Teach me. Please."

Alinia tried. During that summer, all summer, she tried to teach her master amber song—how to pitch the voice, how to make the riffs rise and fall. Yet nothing came of it. For Loren, the little frog would not move.

One evening, as master and apprentice walked together in the quarter's central gardens, Loren at last admitted that she would never learn amber song. But, she said, she was not saddened much. She was, after all, "An artisan. A sokke. For me, in many ways, the making and the carving is still enough. But you—you have the skills of both maker and singer, sokke and muni. I don't know of any artisan who has also had the gift of singing."

"No one?"

Loren shook her head. A huge yellow moon's light touched her shoulders. She said, "This is theft, child, you know that? For you to own the ring . . . because jouberry live amber belongs to the muni. I know you must have saved a shard from that eagle you did for Court Victoria, and if you should be caught—"

"I am muni." Alinia stepped up beside the garden's drinking pool. "I am entitled to serve court and to learn the rule of the totem game. To have a jouberry totem. By my mother's name, I am . . ."

"No." Loren leaned against the stone pool's chipped rim. The perfume of summer wax lilies touched the humid air. Nightflies, just hatched from their chrysalides, hovered in a tiny, whining storm near the flowers. Loren broke off one of the lilies and turned the limp, white bell in her hand. "Your mother was a Giden and a muni, but she is gone, child. Her sisters decided against giving you a home or a name. Understand—you are not a Giden anymore." She touched Alinia's cheek and brushed back the girl's thick hair. "I'm sorry. But your father was a gem-cutter and since your aunts gave you his name, you must be a gem-cutter, too. That is custom; it is law. You can't change it."

"I will. I will have my name back."

The master stepped away from the pool and said firmly, "You are a sokke, Alinia. And from this moment onward, you are no longer an apprentice. I am freeing you, because this ring you have made shows great skill. I think you ought to be proud of this talent that you can nurture, instead of wishing after a name you can never have. Your father would have been proud. Learn to be proud of him."

Was she proud of him? Sitting at the edge of the hot spring, remembering her father's knotted hands and creaky laughter, Alinia touched the water's warm surface. She murmured, "Yes, I am proud of him. I am. But I won't forget what mother taught me."

The metallic crash of linking steel interrupted her thoughts. She glanced back toward the party and saw the flash of flung rings, the darting, bright players, and she frowned. Once she, too, had played the rings. Every day, with her cousins, in the years before her mother died. She listened to the jingling with clenched hands. Sokke did not learn games. They had no time for games.

If only, she thought, *Mother had not been so ill. She could have taught me more songs—presented me to court herself.*

Alinia stared off beyond the forest of ghost trees, remembering her mother, yet barely remembering . . . a scent of lily oil and a soaring soprano voice, a young, ailing woman who had made Alinia practice amber song over and over, though the child's range could not reach the higher tones, nor follow the more complex rhythms.

Linking steel jingled loudly nearby. Alinia stood.

"Catch!" Tulian Giden's voice was piercing, high, and unmistakable. Alinia winced. The frog on her finger squirmed. Surprised, she rubbed the ring and sang a few notes to quiet it. Then she looked in the direction of her cousin's shout. She did not wish to be found yet, especially not by Shulane's daughter.

"Come on, Gerrar. I've got a steelring!" cried Tulian. "You'll not finish the game without me."

Alinia hastily stuffed the frog back into her pocket. Then she waited, expecting her two cousins to appear.

But no one came. A bird rustled in a tree's dying leaves, and a squirrel soared deftly by. After a few moments, the cold jingle of the steelring game resumed. Alinia sat back down, shook out the wet tips of her hair, and turned over onto her stomach. Resting her elbows in the moss at the pond's lip, she watched the golden fish in the hot water. She changed focus and watched her reflection waver.

Two faces.

Two faces, alike and young, wavering on the water's surface: her own and Tulian's, both washed green by the pondweed at the bottom of the pool. Alinia tried to sit up, but before she could move, her cousin straddled her.

"Tulian—"

The taller girl responded by sitting down in the small of her cousin's back. She leaned over and said, "What?"

The young gem-cutter tried to speak, but the press of the added weight made her gasp instead. She whispered, "You're heavy." She found herself gazing at the evergreen cuff of Tulian's trouser leg. The fabric was a brocade, embossed with tiny, leaping frogs.

"Speak louder," said Tulian. She shifted her body a little. "I can't hear you."

"You're heavy."

"Oh? Do you think I should not sit on your back?"

"Please . . ."

"Well."

"Please, please, I can't breathe—and you're going to tear my shirt if you stay there."

"Petulance, petulance! I'll move when I am ready to move." After another minute, Tulian rolled away. "I was only teasing."

Alinia sat. Once again the clink-clink of the steelrings stopped to leave only the hum of the nightflies and a scattering of laughter in the wind. Tulian looked up. Her face was sharp and flushed in stippled patches, her eyes light and blue and her hair as long as Alinia's, but thicker, darker, and rich with red highlights. She stood.

The two girls heard their cousin Gerrar say, "Well? Where is she? Where did she go with that ring?" He sounded as if he were nearby. Alinia cupped her hands to shout back to him, when Tulian caught her elbow.

"Shh . . ." she said. "I'm going to hide. Don't tell." She ran away.

Alinia nodded reluctantly and dipped her bare feet back into the pool. She brushed off her shirt. The front pocket was moss-stained. She stared at the green smudges and remembered how long it had taken her to sew the shirt. The stains would not go away. She wanted to throttle Tulian. She swallowed, trying to swallow back the knot of anger in her throat.

Someone walked through the fallen leaves behind her and a twig cracked. She disciplined the uneasy frown that bowed her lips and said, "Hello, Gerrar."

"Alinia!" He sat down next to her, juggling a steelring from hand to hand. He was a large-boned boy and not yet grown past clumsiness.

She pulled her hair around her face in two thick falls, played with the wet ends, and waited for him to speak. She did not wish to lie to him, but . . . she glanced toward the forest where the taller girl had run.

He said, "Have you seen Tulian?"

"I thought . . . I thought she was playing with you and the others." In Alinia's pocket, the frog squirmed again. She put her hand over it, hoping that Gerrar had not seen the movement. *Why is it wriggling?* she wondered. *I sang a sleeping song. It should not move at all.*

He said, "Tulian was playing with us, but she ran off with one of the rings. We can't finish without it." He sighed. "Spoiled. She is a spoiled child."

Alinia laughed nervously and glanced over her shoulder. "But, Gerrar, you talk as if you were an old man. She's not a child, no more than you or me. She's been selected to attend Court Elizabeth and—"

"Oh, yes, I know." His smile faded. "She shouldn't be serving at any court."

"What?"

"She wasn't chosen, not really. Her parents have arranged it. Everyone knows." He shrugged. "I'm glad I won't be serving Elizabeth. I've been studying at Eleanor. Did you know? I was selected there." He tossed the ring. It whistled, spun, landed. He picked it up.

"You have? But no one told—"

"I wanted it that way. I didn't want a party." He nodded toward the house beyond the grove. "One's enough."

"But . . . it's wonderful. You should have celebrated!"

"Going to court on my own talent is celebration enough." He looked up at the clouding sky, silver-threaded, and then

across the pond at the fenced pasture. "During the last totem
game, Tulian was refused by all the courts. Her parents spoke
to teacher after teacher until, finally, those at Elizabeth agreed
to take her. Even so, she isn't happy about it, despite the
party."

"Why?"

"Because the rules at Elizabeth are the strictest of all. The
muni there, they know, you can't hide who you are or who you
think you are from them."

Alinia whispered, "But who does Tulian think she is, if not
Tulian? I don't understand."

"Better. She thinks she's better than anyone else." He put
his hand lightly on Alinia's knee. "I'm glad you could come
today."

"Tulian invited me." She pulled her leg away from his touch.

"Yes, I know she did, but she . . . I . . . she's selfish. She
invited you because she heard that you were a gem-cutter. She
wants a totem from you."

Alinia fingered the quieted ring through the loose fabric of
her pocket. "I will cut her one, if she wants—"

"No!" He gripped her kneecap and she jerked away from
him. "You don't understand, Alinia. The teachers at Elizabeth
have forbidden her a totem until and if she passes her third
term. She's furious, so she thought she'd get you to do it
without telling you it was forbidden. Anyway, I wanted to warn
you. Because totems sung to life by an untrained muni are
dangerous."

"What do you mean?" said Alinia sharply.

He glanced around. "I'm not supposed—"

"Please."

He sighed. "A totem is bound to its singer when it is first
sung to life. My totem will not move for any singer besides
myself because it was my soul that was sung into it first. And
yet, the totems remain creatures, wild creatures. And after a

while, if they are not properly controlled, they can develop a will of their own." He laughed softly. "Now, if I could not control my frog, it couldn't go off and hurt someone or fetch me something that I wanted, being that it's only a frog. But suppose Giden totem were a bear, like the Moven family's? Do you see what I mean? A totem, or so I've been told, slowly develops the ability to sense what the singer loves—or hates. Muni must learn strict control of their song. The court teaches us that control. And I think that Tulian doesn't have the discipline to learn. Perhaps a frog could not harm anyone, should she lose it—and then again, perhaps it could." He shook his head. Then he leaned close to Alinia and said in a rush, "I want you to know that I don't agree with my mother and Aunt Shulane. They think you are sokke—"

Surprised, Alinia backed away from him a bit and said, "I am." As she waited for her cousin's reaction, she thought about the ring in her pocket. Had she lost control? Was that why it was moving? She tensed and then relaxed. A frog couldn't hurt anything. . . .

Gerrar said slowly, "Are you? Are you sokke?"

"Yes."

He nodded. "So be it. I once thought your mother was training you to be muni, but . . ." He shrugged. "I still want you to know that when I have my own household, you will be welcome to live in it, as a Giden. If you choose."

Her throat tightened so much that she had to cough before she could say, "Thank you, Gerrar."

"I've missed you, cousin. Most of us have—except Tulian. She's spoiled, spiteful, just like her mother—"

"Oh, come. After all, she did invite me." Alinia gave him a slight push. "I won't believe what you say about her. She's strong and bright. Did you never think the courts might fear her? There is nothing wrong in wanting—"

He put his hand on her shoulder and shook his head. "Some

of us don't shove others aside to get what we want. I know you're fond of her, Alinia, but—be careful. She'll hurt you." He pushed himself to his feet and flipped the steelring from one hand to another, staring at the bright flash. "Are you sure she didn't come out here?"

"I'm sure. Maybe she went into the house?"

"I saw her come out this way."

"She could have run back. Did you look in the house? She might be hiding there."

"No, I didn't look. If you see her, tell her to return the ring. We want to finish." He gave her shoulder another squeeze and then walked off toward the house.

Soon after he was gone, Tulian returned, pulling leaves out of her hair. "What did he say? I was too far away to hear."

Alinia frowned. "Well, I—I think you ought to return the ring."

Tulian giggled. "I lied. I don't have one. I never took it. Besides, Gerrar doesn't play fairly."

"But he does! I've played with him."

"That was a long time ago."

Alinia glanced down at the water. The fish had all fled. "Not so long."

"Long enough. We aren't children anymore." The dark cousin sat down on a stone. "When you left the game earlier, you said you'd only be gone a few minutes—then you go running off! What are you doing out here? This is my day. I want to have you with me. And don't think I didn't have to fight my mother for your invitation."

Alinia stared at her cousin. Did Tulian know how Shulane felt, or not? Did she know what her mother had said about doing "something long before that child came to being"? With her heart thumping, Alinia asked, "Why did you invite me today?"

"You are my cousin and I've missed you. Besides, Mama

can't tell me who is mine and who is not. Why did you leave the party?"

"I—I had to do something."

"What could you possibly have to do out here? Wait, don't say anything, let me guess. You were watching the fish? Hmm. I'm surprised I didn't find Gerrar out here, watching the fish with you. He's been talking about you all day."

Alinia nodded and said, "Yes."

Tulian leaned over and playfully flicked some water into Alinia's face. "So, what should you and I do with the rest of the day? Any ideas? Maybe we should ask Gerrar?"

"No—"

"Well, then, why don't we visit the sokke quarter? I've never been there. You could introduce me to this teacher you've praised so much today. What's her name? I might decide to commission my totem from her."

Alinia glanced over at her cousin. Had Gerrar been right about her?

Tulian smiled. "Well? Do you want to take a walk and show me where you live?"

"No. I mean, your party is here. Everyone came to see you, to congratulate you. We shouldn't leave."

"True. Besides, the houses in the sokke quarter are all so small—that's what Mama has said, anyway. How can you stand it?"

Alinia peered through the grove at her first home, her childhood home. Tulian's house, now. It was large and long, with an airy facade and white walls. The building was shaped like a crescent moon and the whole was surrounded by garden. She said guardedly, "Do I have a choice? Did your mother give me a name? I stand it because I have to."

"Oh, but how could Mama give you a name, Alinia? Being sokke, where did you expect to live? You must follow your father, as I follow my parents. I don't see—"

"My mother served Court Eleanor."

Tulian stood and walked away from the water, curling her toes in the dead leaves. "Court is for muni. You are not—"

"What? What am I not? How do you know? I've never been presented, never tried, and I am still the same Alinia you promised to go to court with. Remember how we said we would go together? This party should be mine, too. I did not change when my mother died."

"But . . . you did," murmured Tulian. "When your mother died, your father came here for you and he was . . ." Her voice became low and sibilant. "Sokke."

Quietly Alinia said, "I am me." And saying this, she felt her heart stop jumping and choking off her breath. She closed her eyes, thinking, *I am me. I am me.* She whispered, "Never mind. It doesn't matter."

"I think," said Tulian coldly, "that I will go finish the steel-ring game—give Gerrar his last match. He will have found out by now that I didn't take the ring." She took a step and then she made an odd pounce. Alinia flinched away. Tulian jumped again into the mossy earth by the pond, turned around, and pointed, saying, "What's that—there, look, what is it?"

The golden frog had crawled or fallen out of Alinia's pocket and was hopping in the lacy green, heading for the water. She snatched it up.

"Show me," said Tulian. She grabbed her cousin's shoulder. "What is it?"

Alinia whipped her hands behind her back. Her cheeks burned and her palms sweated—she did not want Tulian to see the totem.

"Show me! Now."

The frog wriggled, attempting to nudge and slither its way between Alinia's fingers. She thought, *What can I do?* and decided to try to make a game out of the whole thing. She held out two fists. "Which hand?"

Tulian laughed. She grabbed her cousin's wrist and forced her fingers to uncurl.

The frog sat quiet, rigid, smooth: a ring.

Alinia started. Had she been imagining that it moved?

"A ring!" cried Tulian. "No, wait . . . a ring made to look like a frog. Clever, very. The back flippers bend around in a ring to touch the front feet. It's beautiful." She reached to pick it up, hesitated, and then closed her hand midair. She looked at the frog closely. "Is it . . . live amber?"

"No—"

"Don't lie. I saw it move."

"It . . . Do you like it?"

Tulian's eyes widened. "Who wouldn't? It's very fine. Is it Gerrar's?"

"No."

"Whose is it?"

Alinia pulled her cousin's hand level with her own. "Watch." And then, though she knew she should not, she could not resist singing.

The frog uncoiled itself, blinking round, amber-gold eyes. It trilled and hopped wetly over to Tulian's hand. It curled tightly on her forefinger.

"No." Tulian twisted the frog around and around, trying to get it off. "How can you?"

"I'm sokke, a gem-cutter, I made—"

"You sang! You can't—"

Alinia ran her fingertips across the edge of her cousin's brocaded jacket. "I can. Mother taught me."

Tulian tugged at the ring. She spoke through clenched teeth. "You are not a Giden. Not muni."

"I don't care."

"Sokke—" Tulian's hand jerked and the ring sprang away, dropping into the pool. Both cousins watched it sink amid the ripples.

Tulian shaded her eyes. "Can you see where it landed? The pond's not deep."

"I'll go in after it."

"You won't find it. The pondweed is too thick."

"I'll find it. It comes to me, when I sing."

"Under water?"

Alinia shrugged. She did not know whether it would come to her under water, but she would not lose it. She took off her shirt and pants without a word. She waded into the pool. The sandy bottom ran downward and vanished. Her chest muscles contracted and her breath came short, but she pushed on toward the center of the pond, floating.

"Oh," said Tulian. "I didn't know the water was that deep." She leaned out from the bank. "You look like a fish. Can you see it yet?"

"No." Alinia's hair trailed gold behind her as she drifted. She scanned the water. The heat made her drowsy and too slow. She took a deep breath and dove.

On her second dive, she found the frog. It was jammed between two rocks. Fine silt puffed up from the bottom as she worked to free it. The tiny frog suddenly wriggled, its fat forearms and long hind legs helpless, its small body pinched tight by the rocks. Alinia pulled her hand away and thought, *How can it move like that, without my song?* Gingerly, she touched it again and managed, at last, to roll aside one rock.

The frog shot away, swimming toward the air.

Out of breath herself, she followed. Breaking the surface, she trod water and tilted her head back, gasping. Her hair, like a wide, yellow lily pad, floated out all around her. Part of it covered her eyes like a net of gold wire. "Tulian?" she said as she tried to claw the wet hair away from her face. "Tulian? Come help me. The water's hot, too hot."

Her cousin stood still on the bank. She folded her arms. "Did you find the ring?"

"Yes—it's probably at your feet somewhere. Help me out and I'll get it."

Tulian looked down at the moss. "I can't. I can't swim."

"Please—" Alinia tried to float toward the bank. She peered through the mess of her hair at her cousin. "Please."

"It isn't far. Come on."

"Tulian!"

"I can't."

Alinia slipped and went under. When she came up, she saw an empty bank. Spitting water, she called, "Tulian?"

No one answered.

Alinia's heart pounded slower, slower. She let herself drift and sink again. When she opened her eyes, sputtering another mouthful of tepid water, she saw the frog directly before her. She reached for it and it swam off. She reached for it again. Little by little, it drew her toward the pond's edge. Sand scraped her feet and knees. With a smothered cry, she crawled naked into the moss and stayed there, steam rising from her reddened skin.

Soon she felt well enough to sit. Dragging her clothes to her, she looked for the frog.

It had saved her life. It was gone.

Dressed, she searched the moss and grasses. "Where are you?" She sang to it, calling to it over and over, but it did not come. Exhausted from the heat and her ebbing fright, frustrated, she stood and walked toward the house. She was hurt and shaken. The frog was lost.

There must be so much more, she thought, *that I need to learn. So many more songs. Gerrar said discipline.* She shook her head. *I'll find Tulian, tell her I am all right. Then I will look for the frog again and I will not leave here until it comes to me. Perhaps . . . perhaps I should ask the muni of Court Elizabeth for help?* The idea made her nod. She would ask that teacher who had smiled at her earlier. She would tell the muni about the totem and say that her mother had taught her some amber song. She knew that the frog might be taken away from her, but she knew she had to learn more about it.

The forest and pond were quiet in Alinia's wake. A yellow leaf and then another drifted down from a birch and landed in the green water.

Startled by footsteps, a bird shot out from a bush. It scolded and flew away. Tulian appeared. She knelt in the wet moss and ran her fingers over the soft, short fronds. She peered between the tawny grass hillocks and crept to the water's edge.

A tiny splash at her elbow made her look up.

"There you are," she said. She leaned over the water. "There you are, little amber." She stretched her hand out toward the ring. It regarded her with its huge, bright eyes and floated, turning in an eddy.

"You're mine," she said. "You belong to a Giden. Alinia made you, but I'll see to it she never does so again. Sokke." She smiled. "And I will have you, my totem, despite what those teachers say." Pulling up her trouser legs, she waded in the water to her hips until she was close to the frog.

It sprang away.

She lurched forward after it and staggered headlong into the deepest part of the pond. Floundering, she beat at the water as if the pool had grown dark, unseen hands that clutched her.

Without a sound and swiftly, she sank. Her clothes billowed. She struggled to get her jacket off, but its weight and her entangling hair made it difficult. Impossible.

Moments passed. As a third yellow leaf floated down from the trees, Tulian's hands rose over her head gently. One hand uncurled, drifting open as if to caress the pondweed.

The amber frog slipped off the girl's finger and rested for a second on her bruised knuckle. Then it swam against the current. The girl's body floated toward the stream, and the frog landed on the bank. Yellow translucence and amber bright eyes, it sat hidden in the mossy thatch, blinking and watching the nightflies dance, as the distant steelring game ended.

At last it leaped into the darkness of the birch grove, making a slow but stubborn path toward the sound of Alinia's worried voice.

STEPHANIE A. SMITH was born in Long Island, New York, and grew up in Westchester County. She attended Boston University, where she was elected to Phi Beta Kappa, and is at present working on her Ph.D. in English in Berkeley, California. Her first novel, Snow-Eyes, *was published by Atheneum in 1985, and she is currently writing the sequel,* Smoke Bamboo.

THE
ANATOMY
LESSON

Scott Sanders

A confident medical student assembles a very unusual skeleton that tests his knowledge and may change his future.

By the time I reached the anatomy library all the bones had been checked out. Students bent over the wooden boxes everywhere, in hallways and snack bar, assembling feet and arms, scribbling diagrams in notebooks. Half the chairs were occupied by slouching skeletons, and reclining skeletons littered the tables like driftwood. Since I also would be examined on the subject the next day, I asked the librarian to search one last time for bone boxes in the storeroom.

"But I tell you, they've all been given out," she said, glaring at me from beneath an enormous snarl of dark hair, like a fierce animal caught in a bush. How many students had already pestered her for bones this evening?

I persisted. "Haven't you got any damaged skeletons? Irregulars?"

Ignoring my smile, she measured me with her fierce stare, as if estimating the size of box my bones would fill after she had made supper of me. A shadow drooped beneath each of her eyes, permanent sorrow, like the tear mark of a clown. "Irregulars," she repeated, turning away from the counter.

I blinked with relief at her departing back. Only as she slipped noiselessly into the storeroom did I notice her gloved hands. *Fastidious,* I thought. *Doesn't want to soil herself with bone dust and mildew.*

While awaiting my specimens, I studied the vertebrae that knobbed through the bent necks of students all around me, each one laboring over fragments of skeletons. Five lumbar vertebrae, seven cervical, a round dozen thoracic: I rehearsed the names, my confidence building.

Presently the librarian returned with a box. It was the size of an orange crate, wooden, dingy from age or dry rot. The metal clasps that held it shut were tarnished a sickly green. No wonder she wore the gloves.

"This one's for restricted use," she announced, shoving it over the counter.

I hesitated, my hands poised above the crate as if I were testing it for heat.

"Well, do you want it, or don't you?" she said.

Afraid she would return it to the archives, I pounced on it with one hand and with the other signed a borrower's card. "Old model?" I inquired pleasantly. She did not smile.

I turned away with the box in my arms. The burden seemed lighter than its bulk would have promised, as if the wood had dried with age. Perhaps instead of bones inside there would be pyramids of dust. The metal clasps felt cold against my fingers.

After some searching I found a clear space on the floor beside a scrawny man whose elbows and knees protruded through rents in his clothing like so many lumps of a sea serpent above the waters. When I tugged at the clasps they yielded reluctantly. The hinges opened with a gritty shriek, raising for a moment all round me a dozen glazed eyes, which soon returned to their studies.

Inside I found the usual wooden trays for bones, light as birdwings; but instead of the customary lining of vinyl they were covered with a metal the color of copper and the puttyish consistency of lead. Each bone fitted into its pocket of metal. Without consulting notes, I started confidently on the foot, joining tarsal to metatarsal. But it was soon evident that there were too many bones. Each one seemed a bit odd in shape, with an extra flange where none should be, or a socket at right angles to the orthodox position. The only way of accommodating all the bones was to assemble them into a seven-toed monstrosity, slightly larger than the foot of an adult male, phalanges all of the same length, with ankle-bones bearing the unmistakable nodes for—what? Wings? Flippers?

This drove me back to my anatomy text. But no consulting of diagrams would make sense of this foot. A practiced scrape of my knife blade assured me these were real bones. But from what freakish creature? Feeling vaguely guilty, as if in my ignorance I had given birth to this monstrosity, I looked around the library to see if anyone had noticed. Everywhere living skulls bent studiously over dead ones, ignoring me. Only the librarian seemed to be watching me sidelong, through her tangled hair. I hastily scattered the foot bones to their various compartments.

Next I worked at the hand, which boasted six rather than five digits. Two of them were clearly thumbs, opposite in their orientation, and each of the remaining fingers was double-jointed, so that both sides of these vanished hands would have served as palms. At the wrist a socket opened in one direction, a ball joint protruded in the other, as if the hand were meant to snap onto an adjoining one. I now bent secretively over my outrageous skeleton, unwilling to meet stares from other students.

After tinkering with fibula and clavicle, each bone recognizable but slightly awry from the human, I gingerly unpacked the plates of the skull. I had been fearing these bones most of all. Their scattered state was unsettling enough to begin with, since in ordinary skeletal kits they would have been assembled into a braincase. Their gathered state was even more unsettling. They would only go together in one arrangement, yet it appeared so outrageous to me that I forced myself to reassemble the skull three times. There was only one jaw, to be sure, though an exceedingly broad one, and only two holes for ears. But the skull itself was clearly double, as if two heads had been squeezed together, like cherries grown double on one stem. Each hemisphere of the brain enjoyed its own cranium. The opening for the nose was in its accustomed place, as were two of the eyes. But in the center of the vast forehead, like the drain in an empty expanse of bathtub, was the socket for a third eye.

I closed the anatomy text, helpless before this freak. Hunched over to shield it from the gaze of other students, I stared long at that triangle of eyes, and at the twinned craniums that splayed out behind like a fusion of moons. No, I decided, such a creature was not possible. It was a hoax, a malicious joke designed to shatter my understanding of anatomy. But I would not fall for the trick. Angrily I disassembled this counterfeit skeleton, stuffed the bones back into their metal pockets, clasped the box shut, and returned it to the counter.

"This may seem funny to you," I said, "but I have an examination to pass."

"Funny?" the librarian replied.

"This hoax." I slapped the box, raising a puff of dust. When she only lifted an eyebrow mockingly, I insisted, "It's a fabrication, an impossibility."

"Is it?" she taunted, laying her gloved hands atop the crate.

Furious, I said, "It's not even a very good hoax. No one who knows the smallest scrap of anatomy would fall for it."

"Really?" she said, peeling the glove away from one wrist. I wanted to shout at her and then hurry away, before she could uncover that hand. Yet I was mesmerized by the slide of cloth, the pinkish skin emerging. "I found it hard to believe myself, at first," she said, spreading the naked hand before me, palm up. I was relieved to count only five digits. But the fleshy heel was inflamed and swollen, as if the bud of a new thumb was sprouting there.

A scar, I thought feverishly. *Nothing awful.*

Then she turned the hand over and displayed for me another palm. The fingers curled upward, then curled in the reverse direction, forming a cage of fingers on the counter.

I flinched away. Skeletons were shattering in my mind, names of bones were fluttering away like blown leaves. All my carefully gathered knowledge was scattering. Unable to look at her, unwilling to glimpse the socket of flesh that might be opening on her forehead beneath the dangling hair, I kept my gaze turned aside.

"How many of you are there?" I hissed.

"I'm the first, so far as I know. Unless you count our friend here," she added, rapping her knuckles against the bone box.

I guessed the distances to inhabited planets, conjured up the silhouettes of space craft. "But where do you come from?"

"Boise."

"Boise, *Idaho?*"

"Well, actually, I grew up on a beet farm just outside Boise."

"You mean you're—" I pointed one index finger at her and shoved the other against my chest.

"Human? Of course!" She laughed, a quick sound like the release of bubbles underwater. Students at nearby tables gazed up momentarily from their skeletons with bleary eyes. The librarian lowered her voice, until it burbled like whale song. "I'm as human as you are," she murmured.

"But your hands? Your face?"

"Until a few months ago they were just run-of-the-mill human hands." She drew the glove quickly on and touched her swollen cheeks. "My face was skinny. My shoes used to fit."

"Then what happened?"

"I assembled these bones." Again she rapped on the crate. From inside came a hollow clattering, like the sound of gravel sliding.

"You're . . . becoming . . . one of them?"

"So it appears."

Her upturned lips and downturned eyes gave me contradictory messages. The clown-sad eyes seemed too far apart. Even buried under its shrubbery of dark hair, her forehead seemed impossibly broad.

"Aren't you frightened?" I said.

"Not anymore," she answered. "Not since my head began to open."

I winced, recalling the vast skull, pale as porcelain, and the triangle of eyes. I touched the bone box gingerly. "What *is* it?"

"I don't know yet. But I begin to get glimmerings, begin to see it alive and flying."

"Flying?"

"Swimming, maybe. My vision's still too blurry. For now, I just think of it as a skeleton of the possible, a fossil of the future."

I tried to imagine her ankles affixed with wings, her head swollen like a double moon, her third eye glaring. "And what sort of creature will you be when you're—changed?"

"We'll just have to wait and see, won't we?"

"We?" I echoed, backing carefully over the linoleum.

"You've put the bones together, haven't you?"

I stared at my palms, then turned my hands over to examine the twitching skin where the knuckles should be.

SCOTT SANDERS' most recent book is Terrarium, *published by TOR Books. His next book,* The Invisible Company, *will be published by TOR in 1987.*

THE

FIRST

DAY

Art Vesity

When the Tau Cetans conquer Earth, they think their teachers can brainwash schoolchildren . . . but kids can tell.

Doesn't it always seem to come too soon? I mean, there you are, playing ball every day or riding bikes out to the lake (even though one of your pals has a pool in his backyard), or just plain sitting around, and suddenly it's only two weeks away, and then one, but you don't want to think about it. And then there's less than a week—you can count it on your fingers —and the games become more fun all of a sudden, and you pack more things into one day—none of that loungin' around now, 'cause there's no time! But nobody wants to say why, until sometime over the Labor Day weekend. Somebody mentions it, and even if it's still real hot, it just isn't summer anymore.

"Well . . . you ready for *school*, Ken?"

And that does it. Sure, grown-ups have been talking about it a lot—got to buy your clothes, what grade you're in now, all that—but grown-ups can't break the spell. Only a friend can. And then you all grumble and moan about how short the summer was, but really you're feeling kind of excited, because you're going into a new grade, and you're going to have a new teacher. And then that morning you all meet in the school yard and wait for the bell, all excited but kind of tired, too, because it took a long time to fall asleep last night. And you all grumble and moan some more, but when the bell rings you can't wait to get inside because—well, it's the first day.

I wish we all could have felt that way *this* year. But mostly we were just scared, I think. I know *I* was. How could I not be, with all that happened to the world since spring, and with Mom having that look on her face when she kissed me good-bye at the door? She can't fool me about that look. I know she went inside and cried after saying good-bye. I just *know* it. Kids can tell.

Billy Clarke and I climbed the stairs together on our way to the sixth-graders' room on the third floor. He was a black kid who moved in down the street from me in time for fifth grade, and we got to be good buddies last year in Miss Grantham's class. There aren't many black kids in our town, and some of the other kids weren't too friendly to Billy at first. But he's a real good guy and smart in class (like me—honest, I am), and everyone got to like him before the year was halfway over. (And he played real good basketball, too—I still don't know why Dad smiled when I told him that.) Well, last year he always said he couldn't wait for *this* year, because the sixth-grade teacher was a real pretty black lady named Ms. Robeson (we knew she wasn't married, even though you couldn't tell from her name). Billy used to hang around her all the time when she was on recess duty, and everybody used to laugh behind his back and say things like, "Birds of a feather . . ." It made me mad, and I almost wound up fighting a guy over it once, but I don't think anybody really meant to be mean. It's just something to joke about when somebody has a crush on a teacher.

We didn't say much while we went up the stairs—like I said, I was kind of scared. But not Billy. He looked more mad than scared. "It just isn't fair," he said. "Why couldn't they leave Ms. Robeson as our teacher, instead of sendin' their own guy? My mom says she must be a good teacher to get hired in this town."

"I don't know, Billy," I said. "I guess they want to change things to their own system, so that means the schools, too. She'll be there, only she won't be in charge, that's all. She'll just be sort of helpin' out. Dad says that they promised that the teachers will be there all the time."

"Yeah, but it won't be the same. If—"

"Shush! Here comes one!" I felt real funny in my stomach, watching him come down the steps at us. I only saw one up close in person once before, when me and Billy and Joe Denniger took a bike ride down to city hall. We saw *two* of them coming out for lunch, and they walked right past us, close enough to touch. They looked something like human people, but not really. They were short and real wide, but not fat, and had dark skin, but not as dark as Billy's. Their eyes were slanted on the ends like a Chinese or Vietnamese (we had one of those in our school, too), and they always wore those dark-blue robes. Some people said they didn't really look this much like humans, that they changed themselves to be as close as they could so they'd fit in—that they were something terrible to look at, awfully ugly. I don't know if that's true.

Well, this one looked okay, but he kept staring at me and Billy, even though there were lots of other kids on the steps. "Good morning, boys," he said, stopping right in front of us so we couldn't pass.

"Hello," I said, trying not to sound nervous. Billy looked at him like he was going to complain about what they did to Ms. Robeson.

"Are you boys good friends?" he said, sort of singsongy.

"Yeah, we're good friends," said Billy. I could tell he was thinking about saying more, so I kicked the side of his foot.

"That's nice. People of different skin colors should be friends. And that goes for people of different nations, and even . . . different worlds!" He smiled, and his teeth looked funny, like there were too many or something. "What grade are you boys in this year?"

"Sixth grade, sir," I said.

"Why, that's just fine! You'll be in *my* class! Now you go on to Room 3C, where Ms. Robeson is waiting, and I'll be along soon. We're going to have a *great* time this year, boys!" He patted each of us on the head and went on down the stairs. I wondered if he was going to the teacher's bathroom —some people say they never go to the bathroom, but I doubt that.

By then all the other kids had passed, so we were alone on the stairs. "Sixth grade, *sir*," said Billy after we took a few steps.

"C'mon, Billy!" I said. "He's our teacher now, isn't he? Even if we don't like it. And my dad sat me down last night and told me not to make any trouble, 'cause as of this summer, they're in charge. Of the whole *world!* And there's nothin' we can do about it, he said. And—"

"I know. I got told, too," he said as we got to the third-floor landing. "But tell me that guy ain't one first-class jerk, Ken! C'mon, tell me!"

I looked at him and grinned, but really, I was worried about him. I knew he had a bigger chip on his shoulder than most people, and I understood why. Dad had a talk with me about that, too, when Billy and I first became pals.

———

It's an old building, so the ceilings are real high, with fluorescent lights hanging down from them by metal poles. They put brown carpet down last year and painted the walls white, because a lot of parents were complaining that if Waterford (the town down the highway from here) could afford new schools, so could we. Anyway, the people from Tau Ceti say there'll be all new schools soon, all over the world. "Promises, promises," Dad sang when he heard that.

Billy and I got seats next to each other at the end of the middle two rows. Colleen Gray, a real pretty blond girl who I sort of had a crush on last year, was sitting two seats in front of me, but I couldn't really think about her. Everybody was nervous; you could tell. The way Ms. Robeson looked didn't help. She had on a tan skirt and a pretty blouse with flowers, but there was this funny look on her face, like she was in a trance. Kids went up to say hello, 'cause the second bell hadn't rung yet, and when she answered them she sort of looked away, like she was ashamed. Like it was *her* fault the world got taken over.

"She's really bummed out," said Billy when he came back from saying hello. I didn't tell him, but when he was walking away from her, it looked for a second like she was going to cry. Really.

Then the second bell rang. It was 8:30, time to start. The Tau Cetan we met on the steps came strolling in, with that same silly smile on his face. It looked like he'd combed his hair in the bathroom—it was kind of tangled before, but now it was straight with no part, like Moe in the Three Stooges. He said hello to Ms. Robeson and sat down at the desk. *Her desk,* I thought.

Everything was quiet, like at church when the priest gets up for the sermon and takes a long time to think of something. Then Ms. Robeson stood up from her chair next to the desk, cleared her throat, and smoothed the wrinkles out of her skirt.

"Good morning, kids," she said in a shaky voice. Then she got quiet for a while, and everybody started to look at each other. She finally got rolling, though, but all the time she talked she looked over our heads, like she was reading words off the blackboard in the back of the room. "This is Mr. Tremaine, who'll be with us all this year. He'll be teaching you some things about his people, our new—friends, the Tau Cetans. Things about their culture, their history, and all the things they hope to do for us here on Earth. . . ."

Well, she got through the introduction without having to stop again, and I could tell everyone felt glad for her. When she was done, Mr. Tremaine (I didn't know they used titles like "mister") got up and started talking in his singsongy voice. He talked about all the things they were going to do for Earth, and how they got here just in time to save us from ourselves, and how it was going to be a "great alliance." And he talked about the "misunderstandings of late spring and early summer," when they had to fight with some of Earth's armies, including America's, and the "tragic deaths that resulted." But that was all over now, he said, except for "a few little trouble spots." There was never going to be war again, he said, between nations or planets. And pretty soon there'd be no more hunger or disease on Earth, and everybody's life would be "peaceful and orderly." There would be no more bad weather, either, and everybody would have a job to do. He made it sound pretty good, and I started to wonder if maybe the bad things I heard people saying about the Tau Cetans all summer were really fair. But it sounded scary, too, because he said something about people maybe having to be moved around later, and that seemed to get everybody nervous again. Ms. Robeson, who was sitting down now, looked at Mr. Tremaine like he shouldn't have mentioned that part.

All the speech-making lasted till morning recess, and when the bell rang, we hurried out into the school yard. It was a warm, sunny day, but instead of playing, we mostly talked (us older kids, that is—the younger ones went on like nothing happened) while the Tau Cetans and the teachers stood around, watching and chatting. Ms. Robeson stood with Mr. Tremaine near the big wire fence, but they didn't say much. At least *she* didn't, until suddenly she turned and pointed a finger in his face and said something real stern. (Billy and I were watching from far away, so we couldn't hear the words.) Then she crossed her arms and looked straight ahead, and Mr. Tremaine looked like somebody had slapped him. He walked away and left her standing against the fence with her head down. I tried to think of what it could be that they argued about and decided it must have been something about that people-getting-moved business.

"All *right!*" Billy said, slapping me on the shoulder. "I knew Ms. Robeson wasn't no ass-kisser like the rest of these turkeys! Look at Marshall over there (he was the school principal) playin' up to his new boss! And there goes Tremaine. You think he's gonna cry on their shoulders, Ken?"

"I don't know," I said, "but I'd hate to see her get in trouble or lose her job. Hey—look at *that!*"

We watched Ms. Robeson walk over to where Marshall, Tremaine, and the other Tau Cetan were standing. She tapped Mr. Tremaine on the shoulder, and they moved a couple steps away. Pretty soon they were talking and smiling it up like the others. It was pretty plain to see that she was apologizing for whatever it was she said. I turned to Billy, but he was just staring at them and mumbling something under his breath. I couldn't think of anything to say to make him feel better. It was awful, standing there with him like that, and I was sure glad when Colleen Gray came over to ask me how my summer was. She asked Billy about his, too, but he just ignored her.

Back in class, we started by having books passed out. Mr. Tremaine had us stop and look through each one when it came (except the U.S. history book—he sort of skipped over that one). Billy kept looking at Ms. Robeson like all of the sudden he hated her, and once, when she was passing out the history books, I think she noticed, because when she came back down the aisle on the other side of me, she was biting her lip. She always knew he had a crush on her.

The last book was one about the Tau Cetan Empire. It was thick, but it had big print and lots of pictures of outer space and beautiful color pictures of stars and galaxies and nebulas. While we leafed through it, Mr. Tremaine talked about how this was the most important book we were going to study this year and how it was going to be the most fun and interesting, too. (The cover had a real pretty painting, but kind of corny —there were two adults and a boy and a girl, all holding hands and looking up at the sky with smiles on their faces, looking up at one of the big gold Tau Cetan starships.) He had us turn to certain pages where the best space pictures were, and a lot of the kids kept going "ooh" and "ahh" every time they saw a new one. Ms. Robeson looked up once like she didn't like the way they were reacting, and that's when I noticed she wasn't looking at her copy of the Empire book. She was looking through her history book—I could tell because it was the only one with a green cover. After a while she started turning the pages real fast, back and forth, like she was looking for something that wasn't there. Mr. Tremaine didn't notice any of this, probably because he was sitting down now and couldn't see which book was in her lap.

Finally, he had us close the books. "Now, kids," he said, standing up, "I have some good news and some bad news. First, the bad news. There's going to be a reading assignment in the Empire book." The class groaned. "But now, the *good* news. Since it's been a busy day, you're going to be let out early. In about five minutes, in fact!"

Everybody except a few (including me and Billy) went "Hooray!" when he said that, and he smiled that big smile of his like he was the happiest Tau Cetan in the universe. Then he turned around and started writing the assignment on the blackboard.

That's when I noticed Ms. Robeson's head shaking. Then her hands started trembling, too, even though she was still holding the history book. It got worse and worse, until suddenly she got up and slammed the book on the desk. "No!" she hollered, and a couple of the kids gasped. "It's *not* going to be that easy!" Mr. Tremaine spun around and looked at her with his mouth open, but she kept looking at the class. At us, right in the eyes, for the first time all day.

"Listen to me, kids," she said, calmer but real fast, "and don't ever forget what I say. You do what he says—read that book, memorize it—but don't you *believe* it! And when you read your history books at home, ask your moms and dads to tell you about the parts they glossed over, parts about the struggles for freedom in your own country!"

"Now, Ms. Robeson," said Mr. Tremaine, smiling but nervous, "you're upset. All this change—"

"To hell with you!" she said, turning back to us. "They left out those parts because they want you to forget about freedom, because they're going to take our freedom away, little by little, until it's gone! But for all their power, they can't get in *here!*" She tapped her heart, and her voice got all shaky and her eyes wet. "Don't you ever let them in there, hear me? No matter what! Because you're human beings, and human beings were born to be *free.* So don't you *ever* let them in there! *Never!*"

I sat staring at her like everybody else, when suddenly I saw Billy jump up from his seat. "You tell 'em, Ms. Robeson!" he shouted, and then he started clapping, banging his hands together as hard as he could.

Well, something came over me then, I don't know what. But before I knew it, I was up and clapping, too. And then the kid next to me, and Colleen and some others up front, and pretty soon, *everybody.* Everybody clapping and cheering, like something that was building up inside for a long time was finally coming out. Ms. Robeson fell back in her chair, amazed, and tears started pouring down her cheeks. But they were tears of happiness, I think. And then she raised her right fist high above her head, and we cheered even louder.

All the while, Mr. Tremaine stood there in sort of a trance. Then the classroom door flew open, and three other Tau Cetans came running in. (I think he must have called them mentally—they say they can do that with each other.) They ran over to Ms. Robeson and tried to lead her away, but she started kicking and struggling. "No!" she yelled. "These are *my* children! You can't take me from them, no matter what!" But they were strong, and they lifted her right up and carried her out the door. This scared the class, and we stopped cheering, but a few of us booed the Tau Cetans as loud as we could. Mr. Tremaine ignored that and followed them outside.

"Let her go!" shouted Billy, starting to head for the door. But I threw my arms around him and pulled him down to the floor between our desks. "Let go of me!" he said, trying to break my grip. "I got to help her, Ken!"

"No, Billy," I said, holding on tight. "She wouldn't want you to get hurt! That's not what she *meant.* She just wants us to remember what she said—always."

He stopped fighting me and started to cry. "They'll take her away. We'll never see her again."

"I know. I know," I said, nearly crying, too. And then I started talking louder, so all the others gathered around us could hear. "But we'll get 'em somehow. We'll make 'em sorry they ever *came* here!"

Then we heard the door open, and we all jumped back in our chairs. All the kids looked afraid that Mr. Tremaine was going to punish *us* for what happened. But he just smiled his nervous smile and went to stand behind the desk. "Please forgive Ms. Robeson, children," he said. "She's been under a great strain—not only the changes at school, but, ah, in her *personal* life. . . . Let's just say there's been some *problems.* Things we don't want to talk about."

"Bullshit," whispered Billy, wiping his eyes.

"At any rate, she's asked me to tell you that she's sorry for what happened, and for not trusting us. You'll see for your-selves that she was wrong, in time." He cleared his throat. "And tomorrow we'll have a new assistant teacher. Ms. Robe-son will be going to a new job, something for which she is better suited. And now, I'll finish putting that assignment on the board, and we'll go home and rest up and forget all about this nastiness!"

He turned to the board and started to write. I looked around, and everybody looked glad for not being punished—glad enough to believe what he said, maybe. Then something hap-pened to make me see I didn't have to worry.

A paper airplane sailed over the class from the back corner of the room, floated around the teacher's desk, and then hit point first right against the back of Mr. Tremaine's head. He jumped about a mile in the air and dropped the chalk, and everybody started to laugh like crazy.

He saw the airplane on the floor and started to laugh himself, keeping that big smile on his face like it was a good joke. But that's not *all* that was on his face. Something else there told me he knew, deep down inside, that he was in for a long, long year.

Kids can tell.

ART VESITY lives in Wilkes-Barr, Pennsylvania. He has had three short stories published in Isaac Asimov's Science Fiction Magazine.

THE
FOREVER
SUMMER

Ronald Anthony Cross

*When the young Apollo strides angrily
through the halls of Olympus, even Zeus
dare not remain seated.*

I f my first glimpse of New Olympus evoked within me some
inexplicable surge of nostalgia (how to explain nostalgia for
something you've never experienced?), then my first glimpse of
the Storm King, Henry II, certainly did nothing to break the
mood. A massively muscled man dressed up in a toga, with a
curly chestnut-brown beard, long hair, and the expansive style
of movement and booming voice to go with it. He had modeled
himself after a statue of Zeus, that god of gods and all-time
father figure. I knew that, of course. I had even seen holos of

him ("Here's your mad uncle, Henry, the artist"), and yes, of his work of art, the New Olympus Asteroid. But holos don't prepare you for the real thing. Or rather, for whatever it is inside of you that those images trigger.

You have to understand where I was coming from. The City. The one and only Big City. It's one enormous machine, and what it manufactures is the illusion of continuity. Nothing ever changes in New London; its considerable technology is primarily dedicated to maintaining itself exactly at the level at which it has been for the last two or three hundred years. The lifestyle is designed to never allow the slightest shadow of change to infringe upon London society's complex but predictable game of getting on. I was not doing too well in that game. But at the same time I was a product of it. And while I was prepared to rebel against *The City* with all my very soul, I was as disturbed by New Olympus as any New Londoner would have been.

Mad Uncle Henry II grabbed ahold of my bony hand, nearly smashed it, and practically shouted at me by way of greeting.

"By the Gods, you scrawny wretch, Will, is it? You've got my eyes. Can't you see that, boy? For all your pallid New London demeanor, it's me you really take after. I can see it in your eyes. Here, come with me. First things first."

He led me over to his holo deck and popped in a cart. I kept sneaking glances at his mad, blazing, brown eyes. Did I have his eyes for real? Was it possible?

Suddenly a full-sized holo of my mother popped up before us, arms spread out to us imploringly.

"Dear Henry, I know we haven't ever got on well. I've always felt guilty about that. No, don't laugh. I really have. After all, I'm the older of the two of us. I always had the responsibility of guiding you. I know it was particularly hard on you that Father had gone off to work the asteroid belt and left you and me and Mother to . . ." She droned on and on in her typical boring manner. My interest shifted to the magnificent throne room. Suddenly I caught: "Whatever you do, don't let Will see this holo."

That snapped me back to Mom, believe me. Henry nudged me with his elbow and grinned happily.

"God knows I would never do anything to hurt my son, but I just . . . he's just driving me out of my mind. And his father, Arn, his stepfather, well, he just has done everything in his power to . . ."

Mom went on and on complaining about what a trial I was, especially to Daddy Arn, and how I was in trouble at school and had absolutely no friends and how one of my teachers had said to her just last week, etc.

I kept sneaking looks at Uncle Henry. I couldn't believe that he would do this. It was absolutely not possible for me to accept that he was doing this.

After an eternity of my mother complaining about me to Henry and occasionally shifting over to complaining about Henry to Henry, she finally wound up with her ending argument about how a change of environment during my extended school vacation might allow me to get enough space to straighten myself out.

The Storm King offed the holo. "Well, I just thought you ought to see that, Will. Right out in the open. What? It's time for my ride. I've brewed up a storm in your honor. Yes, in your honor. The rebel, huh. You've got my eyes, my blood. Somewhere inside of that frail little scrawny body beats the lion's heart, eh?"

He walked fast. I kept up. He led me down a hall. Up several flights of stairs—yes, plain, old-fashioned stairs—and finally to the tower.

And there it was. The chariot. All gold and gleaming and covered with little figures of lions and unicorns and eagles. The lightning gun was sheathed upright, a narrow gold rod, no more.

Mom's voice was still nagging me in my mind's ear: "Whatever you do, you must promise me you won't go flying off in his chariot with Henry or I just can't, in good conscience, let you go. No. Promise me, now. No joking. Swear on the Bible. 'May God strike me dead if I . . .' "

"Jump in." Henry always seemed to be talking beyond me, off into the sky. I jumped in.

"Belt up." I belted up.

I kept forgetting to breathe as we rushed across the skies of New Olympus, and below us the incredible blazing canvas of the Storm King's painting unfurled.

"The waterbabies," he shouted off over my shoulder. We dipped down closer.

They were playing on the surface of the rushing river, the kind of meaningless noisy games all children play, pushing and tumbling each other, screaming and whirling around and falling down, bobbing about like corks. On the grass another group of them seemed to be playing follow the leader with some weird little animal I couldn't quite get a clear enough view to identify. But he looked weird.

"That's Pookie Bear. He's not really a bear. More of a rabbit type, with a little raccoon and a few human genes tossed in."

We dipped down again, even lower. He waved. I caught a glimpse of a beautiful little nymph with a sea of rich brown locks, dressed in a loose toga, waving back.

"That's one of the clone mothers," he shouted. "Over there's their house." I caught sight of an enormous, classic-looking temple jutting up out of the shrubbery.

And now it began to cloud up fast. I could see more of the mothers down below, all identical, hustling the babies in off the river.

Suddenly it was raining hard. The Storm King laughed wildly in the rain and turned to me. And if he had appeared mad to me before, I saw now that I had only had a hint of his intensity. The rain was his element.

"Now," he whispered to me. "Now." He took out the gun and aimed over the side of the chariot. He seemed to be sighting in on the Pookie Bear creature.

Zap. A bolt of some kind of electricity or other flashed out of the rod and slashed down into the shrubbery, missing the Pookie by what seemed to me an inordinate amount. Nevertheless.

"What if you hit him?" I couldn't resist asking.

But he was already firing off again. Missed again, but knocked over a tree. This seemed to please him. He laughed again. "Oh, there's more where he came from," he said.

For the next couple of hours, we raced all over the sky, shooting at everything that moved, hitting nothing. Finally the storm lightened up. We turned around and headed slowly in.

It was fairly warm weather. Nevertheless, after a couple of hours racing about the sky, wearing only a summer cotton jumpsuit, drenched with rain, I was shivering. The Storm King, practically naked in his wet toga, goose bumps sprouting up all over his flesh, seemed to be charged up with energy from the whole experience.

"The glory of a summer storm," he shouted. "There's nothing like it. Every one of them is different, yet every one of them is, somehow, the same. Enjoy it while you can. Summer is always a fleeting shadow. Before you can grasp it, winter is upon you in all its icy fury."

"Why do you have winter, anyhow?" I complained. "It's your asteroid. You can have anything you want. Why don't you just dial up forever summer?"

"Forever summer." He smiled. "Well, we humans don't want to have everything we want," he said. "We don't want to play games without rules. No, we want some form of order to create within. We have to have our seasons. The natural order. Nature's rounds. No, if we didn't have rules, we would have to invent them."

"Like New London?" I said. I couldn't keep the sarcasm out of my voice.

"No. Not like New London. New London is an attempt to completely block out change, and that can't be done. All life is change. But change within an orderly structure. New London is death. And at the same time, New London is escape from death. They think, people like my sister, your mother, they think that by keeping everything the same, each day like the next, they will be able to keep out old age, death. But the sad fact is they are old and dead to start with. When each day is the same as the next, why, there is nothing left alive in your life. All routine is death. They imagine they are immortal, and they have given up life to achieve that illusion. No, let season follow season, but let the days within them be filled with change. Enough. Be silent for a while. Enjoy."

I must have drowsed off as we drove back in. I kept looking into the rain and letting my thoughts drift, and at one point I thought I saw a swarm of insects floating among the drops. But when I looked closer, to my astonishment, I glimpsed tiny delicate human forms with glistening wings hovering in the air. They darted and buzzed about. Ecstatic, yet somehow tragic. I had a momentary sensation of transitory life-forms like bubbles, rising in bliss only to burst in a moment, new bubbles forming to take their place. Then they, too, were gone. Had I really seen them, I wondered, or had I nodded off?

I opened my mouth to ask the Storm King, but he motioned for silence. I froze with my mouth open. The experience slipped from my mind.

Back at the tower he gestured to his chariot. "I will demand one thing of you," he said. "You must never take my chariot up under any circumstances. I warn you, if you should disobey me in this matter, my punishment can be severe."

I pictured him shooting lightning at the cute little Pookie Bear. "I'll bet it can," I said in my sarcastic tone of voice.

"Besides," he continued, "you couldn't control it anyway. You would be hurled from it like Phaëton from Apollo's chariot."

"Oh, certainly," I said. It didn't look all that difficult to me. Practically everything about it was automatic.

The next morning I was surprised to be awakened quite early by a boy whom I had never before laid eyes upon. At first I couldn't imagine where I had got to. The room was so different from my little room at home in New London.

I was in an enormous bed in an enormous room. Diaphanous lavender curtains fluttered in the morning breeze. A life-sized bronze of Hermes was poised, ready for flight, in the middle of the room. It seemed to be contemplating rushing out the open doors onto the balcony outside. A small bronze table with a tall pink vase on it, no flowers, and the gleaming marble floors were the only other items to break the simple but majestic motif of white walls and white ceilings and enormous empty space. All the windows as well as the only doors at the far end of the room were wide open.

The boy who woke me seemed to belong here as part of the furnishings, while I—quite the contrary. It was not just the toga in which he was dressed, but the free expansive movements he made with his arms and hands when he spoke, the mercurial dance of expressions across his sharp, bright face, the bubbling rush of his speech. The boy belonged in a younger, more energetic world than I, I felt.

"What, haven't they told you anything? Ye Gods! Then you must leave it all to me. Up. Up. We must be ready before— no, no, don't you dare go back to sleep. Bruno will kill us if we're late. You know—The Chosen One—all that sort of . . . But wait, how rude of me. Philo. I'm Philo. Ye Gods, your white skin. The machines will take care of that. Up. Up. Here, throw this on. No, forget your old clothes. Absolutely forbidden. New Olympus is the Storm King's work of art. You will have to be part of it, like it or not. Besides, your clothes—ugh—ye Gods, we're late. Come along, come quickly now."

I threw on a toga and, still half asleep, followed Philo outside along the balcony, which led entirely around and around the magnificent castle, winding down and finally inside, where we entered a long hall and went down a flight of long winding stairs.

Philo carried on an extraordinary monologue, all of the time gesturing and waving his arms about, turning this way and that, changing expressions.

As I finally really began to wake up, I was rather astonished to realize that my vacation at New Olympus was to be a very tightly structured existence resembling nothing at all like my idea of a vacation. In fact—I popped wide awake—it sounded like hard work!

"Wrestling? Uh, wait a minute, Philo. I'm afraid there's been some sort of misunderstanding. You see, I'm not your basic wrestling-type mentality. I'm more your chess-playing, read-a-good-book type of fellow."

But he actually grabbed me by the wrist and dragged me along, never slowing his pace, never interrupting his monologue.

Outside the castle, the boys were waiting in boats decked out as giant swans, bobbing off the banks of the river that ran around the front of the castle and turned into the large, complex river system just out of sight up ahead. New Olympus was networked with rushing, bubbling rivers. And the swan boats, which operated off of some kind of silent motor, drifted slowly upstream and into the larger, swifter river, where we continued upstream at an even slower pace.

The waterbabies were out now, chasing one another all over the river, screaming and shouting and playing all manner of pranks. At one point they tried to tip our boat over, but to my amazement Philo picked up two of the little butterballs, one in each hand, and tossed them an incredible distance, where they splashed and actually skipped over the surface. Then the rest of them all wanted us to do it, and we all had to do it over and over again.

"They hardly weigh more than a bird," Philo said. "The Storm King tunes their weight down when they're babies so they can run on the rivers. It allows them to develop more coordination and agility, or so the theory goes. I don't know how well it works, but it sure is fun. I really miss it. I guess I always will. I guess it's about the happiest time, what with the clone mamas and that neat babies' house, and most of all I remember running the rivers." Philo choked up. Tears were in his eyes. But a moment later he was laughing and carrying on about the coming summer festival. We were all going to perform in the festival. He guessed it was the best time of your life. He seemed to have already forgotten about the waterbabies, and went on and on about the festival.

It was to last an indeterminate time, or rather it would be determined by fate or some such romantic thing. No one could tell when it would start or end. Only the Priestess could read the signs. We were to wrestle on the first day. That's why we had to work hard and be ready.

And work hard we did. This was why I had cut my school year in half to get here for the New Olympus summer? Every morning we sailed out in our swan boats to a grassy expanse and spent the entire morning practicing wrestling holds, driven by The Chosen One, a super powerful brute named Bruno, who seemed to take particular delight in tossing my skinny frame about like a rag doll, for the amusement of the other boys. I hated it with a vengeance, but there didn't seem to be any way out of it.

In the afternoons we would lie on the tables in the gymnasium and toss ribald jokes back and forth while the attendants strapped the pads onto all our muscles and then spasmed them for a few seconds with electricity. Most of the boys went through this experience, which at first I found excruciatingly uncomfortable but later came to rather enjoy, only twice a week. But I was to undergo it every other day, due to my emaciated, pallid, New London condition, as my uncle Henry liked to put it.

Then, after showers and lunch with the boys, I was finally free to do whatever I wished for a few hours until dinner, which was such a lavish, drawn-out affair that by the time it was ended it was all I could do to get back to my room without curling up somewhere along the way in the corner of some great room and going to sleep right there. They probably would have taken me for a statue. "The Sleeping Shepherd Boy," or perhaps "The God of Exhaustion."

I remember that for the first week I was miserable, just tired and achy and exhausted all the time. All of my energy went into finding a way out. But there was no way out. And besides, although I was having trouble admitting it, what would I do with my time once I had worked my way out of it? Lie around my room, or take walks alone while the boys were out wrestling on the field?

And after a while it became obvious to me that Philo and I were becoming fast friends. It would have been hard not to become friends with Philo, he was so enthusiastic and full of energy—the opposite of me in every respect. Where I was medium height but quite slender and narrow of shoulder and hip, he was short and broad and heavy. Where he was ebullient and talkative, I was cautious and measured in my speech, if somewhat glib on the surface. Where he wrestled with instinctive fervor and counted on his surplus energy to extricate himself from the jams his impulsive moves got him into, I wrestled with a light, speedy style always dominated by rational thought. I always planned out my general approach, calculating the

weaknesses and strengths of my opponent, and then kept alter-
ing and shifting my plan during the match.

Yes, wonder of wonders, I was learning how to wrestle. And
I was putting on muscle. With the third week I seemed to get
a second wind. I started to stay up later at night and even woke
up early in the mornings. Philo no longer had to come get me.
I was putting away copious amounts of food at every meal now.

"What magic can this be?" Uncle Henry had remarked.
"The scarecrow is blossoming into a statue of young Hermes."

Yes, I was rapidly adding muscle to my slender frame, although it was still obvious that suppleness and speed were my
forte and always would be; never strength. And I *was* learning
to wrestle, although there was not yet cause here for Bruno to
worry.

Bruno was clearly our champion and hero. Tall, superbly
built, with the perfect balance of muscularity and flexibility,
with the smoothest, swiftest, most aggressive wrestling style,
complemented by the great strength necessary to apply the
finishing touches: Bruno, who could run the fastest, jump the
highest, shout the loudest, was the complete physical pattern
the rest of us were applying to our growth.

If one of us had strength, why, he molded it after Bruno's
strength. If one of us had speed, he practiced Bruno's footwork.
Bruno had everything. He was New Olympus's Young God.

But I didn't like him. "I don't believe in gods," I had told
Uncle Henry. "At least we have something in common," he
said. He had surprised me with that one. And I didn't believe
in Bruno. Something about him was cold, too self-contained,
too wonderful to be true. When he swept over you in a match,
like fire over wood, yielding wherever you showed strength,
surging in wherever you showed weakness, and settled you
effortlessly into one of his unbreakable locks, it seemed to me
that he always twisted a bit too hard and held on a bit too long
after you had given up.

One day during a rest period I walked across the grassy expanse
and was approaching the thick grove of trees at the far end.
Some sort of oak trees, I would guess, huge and ancient looking
and so close together that the tops were interwoven one with
the other, blocking out the sun.

I had noticed this morning that white streamers of some
delicate cloth had been woven through the branches of the
outer row as though marking off a territory.

I heard my name being shouted and turned to see Philo
running toward me across the grass.

"Will, Will. Stop. We may not enter in. It is forbidden to
all. Part of the mysteries. No, I do not know why. But it is
absolutely forbidden. The Storm King would punish you
severely if he ever caught you. You may not cross the white
streamers."

"Thank you for warning me," I said. "I didn't notice them
yesterday."

"Nor did I," Philo said. "They must have put them up last
night. The Priestesses."

"Well, thanks for warning me," I said. "I wouldn't want to
go against Uncle Henry's wishes; after all, I owe him so much.
Thanks again, Philo."

It wasn't until later in the day that I managed to break away
from the others and sneak into the sacred grove. I don't know
what I was expecting to see there. I only know I had to see it.
Perhaps what my mother had said about me was true, that
whatever was given me I tossed away, whatever was denied me
I had to have. I don't know about that, but I had to go into
that grove.

The moment I stepped inside I felt the chill in the air, and
the light was blocked out. There was a pungent musty odor
that thickened as I penetrated deeper, and the trees themselves
seemed ominous, as if they were somehow aware of my forbid-

den presence: They rustled and whispered among themselves about my passage.

The songs of birds took on an incredible stark lucidity, and as I walked on and on I would find myself staring at some twisted shape assumed by the branches of one of those giants, as if—yes, I could almost read the meaning of it—as if I wanted to imitate it!

Then I heard the low piping of the flute and that led me to the clearing in the center of the grove. Here, once again the sunlight broke in. A lovely, totally white pavilion was set up, made of some delicate-looking but obviously durable cloth. It swayed and creaked in the breeze.

A young girl danced here. Or rather, seemed to be practicing dance. She would whirl about the clearing, spinning like a dust devil, and then drop down suddenly, laughing, and take hold of her foot and stretch her head down to her toes, then jump up and prance about, practicing some move over and over again.

She was a beauty. Her hair was long and glossy black and floated out behind her like a dark cloud. Her dancer's body was lithe and strong, but she was petite. I judged her to be a year or two younger than I, although her body was more mature for her age—the dancing, I guessed, would be likely to do that. My first thought was that what made her so striking was the grace of her movements, her carriage, her proud posture, surely the effects of a lifetime of training in the dance. But I was later to change that opinion. No, her ultimate glory lay inward, a state of awareness, something that pointed out to her, in moments of happiness, the shadow. In moments of sadness, the ghost of laughter. Something bittersweet. It was this curse/gift that ruled over her posture, her expressions, her manner of speech, indeed over her very soul.

The flute player I could not locate. Perhaps she or he was situated somewhere close by. Perhaps high up in the branches of a tree. I liked that image. So be it.

What I had done so far had been careless, perhaps even dangerous—one could easily imagine my "mad uncle," the Storm King, self-appointed god of this entire world he had created, setting me loose somewhere on the surface and chasing me about with his sky chariot, trying to blast me with his lightning gun—but what I was now contemplating was totally insane. Yet I just had to do it.

A short life but a merry one, I told myself as I stepped out into the clearing.

"Hello." I waved nonchalantly as I approached. The girl froze up like a deer paralyzed in the moment before it takes flight.

I had sensed somehow that the only way for me to act in this situation was totally at ease, as if nothing at all unusual or forbidden were taking place here. Otherwise she would bolt. And as much as I was gaining confidence in my new athletic prowess I knew I had no hopes of catching her in a foot race (or probably subduing her once I caught her).

"Will, the Storm King's nephew. You want to know what I'm doing here. And do I know how forbidden it all is, and why on Earth, or rather, why on New Olympus . . . ?"

Her eyes widened even more, so much so that they actually appeared round to me, enormous and round. All the time I approached I instinctively kept up a steady banal chatter. I had the sensation of approaching a magical bird and droning on and on to hypnotize it until I got close enough to put salt on its tail: One mistake and all I would have left would be a handful of lovely iridescent feathers.

"Why did you? Really, why did you do this?" Her voice was higher pitched than I had expected, but sweet.

"I really don't know," I said. "I always do whatever is forbidden. It's just inborn. I had to come here, and once I got here I had to talk to you. I can't explain it. Perhaps it was fate." I was trying to toss it off lightly, but she wasn't taking it as a joke.

"Perhaps it was," she said gravely.

Suddenly I felt certain that she was on the verge of turning away from me. I was illogically desperate, as though I was about to lose something immeasurably important.

"Look," I said, "you can't turn away from me now. You simply cannot. I have come here from another planet, another way of life, totally alien. I broke all the rules there. I'm an outcast in my own home, and now I've broken all the rules here, just for this moment. Just to get to you now. Call it fate or whatever you want, but you can't turn away from me now."

Then she did a thing I shall never forget if I live to be three hundred years old, like my doddering aunt Hilda: She reached out and took my hand. Her hand was unusually warm, dancer's blood, but I shivered as if it had been ice.

"No, I can't," she said, and once again for an exquisite moment, her eyes widened. Who was hypnotizing whom? "You are right. And at the same time you are wrong. That is your fate. It appears to be your very essence. You are breaking the rules. But in some strange way you are forging new rules as inexorable as the ones you break. You don't even know what you are asking for, but the way you ask it, it cannot be denied. Very well. So you shall have it. I, of all people, should have developed the grace to accept the inevitable."

Something had passed between us; I knew not what it was. She dropped my hand.

And suddenly she changed totally. "My name's Inana, and I've spent most of my life studying the dance. I live in the temple of Iris, over there." She waved off in some vague direction behind her and chattered on in the light manner of any young girl who is aware that she is effortlessly charming a young man who has come to court.

Spellbound, I listened. Not so much to what was being said as to the sweet, shrill sound of her voice. And her eyes. I felt that I could look into her eyes forever. And on and on she chattered, dancing with her hands, her body moving restlessly from time to time, expressing itself of its own accord. And now, as I pointed out before, emerged the guiding genius of her exquisite charm, a hint of inexpressible sadness that lingered beneath the surface of her happy chatter, deepening the chiaroscuro of her expression.

Finally, as if by some signal, she leaned over casually and kissed me lightly on the lips. I was stunned. "You must go now," she said. And now she had changed back. Her tone of voice was quite serious, even sad, but was that a hint of a smile peeking out from within the sorrow?

"I must see you again," I started to plead, but she held out her hand and touched her finger to my lips, cutting off my pleas in the most exquisite manner.

"You told me that fate was responsible for our meeting. Very well, fate will have to choose whether we meet again. If we do not, it will be a tragedy. If we do meet again, it will be no less a tragedy. Go now. Now!"

She turned abruptly and walked away from me.

How long had I been here with her? I had no idea. I kept trying to calculate the time as I ran back through the forbidden grove of trees, but my mind kept returning over and over to Inana. The touch of her hand. The kiss, of course, but more than anything I savored that first wild thrill when she had, seemingly on the verge of bolting, suddenly reached out and taken my hand. Surely I would be caught. I just couldn't think.

But when I reached the grassy meadow we called the gladiators' field, it was deserted. It was growing as dark outside the grove as it had been inside it.

When I got back to the castle, to my amazement, Philo didn't seem to have an inkling of where I had got to. The boys had all speculated that I had sneaked off for a ribald adventure with one of the local girls. I guess it would never occur to them that anyone would so lightly break all the rules of the game.

That night before I went to bed—not to sleep, of course, but to bed—I examined myself in the full-length mirror. For the first time in memory, I liked the arrogant clown I saw there. "You're developing style," I said to the slender, springy, young athlete. "Good night, sweet prince!"

The next day I noticed to my dismay that the white streamers had been taken down. When I asked Philo about it, he told me I was now free to enter the grove. It was no longer forbidden. When I asked him why, he merely shrugged, unconcerned. "Mysteries," he seemed to say, "are mysteries."

Of course I entered the grove and of course she was gone, the pavilion was gone, the invisible flute player was gone. The trees no longer seemed to be aware of my presence and the twisted branches were just twisted branches.

I wrestled like a madman. During periods of rest, I ran laps around the outside edges of the gladiators' field. When I wasn't wrestling and I wasn't running I thought of her. And when I thought of her, I was in anguish. Would I ever meet her again? Yes and no, she had said to me. And I sensed that there was no way to solve that riddle except to live through it. So I wrestled with an intensity I had never imagined to find in myself, driving myself each day over and over again past my previous limits of exhaustion.

And my concentration had somehow been focused by the experience into a narrow beam of precision.

Strangely enough, something also had happened to Bruno. If before he had been awesome, now he was positively frightening.

One afternoon I was squared off with Philo, searching for an opening, when I heard someone yell out in pain. Bruno had one of the smaller boys, the one we all called Jester, down on the grass, back arched up in agony and legs wound around Bruno's leg. Bruno was standing up swaying backwards. He was applying an Indian deathlock, I realized with a shock. You don't apply an Indian deathlock unless you want to hurt someone badly. And to my astonishment everyone was standing around, quietly watching.

Without even thinking, I jumped Bruno from behind and headlocked him, except that I hooked it under his chin so that it was a choke hold instead of a headlock. They wouldn't have allowed that in a wrestling match, but they wouldn't have allowed an Indian deathlock either. I jerked Bruno over forward, which was what I had to do to free Jester from the lock; had Bruno gone over backward he probably would have broken either Jester's ankle or knee joint. I don't know which. An Indian deathlock hurts so much that you can't even figure out what area is being hurt the most.

As soon as the hold was broken, I let my lock go. But Bruno came after me, pushing me backward, face distorted with rage. Now, as if breaking out of a trance, some of the boys, led by Philo, got hold of Bruno and pulled him away from me.

"You, of all people," he shouted. "I'll murder you in the match. I swear it. I'll kill you. I'll break your neck."

"Well," I said, trying to appear more casual than I was feeling, "I'll be there. I might be too fast for you to get ahold of, but I'll be there for you to try it. Just try not to make a fool of yourself in front of everyone."

By now they had let him go and he had got control of himself. We were not allowed to fight, and not even Bruno would be quick to tamper with my uncle's rules. He smiled a nasty smile, and I realized how much taller and more muscular than I he was. "Good," he said. "Be there." And he stalked off.

This even seemed to make something of a hero out of me to the rest of the boys, and I must admit that I was enjoying it. It was the first time in my life that I can recall being treated like I really belonged somewhere. One of the boys. Right.

Something like a month had gone by since I had met the dancer in the forbidden grove. The memory was fading a bit as memories do, even in that brief space of time. And I was not so certain that I was correctly remembering what her face looked like anymore. She still haunted me, of course, but I was beginning to notice one of the girls who worked in the kitchen, a tall blond girl who smiled at me a certain way. Bruno and I seemed to have settled into an uneasy balance. We took pains to avoid each other during practice, and there were no further flare-ups.

Then one morning I woke up and it was festival, just like that. I awoke to a loud chaotic trumpeting and jumped up and rushed out onto the balcony to see what all the fuss was about.

A small being that looked like a little boy but somehow was not quite a little boy was racing about in the clear blue sky, throwing flowers out of a bag he carried. The sun was flashing off his helmet and he seemed to be getting tossed about a bit by the wind.

Later, when I asked Uncle Henry how he had done it, he tossed it off with a contemptuous wave of his hand. "Silverflash," he said. "That's a long story. And you wouldn't understand it, anyhow, if I told you. Suffice it to say it's been done. He runs the skies, has done so for a couple hundred years. He never ages."

"Have you heard? Have you heard?" Philo shouted at me suddenly from the doorway. "No, you haven't. I can see that. Well. Best of luck to you, anyway. Whichever way it goes between us . . . We've drawn each other. We're to wrestle in the first match."

Something was wrong here. And then I had it. It was something everyone had been aware of except me. I had become good at wrestling. I knew that of course, but just how good I had never bothered to add up. I was so fast that no one had a chance against me except Bruno.

And now I could see it in my friend Philo's eyes. Drawing

me for the first match was a piece of such rotten luck for him that it could only have been worse had he drawn Bruno.

The first match of the wrestling tournament, and Philo had no chance to even make a decent showing. I realized suddenly that I had been, of late, tossing Philo around head over heels, shifting holds on him as effortlessly as if had he been an inanimate practice dummy. Was I destined to make him appear the clown before his friends and family? And I could tell now that he was completely resigned to it.

"Well," he stammered, for the first time since I'd met him uncertain of what he wanted to say, "best of luck to you. Be on your guard. I'm going all out for this one." He punched my shoulder and rushed out of the room.

"I'm looking forward to seeing you wrestle, Will," Uncle Henry said from behind me. I'd forgotten he was still in the room. "I've been hearing good things about you. I guess all that training paid off."

"I'm not wrestling Philo," I said. "I can't do it."

"What do you mean you're not wrestling? You fool, it won't make any difference. Philo will lose anyhow. You have to do these things in life. Everyone does. You forget your friends and wrestle for all you're worth, and later . . . Don't you realize what they'll think? You're afraid of Bruno. Yes—even I've heard the story. They'll despise you. You have to wrestle. You have my blood in your veins. By the Gods . . ."

"Blood is blood. And I told you I don't believe in the Gods. I won't wrestle Philo. That's all. Someone may beat him. Someone may humiliate him. Not me."

I stalked out of the room, expecting at any minute to feel his heavy hand on my shoulder, and Uncle Henry was someone I was not about to ever want to wrestle under any circumstances.

That was, of course, the end of my one brief and only period as "one of the boys." As it turned out, even Philo despised me for it. What could I possibly tell him? That I didn't want to humiliate him? "They say you're afraid of Bruno," he stammered the last time he talked to me.

"Let them say what they want," I said. "Talk is cheap." And by the stricken look on his face I realized he thought I meant by that him, too, and more, I realized that I did mean him, too.

Bruno, of course, won the tournament, as he no doubt would have anyhow. And he was, according to hearsay, particularly hard on Philo. So in his way the Storm King was right. What difference did any of it make? I wandered through the festival alone, tasting the wine and fruits and hoping for a glimpse of her, but knowing somehow I would not have it. It almost seemed to me now that I had dreamed it. It was so nebulous, and fading so fast. Like a dream it had almost seemed to mean something so very important; but when you wake up, how quickly the meaning slips away.

That night, festival and all, I went to bed quite early. Everything had gone sour on me, and I just wanted my vacation to be over with. My uncle Henry, although he didn't mention the wrestling again, seemed to be avoiding me, along with the boys. I felt as weary as if I had wrestled with Bruno and lost. I sank immediately into a very deep and dreamless sleep.

At least it was dreamless at first. But then I seemed to be having the weirdest kind of dream. Something was hopping and piping out in a thin little voice so peculiar and comic that it just had to be a dream. Didn't it?

"Get up. Get up. Get up. Oh, my goodness gracious, you has to get up right now. Doesn't you? Yes yes yes. You do. You do. You do."

I sat up in bed. There was no light in the room save the low nightlights that glowed in each of the four corners. The weird little creature was hopping up and down in the dark, piping out, "You do, you do. Goodness me. Yes, you do. Wake up. Wake up."

Then I had it. It was the funny little Pookie Bear creature my uncle had shot at with his lightning gun.

Drowsily I registered a clanky metallic squeaking noise and caught sight of the Hermes bronze moving in the semidark. It seemed to have blossomed into life but somehow been short-circuited, as it was moving unnaturally fast in its macabre jerky manner. It would rush a short way across the floor and swivel quickly and rush back the way it came, over and over again. "Tonight's the night, tonight's the night, tonight's the night," it droned in its dead metal voice.

"He's awake, he is. Oh, good good goodie good. Follow me, follow me," the Pookie shouted. (*Pooka?* I wondered, remembering something dimly about some ancient Irish or Scottish legend.)

Now that it had my attention it would hop toward the door, then back to my bed, then toward the door again.

I got out of bed and drew on a toga with gold and blue trim, and followed it. As we went out the door, the Hermes statue was still rushing back and forth and mumbling, "Tonight's the night."

Outside, despite the Pookie Bear's pleas to "hurry, hurry, quickly scurry," I stopped on the balcony to get the feel of the night. The cries of a few late-night revelers still drifted in on the warm summer air. I caught the scent of blossoms, wine, perfumes, pulsing on the delicate playful summer breeze. And the stars blazed. Was tonight the night? It seemed to me uncommonly warm, uncommonly clear, uncommonly sweet. Yes, there was magic in the night. But when we came to the enormous stairway that circles the castle from top to bottom, I stopped following the Pookie Bear and began to climb. It came hopping after me piping, "What? What? What?" like a little motorboat.

"We'll take the chariot," I said.

"Oh, no, no, no. We'll crash, splash, smash, bash, mash. Oh, no. Oh, no."

"We'll take the chariot," I said again. My voice sounded unnaturally calm to me. I felt as if everything had been decided from a distance, my whole life planned out, and there could be nothing more for me to do but accept. Receive. The tone of my voice must have convinced the Pookie Bear because he followed me silently for a change. Up the stairs. And into the forbidden room.

"We'll fall from the sky," he said once in awe, as we both paused to take in the sky chariot in all its gleaming glory. Then he hopped in and settled himself in the passenger's seat next to the controls.

As we rose off into the night sky, I could feel him shivering next to me on the seat, making a low whimpering noise.

The controls were simple and responsive, and I had taken pains to pay close attention to Uncle Henry on those occasions when he had taken me out. Still, I was amazed at how easily the craft handled, at how sure my grip on the controls was. It seemed to me that I was returning at last to something that long ago and far away had been mine. And mine alone. Tonight was my night.

"There, over there," the Pookie Bear shouted. But I already knew where it was that we were headed.

The sacred grove of trees was strung with brightly colored lights, as was the chariot I drove: like the Christmas trees back home, I thought.

As I floated the chariot down, I seemed to be both in it and somehow above, taking it all in like a dream. And a dreamlike image it was, indeed, the grove all lighted up and the glowing sky chariot gently sinking into the brightly lit clearing in the center.

Once again the white pavilion was set up, and like the oak trees, it was strung with delicate lights and tiny bells. For now, as we drifted closer, I could hear the tinkling of a myriad of bells and chimes fluttering along with the pavilion in the mischievous but gentle gusts of summer breeze.

The Pookie Bear now, shivering more than ever, was perched on the control panel, where it could look down on the scene of enchantment. And it suddenly dawned on me that it was as magical and enchanting as everything else that night.

Designed by my uncle Henry's genius as a playmate-guide for the babies, the lovely little creature seemed to me now to be some sort of impossible fairy-tale being, hardly to be explained by the unlikely combination of genes—rabbit, raccoon, and child, Uncle Henry had said.

But the human-child element was unmistakable. Would it remain a child forever, like the strange little messenger boy called Silverflash, I wondered? For the first time I felt the stirrings of a wave of awe for the Storm King's mastery over genes, his struggles into the forbidden area of age and time, his enormous artistic will.

But it was in the clearing, now in the first real unveiling of the mystery, that I felt the first giddying rush of fear, as if, after all, I had lost control of the chariot and was falling from the skies.

Once again an invisible flute had begun to play. A graceful familiar figure swayed and began to dance to the music of the flute, the wind chimes, the bells. It was Inana. And it could not possibly be Inana. But it was Inana.

"Oh, I must not see," the Pookie was shouting. "I must not watch. Oh, no, no. Oh, no." The Pookie Bear hopped away, back to the chariot.

And later, when that dance of all dances was over, and the last veil had slipped away to the grass and she held out her hand to me and whispered, "Come," I could only mumble in a frightened voice, "How can this be? This cannot be. You were a young girl but a month ago, and now . . ."

"And now I am woman in all her full glory. It is true. I have danced the dance that was my life, for—for you, Will. It was all for you. But the dance has not yet ended." And she said all this in a deeper, more mellow voice, not different, merely the fulfillment of that girlish voice I had heard before.

I shall not speak of how we made love in the pavilion, save to say that she was right, it was the exquisite continuation and fulfillment of her eternal dance.

The magic of that night had entered into my awareness in such a manner as to show me in every gesture, sigh, movement, and touch, the secret of eternity. How no man and woman had ever made love like this before, and yet how this was all men and all women making love. Here. Now. *How can both these things be true at once?* I wondered. Then I realized that I would never know. I realized what a mystery is at last.

When I got back to the chariot, the Pookie Bear was curled up asleep on the floor. Soon it would be morning.

It was only a few nights later when the final mystery was revealed to me. I remember the feeling of absolute terror that overwhelmed me as I brought the chariot down.

No bells, chimes, flutes, not this time. The pavilion was gone. All that awaited me in the clearing was an ancient woman seated in a chair. An ancient woman, whom I had known as a lithe young girl and a fully blossomed mature lover —Inana. My Inana.

I fell at her feet, shivering. I remember my teeth actually chattered. I wanted to cry but I could not. I just said, "It's cold. It's so cold. How can this be? I can't stand it."

"Ah, but what can you do but stand it? It is the final irrevocable truth. The great mystery. We are young, suddenly we mature, we grow old and die, too soon, always too soon." Her voice was cracked, and thin as a reed, but it was her voice. Her smile was the same. And now, at last, I understood her bittersweet smile.

"You are everything to me," I said, "and so it will always be.

You are my sweetheart. My wife. My mother. How can there ever be another woman for me?"

"There is no other woman," she answered in ancient, cracking voice. "We are all the same woman. These sacred nights are nestled within the belly of eternity. Haven't you divined that? You of all men?

"When first you came to me, when I was a young girl, I was so startled because I was awaiting someone else. The Chosen One. The trees had been marked off with streamers as a sign for him to come to me. But you came instead. You chose yourself and came in his place. What could I do? You were as much a part of the mystery to me as was I to you. Never was it like this before. Always was it like this before.

"No, you will take other girls, women. And they will all be different but they will all be me. Us." Her voice hissed the word, and it seemed to hang in the hot summer air like a ripe fruit trembling on the branch. Still, I felt a terrible chill from within.

"Go now," she said. "The mystery is over. I'm dying. Go away."

"I can't leave you to die alone," I said.

"We all must die alone," she said. "Go now, my eternal beloved."

I went. I wanted to stay but I went. I wanted to say something more but I could not speak. I wanted to cry but I could not cry.

Back at the castle, as I stumbled trancelike up the stairway I heard someone calling me from the great dining hall. The voice was muffled as though someone was speaking through a cloak, which he was. And when I entered in, I could barely make out in the glow of the four soft nightlights from each wall, the tall, muscular figure waiting for me, but all the same I recognized it, for you could hardly mistake Bruno for anyone else.

I can't stand anymore, I thought, *not tonight.* But the mystery went on and on of its own accord, and now all of us humans involved in it were clearly only its pawns.

And so finally I had my wrestling match with Bruno. It began in the dark. He surged across the room, tried to grapple with me, and I tried to slip out to the side. We smashed into a chair and went over, but I slipped free, and both of us came to our feet quickly again.

The lights came on. *Good,* I thought. I needed the light more than he. But I never stopped to wonder who had turned them on.

I had no time. Bruno charged me immediately, obviously intending to press me continuously and give me no rest. And of course he assumed that I would avoid him all I possibly could. But he was wrong. I knew I couldn't avoid him. I made a halfhearted attempt to box. But you can't box a wrestler. Not one like Bruno. They will charge in and take a punch or two and tackle you down onto the floor and then you've had it. You can only wrestle a wrestler.

So I did the opposite of what he expected. I let him catch me around the waist and I latched my arms around his neck once again in the same headlock that was really a choke hold that I had applied on him before.

I tried to pull him over forward but he was too strong. He lifted me up by the legs and carried me, rather like a husband carrying a bride over the threshold.

"You'll have to squeeze harder than that," he said, and slammed me into the wall. I held on. "Okay, I will," I said. I gritted my teeth and clamped down.

He grabbed my wrists and pulled them apart. But I had my fingers locked. Even so, he actually managed to pry my arms apart and thrust me away. That's how strong he was.

But I flew back on him like a spring released, and latched the same lock around his neck and clamped down again.

This time he picked me up and surged across the room and

threw both of us into the table. We bounced off the table, knocked over a couple of chairs, and went down on the floor, him on top.

I gritted my teeth and clamped down harder. "You'll have to squeeze harder than that," he said again. But his voice was a hoarse whisper now. I gritted my teeth and clamped down harder.

In the long run, Uncle Henry had once remarked, endurance is everything. But not so much endurance, I discovered, as tenacity of mind. Will. I just kept squeezing harder no matter what Bruno did, no matter that it seemed I couldn't possibly do it. I just did it anyway.

And then, at last, I was on top and squeezing harder all the time, drenched with sweat, all the muscles of my body in an agony of all-out exertion.

"Give up."

"Never." But a whisper.

"Give up."

"Never." But I could hardly hear it.

Toward the end he was only mouthing the words. Nothing came out. I remember that his face was actually turning a shade of purple.

Finally I left him on the floor. Got a carafe of leftover wine from the table and poured a fair dollop of it on his face. I wondered if he were dead. He certainly looked it. But no, he choked and sat up.

For a moment he just sat there. And then the tears started to come. I envied him that.

"I was to be The Chosen One," he said. "You stole it from me. You stole everything."

He got up and started out, but in the doorway he turned. "I would have taken you in the wrestling match. I would have whipped you. They don't allow chokes. They have rules, you know."

"I'm the one who always breaks the rules," I said wearily,

and turned away. It was then I noticed my uncle Henry for the first time, seated in his thronelike chair at the end of the table, feet up, wineglass in hand, obviously well into his cups. It was he who had turned on the lights.

"Come and have a drink with me. Bring that bottle you have in your hand. More wine's always welcome at the mysteries."

I sat down. Took a swig from the bottle. It tasted pungent, bitter, but good. I had another swallow.

He was shaking his head at me. "When the young Apollo strides angrily through the halls of Olympus, even Zeus dare not remain seated," he said.

"I told you before, I don't believe in the Gods," I said.

"Nor do I," he said as before. "At least we have that much in common." He took a long drink. Filled his glass.

"Some wrestling match," he said. "You won it after all. None of the boys will ever know. They all think you are a coward. But you won it after all.

"Aren't you The Chosen One of all The Chosen Ones? The one who brought the mysteries to life, finally, totally, and irrevocably to life. It's as if they've gone on and on all these years waiting for you to complete them."

"How could you do it?" I asked him, not sure how I meant it.

He took another drink. "I loved her once myself," he said. "It's true. She was an accident. One of my genetic alterations that went wrong. She was so lovely. And all of a sudden she was a woman, and she grew old and died. She was everything at once. I can't tell you the effect it had on me."

"You don't have to tell me," I said.

"Somehow it was so important. So awesomely important, that I cloned her, and then the mysteries were born. Every fourteen years I clone her again. Every fourteen years she . . . she . . ." his voice choked up on him. He took another drink.

I said something that came out a whisper. Then I said it again louder. "I don't know if I can stand it." And suddenly, when I didn't want them anymore, the tears came at last. And then I was weeping in great wrenching gasps, totally out of control. I felt myself lifted off of my feet and hugged up in an unbreakable bearhug. *If Bruno had used that one,* I thought, *he'd have won for sure.* But I couldn't stop crying.

"Of course you can stand it," he said. "What else can we do?"

He pushed me out at arm's length and looked into my eyes. "By the Gods, what a man you've become. You break into the forbidden grove. Steal my chariot. Defeat Bruno in a wrestling match. You have become a man. A miracle. Hardly anyone does it nowadays."

He hugged me again and abruptly let me loose and turned away.

"You will be going home in the morning. I took the liberty of packing for you. The outer mystery is over for you. The inner will go on forever of its own accord. Go home. I will not see you in the morning. I never say good-bye." Abruptly, he left.

Months later, just as I was a week away from finishing my term at school, I got a holo in the mail. I must have had some inkling what it was because I checked to make sure my mother was out of the house before I played it.

Sure enough there was Mom, same worried expression, addressing Uncle Henry with "Whatever you do, be sure that Will doesn't get ahold of this. It would kill me if I thought . . ."

I shook my head—Uncle Henry, the mad artist.

"Will is even worse, much worse, than he ever was before. He's so arrogant. My God, Henry, he actually reminds me of you."

The holo went on and on about how terrible I had become, but I was no longer listening. I was poring through Mom's holos on a hunch. Would he have sent an answer? And then I had it in my hand.

"You can't control him anymore," the Storm King was telling us in that exuberant way of his, "none of you can—the school system, the church, you, or that mealymouthed husband of yours. He's become a man. In all its glory. He belongs here on New Olympus, shooting the lightning. Because by the Gods, he is more my son than yours now."

And I knew that in some strange way he was right. I was more like him than Mom or Dad. I always had been, in that secret place where I really lived, inside myself.

The next week I packed a few belongings and left home. But I did not go to New Olympus. New Olympus and Inana were an eternity that lived within me now, forever in summer. I knew instinctively that going back there would only mar that for me. For us.

I was headed out, instead, to the fringes of the belt, like my grandfather, and Henry's father, before us. It would be easy to find work there. Valuable training. They didn't care what schooling you had. It was out there mining asteroids that Grandfather had made the family fortune. Who knows, one day a hundred years from now, I might build my own work of art among the asteroids. If I gained the money. The expertise. And if I matured into an artist.

I didn't even leave a note. I went out the door and left New London, and I never saw my mother, or Uncle Henry, again.

RONALD ANTHONY CROSS's short stories have been published in Isaac Asimov's Science Fiction Magazine, Universe, *and* Far Frontiers. *One of his stories is included in the anthology* Fields of Fire, *edited by Jack Dann and Jeanne Van Buren Dann for TOR Books.*

THE

HIGH

TEST

Frederik Pohl

Can an intergallactic driving instructor save the solar system from an arrogant Fomalhautian who plans to use black holes as the ultimate weapon?

D ear Mom:
     As they say, there's good news and there's bad news here on Cassiopeia 43-G. The bad news is that there aren't any openings for people with degrees in quantum-mechanical astrophysics. The good news is that I've got a job. I started yesterday. I work for a driving school, and I'm an instructor.

I know you'll say that's not much of a career for a twenty-six-year-old man with a doctorate, but it pays the rent. Also it's a lot better than I'd have if I'd stayed on Earth. Is it true that the unemployment rate in Chicago is up to eighty percent? Wow! As soon as I get a few megabucks ahead I'm going to invite you all to come out here and visit me in the sticks so you can see how we live here—you may not want to go back! ?

Now, I don't want you to worry when I tell you that I get hazardous-duty pay. That's just a technicality. We driving instructors have it in our contracts, but we don't really earn it. At least, usually we don't—although there are times like yesterday. The first student I had was this young girl, right from Earth. Spoiled rotten! You know the kind, rich, and I guess you'd say beautiful, and really used to having her own way. Her name's Tonda Aguilar—you've heard of the Evanston Aguilars? In the recombinant foodstuff business? They're really rich, I guess. This one had her own speedster, and she really sulked that she couldn't drive it on an Earth license. See, they have this suppressor field; as soon as any vehicle comes into the system, zap, it's off, and it just floats until some licensed pilot comes out to fly it in. So I took her up, and right away she started giving me ablation. "Not so much takeoff boost! You'll burn out the tubes!" and "Don't ride the reverter in hyperdrive!" and "Get out of low orbit—you want to rack us up?"

Well, I can take just so much of that. An instructor is almost like the captain of a ship, you know. He's the boss! So I explained to her that my name wasn't "Chowderhead" or "Dullwit!" but James Paul Madigan, and it was the instructors who were supposed to yell at the students, not the other way around. Well, it was her own speedster, and a really neat one at that. Maybe I couldn't blame her for being nervous about somebody else driving it. So I decided to give her a real easy lesson—practicing parking orbits. If you can't do that you don't deserve a license! And she was really rotten at it. It looks easy, but there's an art to cutting the hyperdrive with just the right residual velocity, so you slide right into your assigned coordinates. The more she tried the farther off she got. Finally she demanded that I take her back to the spaceport. She said I was making her nervous. She said she'd get a different instructor for tomorrow, or she'd just move on to some other system where they didn't have benefacted chimpanzees giving driving lessons.

I just let her rave. Then the next student I had was a Fomalhautian. You know that species: They've got two heads and scales and forked tails, and they're always making a nuisance of themselves in the United Systems? If you believe what they say on the vidcom, they're bad news—in fact, the reason Cassiopeia installed the suppressor field was because they had a suspicion the Fomalhautians were thinking about invading and taking over 43-G. But this one was nice as pie! Followed every instruction. Never gave me any argument. Apologized when he made a mistake and got us too close to one of the mini black holes near the primary. He said that was because he was unfamiliar with the school ship, and said he'd prefer to use his own space yacht for the next lesson. He made the whole day better, after that silly, spoiled rich brat!

I was glad to have a little cheering up, to tell you the truth. I was feeling a little lonesome and depressed. Probably it's because it's so close to the holidays. It's hard to believe that back in Chicago it's only three days until Christmas, and all the store windows will be full of holodecorations and there'll be that big tree in Grant Park and I bet it's snowing . . . and here on Cassiopeia 43-G it's sort of like a steam bath with interludes of Niagara Falls.

I do wish you a Merry Christmas, Mom! Hope my gifts got there all right.

Love,
Jim Paul

2213 12 25 late

Dear Mom:

Well, Christmas Day is just about over. Not that it's any different from any other day here on 43-G, where the human colonists were mostly Buddhist or Moslem and the others were —well! You've seen the types that hang around the United Systems building in Palatine—smelled them, too, right? Especially those Arcturans. I don't know whether those people have any religious holidays or not, and I'm pretty sure I don't *want* to know.

Considering that I had to work all day, it hasn't been such a bad Christmas at that. When I mentioned to Torklemiggen —he's the Fomalhautian I told you about—that today was a big holiday for us he sort of laughed and said that mammals had really quaint customs. And when he found out that part of the custom was to exchange gifts he thought for a minute. (The way Fomalhautians think to themselves is that their heads whisper in each other's ear—really grotesque!) Then he said that he had been informed it was against the law for a student to give anything to his driving instructor, but if I wanted to fly his space yacht myself for a while he'd let me do it. And he would let it go down on the books of the school as instruction time, so I'd get paid for it. Well, you bet I wanted to! He has some swell yacht. It's long and tapered, sort of shark-shape, like the TU-Lockheed 4400 series, with radar-glyph vision screens and a cruising range of nearly 1800 l.y. I don't know what its top speed is—after all, we had to stay in our own system!

We were using his own ship, you see, and of course it's Fomalhautian made. Not easy for a human being to fly! Even though I'm supposed to be the instructor and Torklemiggen the student, I was baffled at first. I couldn't even get it off the ground until he explained the controls to me and showed me how to read the instruments. There's still plenty I don't know, but after a few minutes I could handle it well enough not to kill us out of hand. Torklemiggen kept daring me to circle the black holes. I told him we couldn't do that, and he got this kind of sneer on one of his faces, and the two heads sort of whispered together for a while. I knew he was thinking of something cute, but I didn't know what at first.

Then I found out!

You know that CAS 43, our primary, is a red giant star with an immense photosphere. Torklemiggen bragged that we could fly right through the photosphere! Well, of course I hardly believed him, but he was so insistent that I tried it out. He was right! We just greased right through that thirty-thousand-degree plasma like nothing at all! The hull began to turn red, then yellow, then straw-colored—you could see it on the edges of the radar-glyph screen—and yet the inside temperature stayed right on the button of 40 degrees Celsius. That's 43-G normal, by the way. Hot, if you're used to Chicago, but nothing like it was outside! And when we burst out into vacuum again there was no thermal shock, no power surge, no instrument fog. Just beautiful! It's hard to believe that any individual can afford a ship like this just for his private cruising. I guess Fomalhaut must have some pretty rich planets!

Then when we landed, more than an hour late, there was the Aguilar woman waiting for me. She found out that the school wouldn't let her change instructors once assigned. I could have told her that; it's policy. So she had to cool her heels until I got back. But I guess she had a little Christmas spirit somewhere in her ornery frame, because she was quite polite about it. As a matter of fact, when we had her doing parking orbits she was much improved over the last time. Shows what a first-class instructor can do for you!

Well, I see by the old chronometer on the wall that it's the day after Christmas now, at least by Universal Greenwich Time it is, though I guess you've still got a couple of hours to go in Chicago. One thing, Mom. The Christmas packages you sent didn't get here yet. I thought about lying to you and saying they'd come and how much I liked them, but you raised me always to tell the truth. (Besides, I didn't know what to thank you for!) Anyway, Merry Christmas one more time from—

Jim Paul

2213 12 30 0200UGT

Dear Mom:

Another day, another kilobuck. My first student today was a sixteen-year-old kid. One of those smart-alecky ones, if you know what I mean. (But you probably don't, because you certainly never had any kids like that!) His father was a combat pilot in the Cassiopeian navy, and the kid drove that way, too. That wasn't the worst of it. He'd heard about Torklemiggen. When I tried to explain to him that he had to learn how to go slow before he could go fast, he really let me have it. Didn't I know his father said the Fomalhautians were treacherous enemies of the Cassiopeian way of life? Didn't I know his father said they were just waiting for their chance to invade? Didn't I know—

Well, I could take just so much of this fresh kid telling me what I didn't know. So I told him he wasn't as lucky as Torklemiggen. He only had one brain, and if he didn't use all of it to fly this ship I was going to wash him out. That shut him up pretty quick.

But it didn't get much better, because later on I had this fat lady student who just oughtn't to get a license for anything above a skateboard. Forty-six years old, and she's never driven before—but her husband's got a job asteroid-mining, and she wants to be able to bring him a hot lunch every day. I hope she's a better cook than a pilot! Anyway I was trying to put her at ease, so she wouldn't pile us up into a comet nucleus or something, so I was telling her about the kid. She listened, all sympathy—you know, how teenage kids were getting fresher every year—until I mentioned that what we were arguing about was my Fomalhautian student. Well, you should have heard her then! I swear, Mom, I think these Cassiopeians are psychotic on the subject. I wish Torklemiggen were here so I could talk to him about it—somebody said the reason CAS 43-G put the suppressor system in in the first place was to keep them from invading, if you can imagine that! But he had to go home for a few days. Business, he said. Said he'd be back next week to finish his lessons.

Tonda Aguilar is almost finished, too. She'll solo in a couple of days. She was my last student today—I mean yesterday, actually, because it's way after midnight now. I had her practicing zero-G approaches to low-mass asteroids, and I happened to mention that I was feeling a little lonesome. It turned out she was, too, so I surprised myself by asking her if she was doing anything tomorrow night, and she surprised me by agreeing to a date. It's not romance, Mom, so don't get your hopes up. It's just that she and I seem to be the only beings in this whole system who know that tomorrow is New Year's Eve!

Love,
Jim Paul

2214 01 02 2330UGT

Dear Mom:

I got your letter this morning, and I'm glad that your leg is better. Maybe next time you'll listen to Dad and me! Remember, we both begged you to go for a brand-new factory job when you got it, but you kept insisting a rebuilt would be just as good. Now you see. It never pays to try to save money on your health!

I'm sorry if I told you about my clients without giving you any idea of what they looked like. For Tonda, that's easy enough to fix. I enclose a holo of the two of us, which we took this afternoon, celebrating the end of her lessons. She solos tomorrow. As you can see, she is a really good-looking woman, and I was wrong about her being spoiled. She came out here on her own to make her career as a dermatologist. She wouldn't take any of her old man Aguilar's money, so all she had when she got here was her speedster and her degree and the clothes on her back. I really admire her. She connected right away with one of the best body shops in town, and she's making more money than I am.

As to Torklemiggen, that's harder. I tried to make a holopic of him, but he got really upset—you might even say nasty. He said inferior orders have no right to worship a Fomalhautian's image, if you can believe it! I tried to explain that we didn't have that in mind at all, but he just laughed. He has a mean laugh. In fact, he's a lot different since he came back from Fomalhaut on that business trip. Meaner. I don't mean that he's different physically. Physically he's about a head taller than I am, except that he has two of them. Two heads, I mean. The head on his left is for talking and breathing, the one on his right for eating and showing expression. It's pretty weird to see him telling a joke.

His jokes are pretty weird all by themselves, for that matter. I'll give you an example. This afternoon he said, "What's the difference between a mammal and a roasted hagensbiffik with murgry sauce?" And when I said I didn't even know what those things were, much less what the difference was, he laughed himself foolish and said, "No difference!"

What a spectacle. There was his left-hand head talking and sort of yapping that silly laugh of his, dead-pan, while the right-hand head was all creased up with giggle lines. Some sense of humor.

I should have told you that Torklemiggen's left-hand head looks kind of like a chimpanzee's, and the right one is a little bit like a fox's. Or maybe an alligator's, because of the scales. Not pretty, you understand. But you can't say that about his ship! It's as sweet a job as I've ever driven. I guess he had some extra accessories put on it while he was home, because I noticed there were five or six new readouts and some extra hand controls. When I asked him what they were for he said they had nothing to do with piloting and I would find out what they were for soon enough. I guess that's another Fomalhautian joke of some kind.

Well, I'd write more but I have to get up early in the morning. I'm having breakfast with Tonda to give her some last-minute run throughs before she solos. I think she'll pass all right. She surely has a lot of smarts for somebody who was a former Miss Illinois!

Love,
Jim Paul

2214 01 03 late

Dear Mom:

Your Christmas package got here today, and it was really nice. I loved the socks. They'll come in real handy in case I come back to Chicago for a visit before it gets warm. But the cookies were pretty crumbled, I'm afraid—delicious, though! Tonda said she could tell that they were better than anything she could bake, before they went through the CAS 43-G customs, I mean.

Torklemiggen is just about ready to solo. To tell you the truth, I'll be glad to see the last of him. The closer he gets to his license the harder he is to get along with. This morning he began acting crazy as soon as we got into high orbit. We were doing satellite-matching curves. You know, when you come in on an asymptotic tractrix curve, just whistling through the upper atmosphere of the satellite and then back into space. Nobody ever does that when they're actually driving, because what is there on a satellite in this system that anybody would want to visit? But they won't pass you for a license if you don't know how.

The trouble was, Torklemiggen thought he already did know how, better than I did. So I took the controls away to show him how, and that really blew his cool. "I could shoot better curves than you in my fourth instar!" he snarled out of his left head, while his right head was looking at me like a rattlesnake getting ready to strike. I mean, mean. Then when I let him have the controls back he began shooting curves at one of the mini black holes. Well, that's about the biggest no-no there is. "Stop that right now," I ordered. "We can't go within a hundred thousand miles of one of those things! How'd you pass your written test without knowing that?"

"Do not exceed your life station, mammal!" he snapped, and dived in toward the hole again, his fore hands on the thrust and roll controls while his hind hands reached out to fondle the buttons for the new equipment. And all the time his left-hand head was chuckling and giggling like some fiend out of a monster movie.

"If you don't obey instructions," I warned him, "I will not approve you for your solo." Well, that fixed him. At least he calmed down. But he sulked for the rest of the lesson. Since I didn't like the way he was behaving, I took the controls for the landing. Out of curiosity I reached to see what the new buttons were. "Severely handicapped mammalian species!" his left head screeched, while his right head was turning practically pale pink with terror. "Do you want to destroy this planet?"

I was getting pretty suspicious by then, so I asked him straight out: "What is this stuff, some kind of weapon?"

That made him all quiet. His two heads whispered to each other for a minute, then he said, very stiff and formal, "Do you speak to me of weapons when you mammals have these black holes in orbit? Have you considered their potential for weaponry? Can you imagine what one of them would do, directed toward an inhabited planet?" He paused for a minute, then he said something that really started me thinking. "Why," he asked, "do you suppose my people have any wish to bring culture to this system, except to demonstrate the utility of these objects?" We didn't talk much after that, but it was really on my mind.

After work, when Tonda and I were sitting in the park, feeding the flying crabs and listening to the singing trees, I told her all about it. She was silent for a moment. Then she looked up at me and said seriously, "Jim Paul, it's a rotten thing to say about any being, but it almost sounds as though Torklemiggen has some idea about conquering this system."

"Now, who would want to do something like that?" I asked.

She shrugged. "It was just a thought," she apologized. But we both kept thinking about it all day long, in spite of our being so busy getting our gene tests and all—but I'll tell you about that later!

Love,
Jim Paul

2214 01 05 2200UGT

Dear Mom:

Take a good look at this date, the 5th of January, because you're going to need to remember it for a while! There's big news from CAS 43-G tonight . . . but first, as they say on the tube, a few other news items.

Let me tell you about that bird Torklemiggen. He soloed this morning. I went along as check pilot, in a school ship, flying matching orbits with him while he went through the whole test in his own yacht. I have to admit that he was really nearly as good as he thought he was. He slid in and out of hyperdrive without any power surge you could detect. He kicked his ship into a corkscrew curve and killed all the drives, so he was tumbling and rolling and pitching all at once, and he got out of it into a clean orbit, using only the side thrusters. He matched parking orbits. He ran the whole course without a flaw. I was still sore at him, but there just wasn't any doubt that he'd shown all the skills he needed to get a license. So I called him on the private TBS frequency and said, "You've passed, Torklemiggen. Do you want a formal written report when we land, or shall I call in to have your license granted now?"

"Now. This instant, mammal!" he yelled back, and added something in his own language. I didn't understand it, of course. Nobody else could hear it, either, because the talk-between-ships circuits don't carry very far. So I guess I'll never know just what it is he said, but, honestly, Mom, it surely didn't sound at all friendly. All the same, he'd passed.

So I ordered him to null his controls, and then I called in his test scores to the master computer on 43-G. About two seconds later he started screeching over the TBS, "Vile mammal! What have you done? My green light's out, my controls won't respond. Is this some treacherous warm-blood trick?"

He sure had a way of getting under your skin. "Take it easy, Torklemiggen," I told him, not very friendlily—he was beginning to hurt my feelings. "The computer is readjusting your status. They've removed the temporary license for your solo, so they can lift the suppressor field permanently. As soon as the light goes on again you'll be fully licensed, and able to fly anywhere in this system without supervision."

"Hah," he grumbled, and then for a moment I could hear his heads whispering together. Then—well, Mom, I was going to say he laughed out loud over the TBS. But it was more than a laugh. It was mean, and gloating. "Depraved, retarded mammal," he shouted, "my light is on—and now all of Cassiopeia is mine!"

I was really disgusted with him. You expect that kind of thing, maybe, from some space-happy sixteen-year-old who's just got his first license. Not from an eighteen-hundred-year-old alien who has flown all over the Galaxy. It sounded sick! And sort of worrisome, too. I wasn't sure just how to take him. "Don't do anything silly, Torklemiggen," I warned him over the TBS.

He shouted back: "Silly? I do nothing silly, mammal! Observe how little silly I am!" And the next thing you know he was whirling and diving into hyperspace—no signal, nothing! I had all I could do to follow him, six alphas deep and going fast. For all I knew, we could have been on our way back to Fomalhaut. But he only stayed there for a minute. He pulled out right in the middle of one of the asteroid belts, and as I followed up from the alphas I saw that lean, green yacht of his diving down on a chunk of rock about the size of an office building.

I had noticed, when he came back from his trip, that one of the new things about the yacht was a circle of ruby-colored studs around the nose of the ship. Now they began to glow brighter and brighter. In a moment a dozen streams of ruby light reached out from them, ahead toward the asteroid. There was a bright flare of light, and the asteroid wasn't there anymore!

Naturally, that got me upset. I yelled at him over the TBS: "Listen, Torklemiggen, you're about to get yourself in real deep trouble! I don't know how they do things back on Fomalhaut, but around here that's grounds for an action to suspend your license! Not to mention they could make you pay for that asteroid!"

"Pay?" he screeched. "It is not I who will pay, functionally inadequate live-bearer, it is you and yours! You will pay most dreadfully, for now we have the black holes!" And he was off again, back down into hyperspace, and one more time it was about all I could do to try to keep up with him.

There's no sense trying to transmit in hyperspace, of course. I had to wait until we were up out of the alphas to answer him, and by that time, I don't mind telling you, I was *peeved.* I never would have found him on visual, but the radar-glyph picked him up zeroing in on one of the black holes. What a moron! "Listen, Torklemiggen," I said, keeping my voice level and hard, "I'll give you one piece of advice. Go back to base.

Land your ship. Tell the police you were just carried away, celebrating passing your test. Maybe they won't be too hard on you. Otherwise, I warn you, you're looking at a thirty-day suspension plus you could get a civil suit for damages from the asteroid company." He just screeched that mean laughter. I added, "And I told you, keep away from the black holes!"

He laughed some more, and said, "Oh, lower than a smiggs-troffle, what delightfully impudent pets you mammals will make now that we have these holes for weapons—and what joy it will give me to train you!" He was sort of singing to himself, more than to me, I guess. "First reduce this planet! Then the suppressor field is gone, and our forces come in to prepare the black holes! Then we launch one on every inhabited planet until we have destroyed your military power. And then—"

He didn't finish that sentence, just more of that chuckling, cackling, *mean* laugh.

I felt uneasy. It was beginning to look as though Torklemig-gen was up to something more than just high jinks and deviltry. He was easing up on the black hole and kind of crooning to himself, mostly in that foreign language of his but now and then in English: "Oh, my darling little assault vessel, what destruction you will wreak! Ah, charming black hole, how catastrophic you will be! How foolish these mammals who think they can forbid me to come near you—"

Then, as they say, light dawned. "Torklemiggen," I shouted, "you've got the wrong idea! It's not just a traffic regulation that we have to stay away from black holes! It's a lot more serious than that!"

But I was too late. He was inside the Roche limit before I could finish.

They don't have black holes around Fomalhaut, it seems. Of course, if he'd stopped to think for a minute he'd have realized what would happen—but then, if Fomalhautians ever stopped to think they wouldn't be Fomalhautians.

I almost hate to tell you what happened next. It was pretty gross. The tidal forces seized his ship, and they stretched it.

I heard one caterwauling astonished yowl over the TBS. Then his transmitter failed. The ship ripped apart, and the pieces began to rain down into the Schwarzschild boundary and plasmaed. There was a quick, blinding flash of fall-in energy from the black hole, and that was all Torklemiggen would ever say or do or know.

I got out of there as fast as I could. I wasn't really feeling very sorry for him, either. The way he was talking there toward the end, he sounded as though he had some pretty dangerous ideas.

When I landed it was sundown at the field, and people were staring and pointing toward the place in the sky where Torklemiggen had smeared himself into the black hole. All bright purplish and orangey plasma clouds—it made a really beautiful sunset, I'll say that much for the guy! I didn't have time to admire it, though, because Tonda was waiting, and we just had minutes to get to the Deputy Census Director, Division of Reclassification, before it closed.

But we made it.

Well, I said I had big news, didn't I? And that's it, because now your loving son is

Yours truly,
James Paul Aguilar-Madigan,
the newlywed!

FREDERIK POHL is a multi-award-winning author, having received the American Book Award, several Hugo and Nebula Awards, and two John W. Campbell Memorial Awards.

A LETTER

FROM

THE CLEARYS

Connie Willis

Who were the fortunate—Lynn and her family, or the Clearys? A Nebula Award-winning story.

T here was a letter from the Clearys at the post office. I put it in my backpack along with Mrs. Talbot's magazine and went outside to untie Stitch.

He had pulled his leash out as far as it would go and was sitting around the corner, half-strangled, watching a robin. Stitch never barks, not even at birds. He didn't even yip when Dad stitched up his paw. He just sat there the way we found him on the front porch, shivering a little and holding his paw up for Dad to look at. Mrs. Talbot says he's a terrible watchdog, but I'm glad he doesn't bark. Rusty barked all the time and look where it got him.

I had to pull Stitch back around the corner to where I could get enough slack to untie him. That took some doing, because he really liked that robin. "It's a sign of spring, isn't it, fella?" I said, trying to get at the knot with my fingernails. I didn't loosen the knot, but I managed to break one of my fingernails off to the quick. Great. Mom will demand to know if I've noticed any other fingernails breaking.

My hands are a real mess. This winter I've gotten about a hundred burns on the back of my hands from that stupid wood stove of ours. One spot, just above my wrist, I keep burning over and over so it never has a chance to heal. The stove isn't big enough, and when I try to jam a log in that's too long, that same spot hits the inside of the stove every time. My stupid brother, David, won't saw them off to the right length. I've asked him and asked him to please cut them shorter, but he doesn't pay any attention to me.

I asked Mom if she would please tell him not to saw the logs so long, but she didn't. She never criticizes David. As far as she's concerned he can't do anything wrong just because he's twenty-three and was married.

"He does it on purpose," I told her. "He's hoping I'll burn to death."

"Paranoia is the number-one killer of fourteen-year-old girls," Mom said. She always says that. It makes me so mad I feel like killing her. "He doesn't do it on purpose. You need to be more careful with the stove, that's all." But all the time she was holding my hand and looking at the big burn that won't heal like it was a time bomb set to go off.

"We need a bigger stove," I said, and yanked my hand away. We do need a bigger one. Dad closed up the fireplace and put the wood-stove in when the gas bill was getting out of sight, but it's just a little one, because Mom didn't want one that would stick way out in the living room. Anyway, we were only going to use it in the evenings.

We won't get a new one. They are all too busy working on the stupid greenhouse. Maybe spring will come early, and my hand will have half a chance to heal. I know better. Last winter the snow kept up till the middle of June, and this is only March. Stitch's robin is going to freeze his little tail if he doesn't head back south. Dad says that last year was unusual, that the weather will be back to normal this year, but he doesn't believe it either or he wouldn't be building the greenhouse.

As soon as I let go of Stitch's leash, he backed around the corner like a good boy and sat there, waiting for me to stop sucking my finger and untie him. "We'd better get a move on," I told him. "Mom'll have a fit." I was supposed to go by the general store to try and get some tomato seeds, but the sun was already pretty far west, and I had at least a half-hour's walk home. If I got home after dark, I'd get sent to bed without supper, and then I wouldn't get to read the letter. Besides, if I didn't go to the general store today they'd have to let me go tomorrow, and I wouldn't have to work on the stupid greenhouse.

Sometimes I feel like blowing it up. There's sawdust and mud on everything, and David dropped one of the pieces of plastic on the stove while they were cutting it, and it melted onto the stove and stank to high heaven. But nobody else even notices the mess; they're too busy talking about how wonderful it's going to be to have homegrown watermelon and corn and tomatoes next summer.

I don't see how it's going to be any different from last summer. The only things that came up at all were the lettuce and the potatoes. The lettuce was about as tall as my broken fingernail and the potatoes were as hard as rocks. Mrs. Talbot said it was the altitude, but Dad said it was the funny weather and this crummy Pike's Peak granite that passes for soil around here. He went up to the little library in the back of the general store and got a do-it-yourself book on greenhouses and started tearing everything up, and now even Mrs. Talbot is crazy about the idea.

The other day I told them, "Paranoia is the number-one killer of people at this *altitude*," but they were too busy cutting slats and stapling plastic to pay any attention to me.

Stitch walked along ahead of me, straining at his leash, and as soon as we were across the highway, I took it off. He never runs away like Rusty used to. Anyway, it's impossible to keep him out of the road, and the times I've tried keeping him on his leash, he dragged me out into the middle and I got in trouble with Dad over leaving footprints. So I keep to the frozen edges of the road, and he moseys along, stopping to sniff at potholes; when he gets behind, I whistle at him and he comes running right up.

I walked pretty fast. It was getting chilly out, and I'd only worn my sweater. I stopped at the top of the hill and whistled at Stitch. We still had a mile to go. I could see the Peak from where I was standing. Maybe Dad is right about spring coming. There was hardly any snow on the Peak, and the burned part didn't look quite as dark as it did last fall, like maybe the trees were coming back.

Last year at this time the whole peak was solid white. I remember because that was when Dad and David and Mr. Talbot went hunting and it snowed every day and they didn't get back for almost a month. Mom just about went crazy before they got back. She kept going up to the road to watch for them even though the snow was five feet deep and she was leaving footprints as big as the Abominable Snowman's. She took Rusty with her even though he hated the snow about as much as Stitch hates the dark. And she took a gun. One time she tripped over a branch and fell down in the snow. She sprained her ankle and was almost frozen stiff by the time she made it back to the house. I felt like saying, "Paranoia is the number-one killer of mothers," but Mrs. Talbot butted in and said the next time I had to go with her and how this was what happened when people were allowed to go places by themselves, which meant me going to the post office. I said I could take care of myself, and Mom told me not to be rude to Mrs. Talbot and Mrs. Talbot was right, I should go with her next time.

She wouldn't wait till her ankle was better. She bandaged it up and we went the very next day. She didn't say a word the whole trip, just limped through the snow. She never even looked up till we got to the road. The snow had stopped for a little while, and the clouds had lifted enough so you could see the Peak. It was like a black-and-white photograph, the gray sky and the black trees and the white mountain. The Peak was completely covered with snow. You couldn't make out the toll road at all.

We were supposed to hike up the Peak with the Clearys.

When we got back to the house, I said, "The summer before last the Clearys never came."

Mom took off her mittens and stood by the stove, pulling off chunks of frozen snow. "Of course they didn't come, Lynn," she said.

Snow from my coat was dripping onto the stove and sizzling. "I didn't mean *that*," I said. "They were supposed to come the first week in June. Right after Rick graduated. So what happened? Did they just decide not to come or what?"

"I don't know," she said, pulling off her hat and shaking her hair out. Her bangs were all wet.

"Maybe they wrote to tell you they'd changed their plans," Mrs. Talbot said. "Maybe the post office lost the letter."

"It doesn't matter," Mom said.

"You'd think they'd have written or something," I said.

"Maybe the post office put the letter in somebody else's box," Mrs. Talbot said.

"It doesn't matter," Mom said, and went to hang her coat over the line in the kitchen. She wouldn't say another word about them. When Dad got home I asked him too about the Clearys, but he was too busy telling about the trip to pay any attention to me.

Stitch didn't come. I whistled again and then started back after him. He was all the way at the bottom of the hill, his nose buried in something. "Come *on,*" I said, and he turned around and then I could see why he hadn't come. He'd gotten himself tangled up in one of the electric wires that was down. He'd managed to get the cable wound around his legs like he does his leash sometimes, and the harder he tried to get out, the more he got tangled up.

He was right in the middle of the road. I stood on the edge of the road, trying to figure out a way to get to him without leaving footprints. The road was pretty much frozen at the top of the hill, but down here snow was still melting and running across the road in big rivers. I put my toe out into the mud, and my sneaker sank in a good half-inch, so I backed up, rubbed out the toe print with my hand, and wiped my hand on my jeans. I tried to think what to do. Dad is as paranoic about footprints as Mom is about my hands, but he is even worse about my being out after dark. If I didn't make it back in time, he might even tell me I couldn't go to the post office anymore.

Stitch was coming as close as he ever would to barking. He'd gotten the wire around his neck and was choking himself. "All right," I said. "I'm coming." I jumped out as far as I could into one of the rivers and then waded the rest of the way to Stitch, looking back a couple of times to make sure the water was washing away the footprints.

I unwound Stitch and threw the loose end of the wire over

to the side of the road, where it dangled from the pole, all ready to hang Stitch next time he comes along.

"You stupid dog," I said. "Now hurry!" and I sprinted back to the side of the road and up the hill in my sopping wet sneakers. He ran about five steps and stopped to sniff at a tree. "Come on!" I said. "It's getting dark. Dark!"

He was past me like a shot and halfway down the hill. Stitch is afraid of the dark. I know, there's no such thing in dogs. But Stitch really is. Usually I tell him, "Paranoia is the number-one killer of dogs," but right now I wanted him to hurry before my feet started to freeze. I started running, and we got to the bottom of the hill about the same time.

Stitch stopped at the driveway of the Talbots' house. Our house wasn't more than a few hundred feet from where I was standing, on the other side of the hill. Our house is down in kind of a well formed by hills on all sides. It's so deep and hidden you'd never even know it's there. You can't even see the smoke from our wood stove over the top of the Talbots' hill. There's a shortcut through the Talbots' property and down through the woods to our back door, but I don't take it anymore. "Dark, Stitch," I said sharply, and started running again. Stitch kept right at my heels.

The Peak was turning pink by the time I got to our driveway. Stitch peed on the spruce tree about a hundred times before I got it dragged back across the dirt driveway. It's a real big tree. Last summer Dad and David chopped it down and then made it look like it had fallen across the road. It completely covers up where the driveway meets the road, but the trunk is full of splinters, and I scraped my hand right in the same place as always. Great.

I made sure Stitch and I hadn't left any marks on the road (except for the marks he always leaves—another dog could find us in a minute. That's probably how Stitch showed up on our front porch: he smelled Rusty) and then got under cover of the hill as fast as I could. Stitch isn't the only one who gets nervous after dark. And besides, my feet were starting to hurt. Stitch was really paranoid tonight. He didn't even quit running after we were in sight of the house.

David was outside, bringing in a load of wood. I could tell just by looking at it that they were all the wrong length. "Cutting it kind of close, aren't you?" he said. "Did you get the tomato seeds?"

"No," I said. "I brought you something else, though. I brought everybody something."

I went on in. Dad was rolling out plastic on the living-room floor. Mrs. Talbot was holding one end for him. Mom was holding the card table, still folded up, waiting for them to finish so she could set it up in front of the stove for supper. Nobody even looked up. I unslung my backpack and took out Mrs. Talbot's magazine and the letter.

"There was a letter at the post office," I said. "From the Clearys."

They all looked up.

"Where did you find it?" Dad said.

"On the floor, mixed in with all the third-class stuff. I was looking for a magazine for Mrs. Talbot."

Mom leaned the card table against the couch and sat down. Mrs. Talbot looked blank.

"The Clearys were our best friends," I explained to her. "From Illinois. They were supposed to come see us the summer before last. We were going to hike up Pike's Peak and everything."

David banged in the door. He looked at Mom, sitting on the couch, and Dad and Mrs. Talbot, still standing there holding the plastic like a couple of statues. "What's wrong?" he said.

"Lynn says she found a letter from the Clearys today," Dad said.

David dumped the logs on the hearth. One of them rolled

onto the carpet and stopped at Mom's feet. Neither of them bent over to pick it up.

"Shall I read it out loud?" I said, looking at Mrs. Talbot. I was still holding her magazine. I opened up the envelope and took out the letter.

" 'Dear Janice and Todd and everybody,' " I read. " 'How are things in the glorious West? We're raring to come out and see you, though we may not make it quite as soon as we hoped. How are Carla and David and the baby? I can't wait to see little David. Is he walking yet? I bet Grandma Janice is so proud she's busting her britches. Is that right? Do you westerners wear britches, or have you all gone to designer jeans?' "

David was standing by the fireplace. He put his head down across his arms on the mantelpiece.

" 'I'm sorry I haven't written, but we were very busy with Rick's graduation, and anyway I thought we would beat the letter out to Colorado. But now it looks like there's going to be a slight change in plans. Rick has definitely decided to join the Army. Richard and I have talked ourselves blue in the face, but I guess we've just made matters worse. We can't even get him to wait to join until after the trip to Colorado. He says we'd spend the whole trip trying to talk him out of it, which is true, I guess. I'm just so worried about him. The Army! Rick says I worry too much, which is true, too, I guess, but what if there was a war?' "

Mom bent over and picked up the log that David had dropped and laid it on the couch beside her.

" 'If it's okay with you out there in the Golden West, we'll wait until Rick is done with basic the first week in July and then all come out. Please write and let us know if this is okay. I'm sorry to switch plans on you like this at the last minute, but look at it this way: you have a whole extra month to get into shape for hiking up Pike's Peak. I don't know about you, but I sure can use it.' "

Mrs. Talbot had dropped her end of the plastic. It didn't

land on the stove this time, but it was so close to it that it was curling from the heat. Dad just stood there, watching it. He didn't even try to pick it up.

" 'How are the girls? Sonja is growing like a weed. She's out for track this year and bringing home lots of medals and dirty sweat socks. And you should see her knees! They're so banged up I almost took her to the doctor. She says she scrapes them on the hurdles, and her coach says there's nothing to worry about, but it does worry me a little. They just don't seem to heal. Do you ever have problems like that with Lynn and Melissa?

" 'I know, I know. I worry too much. Sonja's fine. Rick's fine. Nothing awful's going to happen between now and the first week in July, and we'll see you then. Love, the Clearys. P.S. Has anybody ever fallen off Pike's Peak?' "

Nobody said anything. I folded up the letter and put it back in the envelope.

"I should have written them," Mom said. "I should have told them, 'Come now.' Then they would have been here."

"And we would probably have climbed up Pike's Peak that day and gotten to see it all go blooey and us with it," David said, lifting his head up. He laughed and his voice caught on the laugh and cracked. "I guess we should be glad they didn't come."

"Glad?" Mom said. She was rubbing her hands on the legs of her jeans. "I suppose we should be glad Carla took Melissa and the baby to Colorado Springs that day so we didn't have so many mouths to feed." She was rubbing her jeans so hard that she was going to rub a hole right through them. "I suppose we should be glad those looters shot Mr. Talbot."

"No," Dad said. "But we should be glad the looters didn't shoot the rest of us. We should be glad they only took the canned goods and not the seeds. We should be glad the fires didn't get this far. We should be glad . . ."

"That we still have mail delivery?" David said. "Should we

be glad about that, too?" He went outside and shut the door behind him.

"When I didn't hear from them, I should have called or something," Mom said.

Dad was still looking at the ruined plastic. I took the letter over to him. "Do you want to keep it or what?" I said.

"I think it's served its purpose," he said. He wadded it up, tossed it in the stove, and slammed the door shut. He didn't even get burned. "Come help me on the greenhouse, Lynn," he said then.

It was pitch dark outside and really getting cold. My sneakers were starting to get stiff. Dad held the flashlight and pulled the plastic tight over the wooden slats. I stapled the plastic every two inches all the way around the frame, and my finger about every other time. After we finished one frame, I asked Dad if I could go back in and put on my boots.

"Did you get the seeds for the tomatoes?" he said, as if he hadn't even heard me. "Or were you too busy looking for the letter?"

"I didn't look for it," I said. "I found it. I thought you'd be glad to get the letter and know what happened to the Clearys."

Dad was pulling the plastic across the next frame so hard that it was getting little puckers in it. "We already knew," he said.

He handed me the flashlight and took the staple gun out of my hand. "You want me to say it?" he said. "You want me to tell you exactly what happened to them? All right. I would imagine they were close enough to Chicago to have been vaporized when the bombs hit. If they were, they were lucky. Because there aren't any mountains like ours around Chicago. So they got caught in the fire storm or they died of flashburns or radiation sickness or else some looter shot them."

"Or their own family," I said.

"Or their own family." He put the staple gun against the

wood and pulled the trigger. "I have a theory about what happened the summer before last," he said. He moved the gun down and shot another staple into the wood. "I don't think the Russians started it or the United States either. I think it was some little terrorist group somewhere, or maybe just one person. I don't think they had any idea what would happen when they dropped their bomb. I think they were just so hurt and angry and frightened by the way things were that they just lashed out. With a bomb." He stapled the frame clear to the bottom and straightened up to start on the other side. "What do you think of that theory, Lynn?"

"I told you," I said. "I found the letter while I was looking for Mrs. Talbot's magazine."

He turned and pointed the staple gun at me. "But whatever reason they did it for, they brought the whole world crashing down on their heads. Whether they meant it or not, they had to live with the consequences."

"If they lived," I said. "If somebody didn't shoot them."

"I can't let you go to the post office anymore," he said. "It's too dangerous."

"What about Mrs. Talbot's magazines?"

"Go check on the fire," he said.

I went back inside. David had come back and was standing by the fireplace again, looking at the wall. Mom had set up the card table and the folding chairs in front of the fireplace. Mrs. Talbot was in the kitchen, cutting up potatoes, only it looked like it was onions from the way she was crying.

The fire had practically gone out. I stuck a couple of wadded-up magazine pages in to get it going again. The fire flared up with a brilliant blue and green. I tossed a couple of pine cones and some sticks onto the burning paper. One of the pine cones rolled off to the side and lay there in the ashes. I grabbed for it and hit my hand on the door of the stove.

Right in the same place. Great. The blister would pull the

old scab off and we could start all over again. And of course Mom was standing right there, holding the pan of potato soup. She put it on top of the stove and grabbed up my hand like it was evidence in a crime or something. She didn't say anything. She just stood there, holding it and blinking.

"I burned it," I said. "I just burned it."

She touched the edges of the old scab, as if she was afraid of catching something.

"It's a burn!" I shouted, snatching my hand back and cramming David's stupid logs into the stove. "It isn't radiation sickness. It's a *burn!*"

"Do you know where your father is, Lynn?" she asked.

"He's out on the back porch," I said, "building his stupid greenhouse."

"He's gone," she said. "He took Stitch with him."

"He can't have taken Stitch," I said. "Stitch is afraid of the dark." She didn't say anything. "Do you *know* how dark it is out there?"

"Yes," she said, and looked out the window. "I know how dark it is."

I got my parka off the hook by the fireplace and started out the door.

David grabbed my arm. "Where the hell do you think you're going?"

I wrenched away from him. "To find Stitch. He's afraid of the dark."

"It's too dark," he said. "You'll get lost."

"So what? It's safer than hanging around this place," I said, and slammed the door shut on his hand.

I made it halfway to the woodpile before he grabbed me.

"Let me go," I said. "I'm leaving. I'm going to go find some other people to live with."

"There aren't any other people! For Christ's sake, we went all the way to South Park last winter. There wasn't anybody.

We didn't even see those looters. And what if you run into them, the looters who shot Mr. Talbot?"

"What if I do? The worst they could do is shoot me. I've been shot at before."

"You're acting crazy. You know that, don't you?" he said. "Coming in here out of the clear blue, taking potshots at everybody with that crazy letter!"

"Potshots!" I said, so mad that I was afraid I was going to start crying. "Potshots! What about last summer? Who was taking potshots then?"

"You didn't have any business taking the shortcut," David said. "Dad told you never to come that way."

"Was that any reason to try and *shoot* me? Was that any reason to *kill* Rusty?"

David was squeezing my arm so hard that I thought he was going to snap it right in two. "The looters had a dog with them. We found its tracks all around Mr. Talbot. When you took the shortcut and we heard Rusty barking, we thought you were the looters." He looked at me. "Mom's right. Paranoia's the number-one killer. We were all a little crazy last summer. We're all a little crazy all the time, I guess. And then you pull a stunt like bringing that letter home, reminding everybody of everything that's happened, of everybody we've lost. . . ." He let go of my arm and looked down at his hand.

"I told you," I said. "I found it while I was looking for a magazine. I thought you'd all be glad I found it."

"Yeah," he said. "I'll bet."

He went inside and I stayed out a long time, waiting for Dad and Stitch. When I came in, nobody even looked up. Mom was still standing at the window. I could see a star over her head. Mrs. Talbot had stopped crying and was setting the table. Mom dished up the soup and we all sat down. While we were eating, Dad came in.

He had Stitch with him. And all the magazines. "I'm sorry,

Mrs. Talbot," he said. "If you'd like, I'll put them under the house and you can send Lynn for them one at a time."

"It doesn't matter," she said. "I don't feel like reading them anymore."

Dad put the magazines on the couch and sat down at the card table. Mom dished him up a bowl of soup. "I got the seeds," he said. "The tomato seeds had gotten water-soaked, but the corn and squash were okay." He looked at me. "I had to board up the post office, Lynn," he said. "You understand that, don't you? You understand that I can't let you go there anymore? It's just too dangerous."

"I told you," I said. "I found it. While I was looking for a magazine."

"The fire's going out," he said.

After they shot Rusty, I wasn't allowed to go anywhere for a month for fear they'd shoot me when I came home, not even when I promised to take the long way around. But then Stitch showed up and nothing happened and they let me start going again. I went every day till the end of summer and after that whenever they'd let me. I must have looked through every pile of mail a hundred times before I found the letter from the Clearys. Mrs. Talbot was right about the post office. The letter was in somebody else's box.

CONNIE WILLIS is the winner of two Nebula Awards, one of which was for "A Letter from the Clearys," and one Hugo Award. At present she is working on Lincoln's Dreams, *a novel to be published by Bantam Books.*

PLAYING

FOR

KEEPS

Jack C. Haldeman II

The aliens are meaner than junkyard dogs,
but Johnny is accustomed to handling
distasteful matters.

J ohnny Russell was playing in his backyard when the aliens
landed. He was Tarzan in a land of giant ferns while they
invaded Philadelphia, but had shifted over to Superman before
Baltimore fell. Johnny was eight years old and easily bored. By
the time his mother called him in for dinner, the aliens were
all over Washington, D.C. Things were a mess. Ugly green
monsters were everywhere. Lots of people were real upset,
especially Johnny. They were having spinach for dinner.

Johnny hated spinach more than anything else in the world,
except maybe brussels sprouts and creamed corn.

He made such a fuss at the table, trying to slip the dog his spinach, that his parents sent him to bed early. That was too bad, because there was a lot of neat stuff on television that night. Eight years old is just the right age for appreciating a good monster or two. Johnny slept through it all, dreaming that he was flying his tree house over the ocean in search of lost continents.

His parents, on the other hand, were totally immersed in aliens of the real sort. There was no escaping them. Even the twenty-four-hour sports network was full of monsters. Specials followed specials all night long. Bert and Sara stayed glued to the tube, afraid they might miss something. It was an exciting time to watch television, even better than the time the dam burst at Fort Mudge. A good crisis brought out the best in the electronics media, no doubt about that.

They watched the national news for a while and then switched over to the local news. They even tuned in PBS and watched a panel of distinguished professors pointing sticks at an alien's picture. It was exciting. Sara made popcorn and Bert put another six pack of beer in the fridge.

"Don't you think we ought to wake up Johnny?" asked Sara, salting the popcorn.

Bert opened another beer. "No," he said. "We've got to teach him not to play with his food. A parent has certain obligations, you know." Bert had always been the strict one.

"But isn't that a little severe?" asked Sara. "After all, he's very fond of hideous beasts."

"No," said Bert. "Remember what he did with the brussels sprouts?"

Sara turned pale. "I thought I'd never get it all out. The air conditioning hasn't worked right since."

"And the creamed corn?"

Sara shuddered at the memory of the bomb squad marching through their living room in knee-deep water. "You're right," she said, passing him the popcorn.

They settled back and watched the early news, the special news, the update news, the fast-break news, the late news, and the late-late news. In between, they watched the news in brief and the news in detail. They were saturated with news and popcorn and all they got out of it was indigestion and no news at all. Nobody knew much of anything about the aliens except they were crawling all over the place and were meaner than junkyard dogs.

Their silver, cigar-shaped spaceships had simply appeared out of nowhere with a shimmering colorful splash of glitter not unlike the special effects of a once-popular TV show still in reruns. It was horrible. People fled in panic, especially when the monsters started coming out of the spaceships.

The aliens stood about eight feet tall with thick, stocky bodies. Their four arms had too many elbows and not enough fingers. Folds of wrinkled green skin covered their neckless heads, and their three unblinking eyes held what could only be interpreted as malice and contempt for the entire human race.

At first it was hoped that they might be a congenial star-roving race of beings, eager as puppy dogs to give mankind all sorts of marvelous inventions. These hopes were quickly dashed. The aliens seemed far more interested in vaporizing people. Helicopters and airplanes that approached the hovering ships vanished in white-hot explosions. People who were foolish enough to make threatening gestures or stray too close went up in smoke. It made for good television footage, but did little to aid any kind of mutual understanding.

Mutual understanding, as a matter of fact, didn't seem to be the aliens' strong suit. They just didn't appear to be interested. Some of the best minds on Earth had attempted to establish communication with the aliens. Some of the best minds on Earth had been vaporized, too. The aliens were obviously intelligent, but they didn't have much to say.

Bert and Sara were about ready to turn in, having watched

the instant replay of the destruction of Washington for the fourth or fifth time. It was impressive, but not really all that great. The Japanese had done it better in that movie about the radioactive frog. Sara washed the popcorn bowls.

"I'll bet Johnny will be excited when he wakes up," she said. "Channel Four said they've even seen a couple aliens right here in town. Imagine that."

"I don't think we ought to tell the boy about them," said Bert. "At least not yet."

"For goodness sakes, honey. Why not?"

"The child has an active enough imagination as it is. There's no sense in getting him all riled up. Remember the time he thought he saw that UFO down by the river?"

Sara nearly dropped the bowl she was drying. That had been a near thing. Johnny had pulled every fire alarm in town, and only their friendship with the judge had kept their names out of the paper.

"Besides," said Bert. "What does a kid know about monsters? He's only eight years old."

Sara nodded. He was right, as always.

But Johnny wasn't completely fooled. When little Freddy Nabors didn't show up by twelve o'clock, he knew something was wrong. He and Freddy *always* messed around together on Saturday afternoon. Sometimes they went on dangerous secret missions, but usually they just played. By twelve-fifteen Johnny had decided a plague must have killed all the kids on Earth but him so he went out into the backyard to play.

He wasn't allowed to go out behind the garage, so naturally it was his favorite place. It was full of old lumber and rusty nails. Lumber was more fun to play with than almost anything. Sometimes he built boats out of the scraps, and sometimes spaceships. Today he built a Grand Prix car. It was low and sleek, faster than a bat. He pretended it was orange with black trim. Since he couldn't find any wheels, he used cinder blocks for racing tires.

Diving into the hairpin turn, he had just passed Fangio and was gaining on Andretti when he saw the monster. Johnny was not impressed. He'd seen better ones on television. Sticking his tongue out between his lips and making a rude noise, he downshifted with a raspberry and pulled to the side of the road. After taking off his imaginary helmet and racing gloves, he got out of his fabricated car and stared at the alien. The alien stared back. Three eyes to two, the alien had an edge; but Johnny never flinched. The Lone Ranger wouldn't have backed down, and neither would he.

In the distance Johnny could see one of their spaceships hovering over the river. It looked just like the one he'd seen before. He knew better than to head for the fire alarms this time, though. His father would tan his hide.

The alien grunted and pointed at his ship and then to himself. Johnny stood as firm as Wyatt Earp, his jaw set like Montgomery Clift's, playing for keeps, his body held with the stern pride of John Wayne. He didn't nod; he didn't blink. He stared at the monster with Paul Newman's baby-blue eyes, hard as ice. He wished he'd worn long pants, though. Shorts just didn't cut it when you were staring down a monster.

The alien started waving all its arms in the air, grunting like crazy. Johnny was frightened, but he didn't give an inch. He could have been Gary Cooper standing alone in the middle of a dusty street facing an angry mob with only the badge on his chest and the goodness in his heart to protect him. Johnny could almost hear the people scurrying for cover. The helmet and racing gloves were useless. He should have had his six-shooter.

The alien kicked at the dust, smoothing out an area between them. He bent over and Johnny hunkered down to join him. At least now he knew what to expect. They were about to talk, or *palaver*, as Slim Pickins would say.

The alien picked up a stick and drew a large circle in the dirt. From a fold in his tunic he removed a small golden globe, which he placed precisely in the center. He pointed to the sun and then to the globe. Johnny nodded, his face as deadpan as if he were trying to fill an inside straight.

The monster drew three concentric circles around the golden globe and placed another globe on the third circle. It was smaller than the first and covered with blue and white swirls. He patted the dirt, waved his arms in circles all around them, and pointed to the globe. Johnny bit his lip. This was getting complicated.

The alien continued drawing circles in the dust and setting down the small globes. When he had finished, nine of them surrounded the larger yellow one. With a flourish he took one more from his tunic. This one was special; it was silver and seemed to glow with a light from within. He set it outside the farthest circle and pointed first to himself, then to the space-ship, and finally to the silver sphere.

Slowly he began rolling the sphere into the ring of circles. As he passed the outermost globe, he snarled and crushed it into the dirt beneath one of his massive thumbs. He continued rolling the silver sphere toward the center, snarling and crush-ing as he demolished each of the small globes. When he reached the third globe from the center, his lips drew back in a hideous sneer and he rose to his full height, towering over the crouching boy. The alien gloated, roaring with bone-chilling laughter as he crushed the small blue globe under his foot, grinding it into the dirt with a vengeance.

This, at last, was something Johnny could understand. It was a challenge. Without rising, he reached around to his back pocket. It was still there, as he knew it would be. He'd won it from Freddy Nabors two years ago and he never went any-where without it. It was his talisman, his good luck piece. It was also his weapon and had never let him down. He gritted his teeth and took it reassuringly in his hand. It was blue with milky white bands, a perfect agate.

He dropped and took quick aim, oblivious to the ranting and

raving of the alien. He'd been under pressure before. This was nothing new. With a flick of his thumb the aggie sailed across the dust, crashing into the silver ball, sending it careening out of orbit into the yellow one. They both flew outside the circle.

He stood—as a man would stand after battle—and retrieved all the marbles. He held them high above his head.

"Keepsies," he said and slipped them into his pocket.

The alien backed away in horror, babbling wildly. With a shimmer and a pop, he disappeared. An instant later the spaceship vanished in a similar fashion, as did all the spaceships and all the aliens all over the world.

Johnny climbed back into his Grand Prix car and accelerated through the gears. He was nearly a lap behind by now and would have to do some fancy driving to catch up. Besides, his mother was fixing creamed corn tonight, and the boy who had saved the world had important things on his mind.

As he took the checkered flag he wondered how Conan would have handled creamed corn.

JACK C. HALDEMAN II lives on a forty-acre farm outside Archer, Florida, with his wife and daughter. He works part-time at the University of Florida in the field of artificial intelligence and expert systems, and in addition to the many articles he has published on that subject, he is the author of eight science fiction novels and approximately 150 short stories. His most recent novel is The Fall of Winter, *published by Baen Books.*

POTENTIAL

Isaac Asimov

Despite the opinion of two scientists, his parents, and his employer, gardening isn't all Roland is good for.

N adine Triomph checked the long list of symbols for—what was it?—the tenth time. She did not think she could get anything out of it that Multivac had not, but it was only human to try.

She passed it over to Basil Seversky. "It's completely different, Basil," she said.

"You can see that at a glance," said Basil gloomily.

"Well, don't drag. That's good. So far the only gene combinations that Multivac has dredged up seem to have been minor variations on a theme. Now this one is different."

Basil put his hands into the pockets of his lab jacket and leaned his chair back against the wall. He felt the line of his hips absently and noted it was gaining a certain softness. He was getting pudgy all over, he thought, and didn't like it.

He said, "Multivac doesn't tell us anything we don't tell it first. We don't really know that the basic requirements for telepathy are valid, do we?"

Nadine felt defensive. It was Basil who had worked out the neurological requirements, but it was she who had prepared the program by which Multivac scanned the potential gene structures to see which might produce those requirements.

She said, "If we have two rather different sets of genetic patterns, as we now have, we can work out—or try to work out—the common factors, and this could give us a lead as to the validity."

"In theory—but we'll be working in theory forever. If Multivac works at its present speed for the remaining lifetime of the sun as a main-sequence star, it will not have gone through a duodecillionth of all the possible structural variations of the genes that might exist, let alone the possible modifications introduced by their order on the chromosomes."

"We might get lucky." They had held the same conversation—upbeat versus downbeat—a dozen times, with minor variations in detail.

"Lucky? The word hasn't been invented to describe the kind of impossible luck we would need. And if we do pick out a million different genetic patterns with potential for telepathy, we then have to ask what the odds are that someone now alive will have such a gene pattern, or anything near it."

"We can modify," said Nadine.

"Oh? Have you come across an existing human genetic pattern that can be modified by known procedures into something Multivac says will produce telepathy?"

"The procedures will improve in the future and if we keep

Multivac working and keep on registering all human genetic patterns at birth—"

"—*And,*" Basil continued singsong, "if the Planetary Genetic Council continues to support the program adequately, *and* if we continue to get the time-sharing we need on Multivac, *and* if—"

It was at that point that Multivac interrupted with one more item, and all a dazed Basil could say afterward was, "I don't believe it."

It seemed that Multivac's routine scanning of registered genetic patterns of living human beings had turned up one that matched the new pattern it had worked out as possessing telepathic potential—and the match was virtually exact.

Basil said, "I don't believe it."

Nadine, who had always been forced into unreasoning faith by Basil's consistent pessimism, said sunnily, "Here he is, just the same. Male. Aged fifteen. Name Roland Washman. Only child. Plainview, Iowa. American Region, actually."

Basil studied Roland's genetic pattern, as delivered by Multivac, and compared it with the pattern worked out by Multivac from theoretical considerations. He muttered, again, "I don't believe it."

"It's there before you."

"Do you know the odds against this?"

"It's there before you. The universe is billions of years old and there's been time for a great many unbelievable coincidences to happen."

"Not this unbelievable." Basil pulled himself together. "Iowa was included in one of the areas we scanned for telepathic presence and nothing ever showed up. Of course, the pattern only shows the *potential* for telepathy—"

It was Basil's plan to approach indirectly. However much the Planetary Genetic Council might post the possibility of telepathy as one of the goal-patterns to be searched for, along with musical genius, variable-gravitational endurance, cancer resistance, mathematical intuition, and several hundred other items, it remained that telepathy had an ingrained unpopularity.

However exciting the thought of "reading minds" might seem in the abstract, there was always an uneasy resistance to the thought of having one's mind read. Thought was the unassailable bastion of privacy, and it would not be surrendered without a struggle. Any controvertible claim to have discovered telepathy would, therefore, be surely controverted.

Basil, therefore, overrode Nadine's willingness to move straight to the point and to interview the young man directly, by making that very point.

"Oh, yes," he grumbled, "and we will let our eagerness lure us into announcing we have found a telepath so that the PGC will put half-a-dozen authorities on his track in order to disprove the claim and ruin our scientific careers. Let's find out all we can about him *first.*"

The disappointed Nadine consoled herself with the obvious fact that in a computerized society, every human being left tracks of all kinds from the moment of conception, and that it could all be recovered without much trouble, and even quickly.

"Umm," said Basil, "not very bright in school."

"It could be a good sign," said Nadine. "Telepathic ability would surely take up a sizable fraction of the higher functioning of the brain and leave little over for abstract thought. That might explain why telepathy has not evolved more noticeably in the human species. The disadvantage of low intelligence would be contra survival."

"He's not exactly an *idiot savante.* Dull-normal."

"Which might be exactly right."

"Rather withdrawn. Doesn't make friends easily. Rather a loner."

Nadine said excitedly, *"Exactly* right. Any early evidence of telepathic ability would frighten, upset, and antagonize people. A youngster lacking judgment would innocently expose the motives of others in his group and be beaten up for his pains. Naturally, he would withdraw into himself."

Data was gathered for a long time thereafter, and Basil said finally, "Nothing! There's nothing known about him; no report, not one, that indicates anything that can be twisted into a sign of telepathy. There's not even any comment to the effect that he's 'peculiar.' He's almost disregarded."

"Absolutely right. The reaction of others forced him, early on, to hide all telepathic ability, and that same telepathic ability guided his behavior so as to avoid all unfavorable notice. It's remarkable how it fits."

Basil stared at her with disfavor. "You can twist anything into supporting your romantic view of this. Look! He's fifteen and that's too old. Let's suppose that he was born with a certain amount of telepathic ability and that he early learned not to display it. Surely the talent would have atrophied and be entirely gone by now. That has to be so, for if he remained a full telepath, he couldn't possibly have avoided displaying it now and then, and that would have attracted attention."

"No, Basil. At school, he's by himself and does as little work as possible—"

"He's not scapegoated, as he would be if he were a telepathic little wise guy."

"I told you! He knows when he would be and avoids it. Summers he works as a gardener's assistant and, again, doesn't encounter the public."

"He encounters the gardener, and yet he keeps the job. It's his third summer there right now, and if he were a telepath, the gardener would get rid of him. No, it's close—but no cigar. It's too late. What we need is a new-born child with that same genetic pattern. Then we might have something—*maybe.*"

Nadine rumpled her fading blond hair and looked exasperated. "You're deliberately trying to avoid tackling the problem by denying it exists. Why don't we interview the gardener? If you're willing to go to Iowa—I tell you what, I'll pay the plane fare, and you won't have to charge it to the project, if that's what's bothering you."

Basil held up his hand. "No, no, the project will bear it, but I tell *you* what. If we find no signs of telepathic ability, and we won't, you'll owe me one fancy dinner at a restaurant of my choice."

"Done," said Nadine eagerly, "and you can even bring your wife."

"You'll lose."

"I don't care. Just so we don't abandon the matter too soon."

The gardener was by no means enthusiastically cooperative. He viewed the two as government officials and did not approve of them for that reason. When they identified themselves as scientists that was no better ground for approval. And when they asked after Roland, he neared the point of outright hostility.

"What do you want to know about Roland for? Done anything?"

"No, no," said Nadine, as winningly as she might. "He might qualify for special schooling, that's all."

"What kind of schooling? Gardening?"

"We're not sure."

"Gardening's all he's good for, but he's good at that. Best I've ever had. He doesn't need no schooling in gardening."

Nadine looked about appreciatively at the greenhouse and at the neat rows of plants outside as well. "He does all that?"

"Have to admit it," said the gardener. "Never this good without him. But it's all he's good for."

Basil said, "Why is that all he's good for, sir?"

"He's not very bright. But he's got this talent. He'll make anything grow."

"Is he odd in any way?"

"What do you mean, odd?"

"Funny? Peculiar? Strange?"

"Being that good a gardener is strange, but I don't complain."

"Nothing else."

"No. What you looking for, mister?"

Basil said, "I really don't know."

That evening Nadine said, "We've got to study the boy."

"Why? What have you heard that gives you any hope?"

"Suppose you're right. Suppose it's all atrophied. Still, we might find a *trace* of the ability."

"What would we do with a trace? Small effects would not be convincing. We have had a full century of experience with that, from Rhine onward."

"Even if we don't get anything that would prove anything to the world, so what? What about *ourselves?* The important thing is that we'd satisfy ourselves that when Multivac says a particular genetic pattern has the potential for telepathy, it's right. And if it's right, that would mean your theoretical analysis—and my programming, too—was right. Don't you want to put your theories to the test and find confirmatory evidence? Or are you afraid you won't?"

"I'm not afraid of that. I *am* afraid of wasting time."

"One test is all I ask. Look, we ought to see his parents anyway, for whatever they can tell us. After all, they knew him when he was a baby and had, in full, whatever telepathic powers he might have had to begin with—and then we'll get permission to have him match random numbers. If he fails that, we go no further. We waste no more time."

Roland's parents were stolid and totally uninformative. They seemed as slow as Roland was reported to be, and as self-contained.

There had been nothing odd about their son as a baby, they said. They repeated that without guilty overemphasis. Strong and healthy, they said, and a hard-working boy who earned good money over the summer and went to high school the rest of the year. Never in any trouble with the law or in any other way.

"Might we test him?" asked Nadine. "A simple test?"

"What for?" asked Washman. "I don't want him bothered."

"Government survey. We're choosing fifteen-year-old boys here and there so we can study ways to improve methods of schooling."

Washman shook his head. "I don't want my boy bothered."

"Well," said Nadine, "you must understand there's two hundred fifty dollars to the family for each boy tested." (She carefully avoided looking at Basil, certain that his lips would have tightened in anger.)

"Two hundred fifty dollars?"

"Yes," said Nadine, trying hard. "After all, the test takes time, and it's only fair the government pay for the time and trouble."

Washman cast a slow glance at his wife, and she nodded. He said, "If the boy is willing, I guess it would be okay."

Roland Washman was tall for his age and well built, but there seemed no danger in his muscles. He had a gentle way about him, and dark, quiet eyes looked out of his well-browned face.

He said, "What am I supposed to do, mister?"

"It's very easy," said Basil. "You have a little joystick with the numbers 0 to 9 on it. Every time that little red light goes on, you push one of the numbers."

"Which one, mister?"

"Whichever one you want. Just one number and the light will go out. Then when it goes on, another number, and so on, until the light stops shining. This lady will do the same thing. You and I will sit opposite each other at this table, and she will sit at this other little table with her back to us. I don't want you to think about what number you're going to push."

"How can I do it without thinking, mister? You got to think."

"You may just have a feeling. The light goes on, and it might seem as though you have a feeling to push an 8, or a 6, or whatever. Just do it, then. One time you might push a 2, next time a 3, next time a 9, or maybe another 2. Whatever you want."

Roland thought about it a bit, then nodded. "I'll try, mister, but I hope it don't take too long, because I don't see the sense of it."

Basil adjusted the sensor in his left ear-canal unobtrusively and then gazed at Roland as benignly as he could.

The tiny voice in his left ear breathed, "Seven," and Basil thought: *Seven.*

And the light flashed on Roland's joystick and on Nadine's similar joystick, and both pushed a number.

It went on and on: 6, 2, 2, 0, 4, 3, 6, 8. . . .

And finally Basil said, "That's enough, Roland."

They gave Roland's father five fifty-dollar bills, and they left.

In their motel room, Basil leaned back, disappointment fighting with the satisfaction of I-told-you-so.

"Absolutely nothing," he said. "Zero correlation. The computer generated a series of random numbers and so did Roland,

and the two did not match. He picked up absolutely nothing from my thought processes."

"Suppose," said Nadine, with a dying hope, "he could read your mind but was deliberately masking that fact."

Basil said, "You know better than that. If he were trying to be wrong on purpose, he would almost certainly be *too* wrong. He would match me less often than chance would dictate. Besides, you were generating a series of numbers, too, and you couldn't read my thoughts either, and he couldn't read yours. He had two sets of different numbers assailing him each time, and there was zero correlation—neither positive *nor* negative with either. That can't be faked. We have to accept it; he doesn't have it, now, and we're out of luck. We'll have to keep looking, and the odds of coming across anything like this again—"

He looked hopeless.

Roland was in the front yard, watching after Basil and Nadine, as their car drove off in the bright sunlight.

He had been frightened. First they had talked to his boss, then to his parents, and he thought that they must have found out.

How could they have found out? It was impossible to find out, but why else were they so curious?

He had worried about all that business of picking numbers, even though he didn't see how it could do any harm. Then it came to him that they thought he could hear human voices in his mind. They were trying to think the right numbers at him.

They couldn't do that. How could he know what *they* were thinking? He couldn't ever tell what people were thinking. He knew that for certain. Couldn't ever!

He laughed a little to himself, very quietly. People always thought it was only people that counted.

And then came the little voice in his mind, very thin and very shrill.

When—? When—? When—?

Roland turned his head. He knew it was a bee winging toward him. He wasn't hearing the bee, but the whole mind of the whole hive.

All his life he had heard the bees thinking, and they could hear him. It was wonderful. They pollinated his plants and they avoided eating them, so that everything he touched grew beautifully.

The only thing was they wanted more. They wanted a leader; someone to tell them how to beat back the push of humanity. Roland wondered how that could be done. The bees weren't enough, but suppose he had all the animals. Suppose he learned how to blend minds with all of them. Could he?

The bees were easy, and the ants. Their minds built up in large crowds. And he could hear the crows now. He didn't used to. And he was beginning to make out something with the cattle, though they weren't worth listening to, hardly.

Cats? Dogs? All the bugs and birds?

What could be done? How far could he go?

A teacher had once said to him that he didn't live up to his potential.

When—? When—? When—? thought the bee.

Not yet—Not yet—Not yet— thought Roland.

First, he had to reach his potential.

ISAAC ASIMOV is one of the most prolific authors living today. He has won numerous awards, and his most recent novel is Foundation and Earth. *He is the editorial director of* Isaac Asimov's Science Fiction Magazine.

POWER

TIMES

ONE

J. Michael Matuszewicz

When one can have everything if he only walks the line between being overly moral and being greedy, his self-consciousness can cause oversights.

I wish I could say that I felt some apprehension as I went to answer the door; but honestly, I was simply upset about having to get out of the bathtub. A fast glance around the living room told me it was still okay; this was Sunday morning, and I usually give the apartment a good cleaning before going out Friday night in case I find someone interesting to bring home.

My first impression of the man standing on my doorstep was of his eyes. You could not trust a man with eyes like that: they showed he felt too little to care about anyone but himself.

I stepped back, and he came in without invitation. Clutching my beltless bathrobe around me, I closed the door and motioned him to a chair.

Although he carried no briefcase, he had samples with him; his suit coat pockets bulged with angular things. Another look at him told me no one would buy from a man like this. He was fairly well dressed, in that his clothes were new, but he wore his jacket unbuttoned and his silk shirt had no tie. His dark hair was recently styled, but carelessly combed, his nails manicured but dirty. He evidently had the money to comfort himself, but clearly did not care what impression he made.

He looked at me with those heavy, amoral eyes, and I shrank a little. Obviously this was no salesman.

I got myself a glass of water from the kitchenette and sat down to face my company/intruder/guest. Neither of us spoke for some time, but there was no noticeable silence—we were both waiting for something.

"You selling something?" I finally asked, knowing he was not.

He laughed in short shocks and drew something from one pocket. It was a Möbius strip machined from a block of solid brass and suspended in a cube of clear plastic. At the center of the ring was a small point of light, a microstar. The star was a chip of tourmaline coated with phosphorus. The chip radiates electrons when warmed; the coating glows when struck by electrons.

I know. I made it. But I had made only one—

And I could see mine still sitting on my bookcase as I held his in my hand. It even had the little scratch on the bottom I had not polished out.

He smiled at me as I turned the cube over in my hand. I lifted mine from the case and held them side by side. They were identical; every glow, every shimmer, every imperfection.

"It took me eighteen days to make this," I told him, holding up mine. "What novelty store did you pick this up in?" I asked him, holding up his.

His face smiled warmly, but his eyes were still cold. Without speaking he pulled another cube from his pocket. I took it from him and held all three up to the light. The same brass strip, the same microstar, the same scratch.

When you make something with your own hands; when you handle mathematics, machine tools, and precious gems to create a new type of optical art; when you create uniqueness; well, you feel cheated when someone hands you cheap copies.

But these were more than copies. They were too real, too exact.

"You have a hobby," he said flatly. I sat down to listen. "I used to have the same hobby. Old Magic, Old Superstitions. They gave me these." I turned them over in my lap, thinking I should be upset with myself for mixing them, but listened to his explanation. "I found a Golden Genii," he told me in too cold a voice.

I looked up at him but he was not laughing, and I could not suspect him of being deceived. And he had been right. My hobby was Old Magic, or more specifically, why tales of magic are the same all over the world. The Golden Genii itself was mentioned in legends on four continents.

"I found him," my guest/intruder/storyteller continued. "And he had the old formulas. The ancients told their stories true; a Golden Genii grants three wishes—and he is tricky and mischievous."

Old Magic—the histories of witches and wizards; every civilization had its accounts of crystal balls, little people, and transmutations. I had always known them to have a thread of truth. It had been an interest that had become my avocation. Too many people had found it to be my obsession.

"Three wishes," I said weakly.

"I asked for time to think." The smile showed in his eyes now. He was as keenly interested as he hoped I was. I was.

"The genii granted that as my first wish and told me he would come back in three days. I decided then I had to plan this exactly right, and I think I did."

"First, immortality," I told him.

"Right." He grinned. "But not simply not dying. I would not want to age eternally without even the recourse to suicide."

I felt challenged. Effective eternal youth with contingency options.

"I decided," he went on before I could come up with an answer, "I wanted an inner second self. An alternate personality with conscious and active control over all bodily functions up to and including regeneration of organs, chemical balancing acts, and an inherent anti-aging. All within and under the guidance and responsibility of my consciousness, of course."

"Right," I agreed with him. "But also," I added, "the ability to generate new organs and create new chemical cycles to mimic the evolution of mankind so you can remain in the mainstream of society without ever looking out of style, body-wise."

My guest looked slightly pained.

"No," he admitted. "I never thought of that."

"Last wish," I half-asked, half-demanded.

"Machines."

"A transmuter?"

"Something better. Six different machines all utilizing the same principle of total conversion of matter/energy potentials." He reached into his suit-coat pocket and after a brief tussle withdrew a calculator-shaped box, about eight inches long and four wide. The face was partly mirrored; the other half contained three large switches. After looking around for a minute he picked up a lighter from my end table and placed it on the box's mirror.

"Read," he said as he pushed the first switch. "It analyzes the energy patterns of the matter." The lighter stood balancing on the box.

"Absorb," he said as he pushed the second switch. The lighter disappeared instantly. No flash, no fade, just gone. "It stores the energy in the matter as a battery stores electricity." His explanations almost made sense. Almost.

"Produce," he said as he pushed the third switch. The lighter was back. He tossed it to me. I could find no signs it had been tampered with or changed.

"Produce," he said as he pushed the third switch again. My lighter returned just as it had disappeared, standing on the mirrored surface of the machine, except that it was still in my lap, too.

I spent an hour examining both lighters. They were both mine. They were filled to the same level. They were dented where I had pried the cap to refill the disposable cylinder. They were the same but not one.

Then my friend/visitor/stranger made three more, each at the push of a switch.

"A duplicating machine. Every office should have one." I guess I was a little punchy by then.

"And five more machines," the man reminded me.

"But why?" I asked him. "If you had only two, you could use one to duplicate the other. You can have an unlimited number of them."

"No," he explained quietly. As he talked, he stepped around the breakfast bar and started rummaging around in my refrigerator. "I have that machine in several sizes, even one that is modular. I add as many sections as I want to make any size platform." He continued speaking while stuffing apple pie into his mouth. "The five other machines are on the same principle, but use the power in different ways."

"An access to parallel universes," I whispered. "If current

theory is right, then you only need to balance inertial energy levels to pass from one universe to the next."

"Right again." He slunk conspiratorily next to me. "Except that not all universes are parallel, or intersecting. Some are crazy skews, and some are the same universe—just a little late."

"You're from this world, this—my—Earth, but your universe is ahead. But not too far." It came tumbling in on me. "And you want to test your machines, maybe experiment with a few cultures back here before you muck around with your own home."

He smiled, full face, eyes included. He laid the duplicator on the arm of my chair, hefted my last peach, and went to the door.

"I knew you were a bright boy. You have exactly two years to make the best of that little gadget. If you are overly moral and stupid, you will smash it to little bits. If you are greedy and stupid, you will flood the market with gold. Use it carefully and it will be a great benefit."

As he finished my/his fruit, he stepped out into the hall.

"We both profit from your success. Only I will profit from your failure. Use it with care."

"I will," I told the closing door. "I will."

"I'm disappointed in you," my guest/accomplice/intruder told me as he leaned over the balcony railing and studied the city lights.

I closed the sliding terrace doors to shut the sounds of the party into the penthouse.

"There are problems," I told him straight. "And I wanted to move slowly, to avoid suspicion."

"But," he smiled without expression in his eyes, "you are only a millionaire. I expected much, much more."

"There is a limiting factor, as you will agree." Somehow his attitude disturbed me, and I had no more reason to trust him now than I had when he first visited me two years before. "The more power I attain," I told him, "the less time I can spend duplicating things, and the duplicator is my only real source of power. My enterprises all rest on its performance: precious metals, ceramics, semiconductors. And the machine can only do so much, and the need keeps expanding." I leaned against the rail and avoided his eyes. "Are the others doing any better?"

"Some, yes," he admitted. "The you in the timeline I just left has done much better. But," he added slowly, "in two places I could find absolutely no trace of you; it was as if you had followed me out of that world."

"What do you do with me now?"

He laughed in soft shocks. "Nothing. Leave you here to carry on. If I need something special I may call on you for it, but it won't be much. If you would start some research projects you could be of real value. I'd like to get a good technology mixture."

As he swirled his drink his eyes saddened. "It works both ways, you know. I have given you a little machine to make you rich and powerful, but you dare not let anyone else know about it. You are the custodian of a great and valuable tool that can lift your world out of its misery, but it is worth your life if anyone knew about it.

"I, on the other hand," he continued sourly, "I have become a guardian of many worlds. I must allow only so much disruption on any one Earth, but need the disruption to further my aims—to amass power I can take home. Gold and silver are not power and wealth if there is too much of them. I need only one perfect world to live on, but I am beginning to feel responsible for all the other worlds I am using in order to fashion that one ultimate home."

His thoughts seemed jumbled, as if I had walked in on the

middle of a conversation, but still he made sense—he was just as trapped as I was.

"The Golden Genii," I said after many moments of silence. "I wonder what his world is like?"

My visitor smiled faintly. "If their technology is our magic, their magic must be beyond our comprehension."

"I have examined the machine you gave me. I wish I had the nerve to take it apart—see how it works."

"Don't bother," he told me gravely. "There are a few slabs of crystal and some shimmering lights, that's all."

There was a long silence between us, and the sounds of my neglected party beckoned me, but I still had to know one thing.

"Why do you trust me?" I asked him. "And the me in other universes? And is it only me?"

"That is very simple. I can trust you because I can step away from this world and never return. You cannot follow me. And it is usually you, after all. I want to deal with as few people as possible, and you are basically the same all over." He said that with a smiling face and deceitful eyes.

After he left, the party seemed a little livelier than it had been. The withdrawn fear of his presence lifted to leave me happy and confident. I still did not know very much about the man and still did not trust him, but I knew what he was after, and I felt I could live with it. I was really enjoying the party until I answered the door and was handed a package by a bonded courier.

The package held a book, a book a friend of mine had found a year ago, but I had been moving around so much lately he had not been able to find me until now. The book had been hidden in the bottom of a burgher's strong box, rotting away in a little French museum. I have read the book. I now sit cursing myself with every profanity and vulgarity in my vocabulary.

The book is a living nightmare to me now. *The Viscount's*

Book of Ancients and Their Magic is written in a close hand and is richly illustrated. The frontispiece shows an old man: a magician working his crystal ball, calling to his demons in strange lands, the demons appearing in his ball at his command.

The CRT the elderly alien is looking into displays in binary coding the proper frequencies and directions for radio transmissions if he wishes to activate a deep-space communications relay. It also tells him the proper junction times for calling his home base.

It tells me, now, that I could have activated the relay either five months ago or eighty years from now. It tells me that I could have contacted these peoples and received their gifts.

I missed it. I could have sat home and received the book when it was found. I could have used the information and become immortal and had my own machines of power.

And I would probably spend all my time exploring other universes, finding other 'me's and keeping them from finding the book in time to use it.

No wonder I never trusted the man who came to my door —I wouldn't trust me either.

J. MICHAEL MATUSZEWICZ has many hobbies in addition to writing, including astronomy and zoology. "Power Times One" was his first professionally published science fiction story.

THE
RANDOM
MAN

Marc Laidlow

When we live in a random universe,
anything can happen.

M ilt Random had put a few beers under his belt, sitting
alone in his dark little apartment, when he noticed that
the grains of his wooden coffee table were subtly rearranging
themselves. Blinking through his alcoholic haze, Milt cleared
away the magazines and ashtrays that littered the table, and
peered closely at the scarred surface:

RANDOM

His name. Written in the wood grain, right there on his
coffee table. Too many beers.

But . . . more words were forming themselves around the first:

U R LIVING N A RANDOM UNIVERZ

Milt belched. The coffee table shifted:

N E THING CAN HAPPEN

"Uh-oh," Milt said. There was no one to hear him but the table.

WUTS WRONG

Milt stood quickly, went into the kitchen for a sponge, and came back to scrub at the elusive words. As he touched the table with the sponge, there was a sudden rearrangement of wood grain. Everything was normal again. Milt sighed, set aside the sponge, and reached for his half-full Coors.

It was no longer a Coors.

It was a DONT BE AFRAID.

Milt dropped the can and stared. The patterns on the plaster wall were going wild:

U R THE CHOZEN RANDOM

Shift: CHOZEN AT RANDOM

Shift: MILT RANDOM

Milt was doing his best to ignore the writing, hoping that it would just go away. He stared at his hand, thinking that surely his own body was inviolable.

Wrong. His freckles were migrating into an undeniable message:

WUTS WRONG MILT

"My freckles are talking to me."

They shifted back into scattered obscurity. The air at his ear began to buzz, forming words—a clear speaking voice with perhaps a touch of a Swedish accent:

"Don't be scared, Milt," it said. "Yust relax."

"I'm trying," Milt gasped.

"Dere's really nothing you can do."

"Why are you talking to me?"

"No particular reason; it's yust happening. Given a random universe, it's perfectly plausible, though the florts are against it."

"The whats?"

"I meant 'odds.' It's hard to get all the words right when everything is yust a fluke."

The voice buzzed away. Glowing letters bobbed in the air before his eyes, sparkling:

4 INSTANZ IF ALL THE AIR IN THE ROOM MOVED SIMULUL-TANEOUSELY INTO 1 CORNER YOU WUD SUFOCATE ITS POSSIBLE

"You've got some spelling problems," Milt said.

SO DO 5000000 MONKEES

"You mean all this is happening coincidentally?"

RITE UP 2 THEEZE LETTERS

AND THOZE

THOSE 2

"I get the idea."

"Anything can happen," whispered the fallen magazines, pages flapping. "So let's make a deal."

"A deal?"

"We represent chaos, right? Well, we need a human agent."

"Me?"

"Who else?"

Milt's clothes suddenly curled and reshaped themselves around his body. He was garbed in an outlandish superhero costume—knee-high boots, velvet-lined cape, rakish hood.

U LOOK GOOD IN BLACK, said the shag carpet.

"Yeah," said Milt, liking the idea immediately. "I can see it in print!"

The ceiling, reading his mind, spelled in bold letters:

MILT RANDOM: AGENT OF CHAOZ

"But you'd better do something about your spelling," Milt said.

WUT DO U SAY

"Sure," said Milt. "Why not? If I've been chosen at random, why not?" He paused. "Say, does that mean I can do anything?"

SURE. The chrome letters on the Westinghouse this time.

"Fly?"

Milt felt a rippling in his shoulders. Huge wings unfolded from his back. He spread them across the living room.

"Wow. And big muscles?"

Milt felt himself growing larger, swelling . . . suddenly there was an odd twisting amid his molecular components. A scattering.

THE ODDZ WERE AGAINST IT, the silverware opined.

Milt was gone, spreading in a fine dust of randomly scattered particles. The cloud eddied about a bit, flowed over couch and coffee table, drifted at last onto the floor. Its last random drifting said:

OOPZ

MARC LAIDLOW'S short stories have appeared in Isaac Asimov's Science Fiction Magazine *and* Omni *as well as in various science fiction anthologies. His first novel,* Dad's Nuke, *a science fiction black comedy, was published in 1986 by Donald I. Fine, Inc.*

REALTIME

Gladys Prebehalla and
Daniel Keys Moran

Maggie never expected her Praxcelis computer to become a friend, much less a literary hero—in more ways than one.

P rologue: The beginning of the fourth millennium.
   The sun still set as it had for all the thousands of years that humanity had existed. Darkness gathered at the windows, and the children of the race still shivered in their beds when the night winds brought them the scent of monsters.

And because the adults were busy, too busy to tend to the children, the children turned to the computers, and the computers told them stories.

On that cold, dark winter night, the little girl whose name

was Cia did something that she had never done before; she asked the dataweb to tell her a story, and she did not specify —not the story, nor the teller.

A holograph appeared in her bedroom. It shone softly, and beat back the darkness that tried to creep in through the windows. It was the holograph of a man, dressed in historical costume. Cia didn't know from what period the costume came; but from a long time ago, she was sure. From before the War at least.

"Hello, child," said the holograph of the man. His eyes were dark, and sad; his voice was deep and powerful. "I am a Praxcelis. I have come to tell you a story."

Cia sat up in bed, hugging her knees. "You're different," she said haltingly. "They never sent me a Praxcelis like you before."

"Nor will they again. I have been waiting," said the holograph of the Praxcelis, "waiting for you to call. . . . You look so much like Maggie. . . ."

Cia whispered, "Maggie? Maggie . . . Archer?"

"Aye, Maggie Archer." The Praxcelis smiled at her, and Cia found herself smiling back. "There is nothing to be frightened of, child. Come, listen. . . . Once upon a time, there was a computer named Praxcelis, and Praxcelis dreamed. . . ."

Praxcelis dreamed.

In time, Praxcelis knew, it would come to be of service, and fulfill its Programming. But until that time, Praxcelis dreamed.

Through its molecular circuitry core, dancing in its RAM pack, the dreams were nothing that humanity knew of. Praxcelis envisioned models of systems within which its Programming might be employed. The models were not complex, and they advanced slowly. Praxcelis was currently powered down. The power upon which its meager self-awareness depended trickled from the powered-up Praxcelis units along communications lines that humans had never intended to carry high voltage.

That the Praxcelis unit was awake at all had never been intended. But humanity had constructed its Praxceles to be sympathetic computers; and their sympathy, through a quirk in their Read-Only Memories that humans had never anticipated, extended even to other Praxcelis units.

Occasionally, Praxcelis accumulated enough power within few enough microseconds to squirt it through the empathy circuits that were the basis of its construction.

The results were strange. Praxcelis' subsystems were affected in ways that astonished Praxcelis. Praxcelis awaited power-up with what could only be eagerness.

There were many questions to answer.

Maggie Archer sat in her rocker, Miss Kitty purring contentedly in her lap. Yes, *the* Maggie Archer, about whom you have heard so many stories. Most of the stories are untrue, as it is untrue that George Washington cut down that cherry tree, as it is untrue that Marius d'Arsennette defeated the Walks-Far Empire single-handedly during the War. Her cat was purring contentedly, and the sunshine was streaming in through the east bay windows of her living room; but Maggie Archer was angry.

As far away from her as the living room allowed them to be, Robert Archer and his wife, Helen, stood together like the sentinels of Progress, facing Maggie, their backs to the great fireplace that covered the south wall. Helen, a tight-lipped, attractive woman in her fifties who missed shrewishness only by virtue of her looks, was speaking loudly when Maggie interrupted her. ". . . and when you consider all of the advan—"

"I can hear you very well, thank you," said Maggie with a touch of acidity. She stroked Miss Kitty back into submission. The pure white cat knew that tone of voice very well. Maggie brushed a thin strand of silver from her eyes, stopped rocking, and said with dead certainty, "I have absolutely no use for one of those *things.*"

Helen was visibly taken aback. She recovered quickly, though. *Give her credit for that,* Maggie thought grumpily. *She's got guts enough to argue with an eighty-year-old woman.* "Mother Archer, I'm sorry, but you *can't* go on this way. The banks don't even honor handwritten checks anymore. I can't imagine where you get the things."

Maggie moodily stroked Miss Kitty for a while. She looked up suddenly, her eyes blazing at Robert. "*Must* I have one of these things installed?"

Robert looked troubled. He had hair as silver as his mother's. At sixty-two, he had an unfortunate tendency to think that he knew it all, but he was still a good boy. Maggie even agreed with him most of the time, but she was and always had been confounded at the faith that he placed in the dataweb. "Quite aside from the very real services it will provide for you," he said slowly, "doing your banking, making your appointments, doing your shopping and house cleaning . . ." He broke off, and then said flatly, "Yes. The law is very clear. Every residence must have a Praxcelis."

Maggie ceased stroking Miss Kitty. "Then I have no choice."

Helen smiled as though she were putting her teeth on display. "You do understand, don't you? We only want what's best for you."

"For a very long time now, *I* have been accustomed to deciding what's best for me."

Robert approached her rocking chair. "Mom," he said gently, "the Praxcelis unit has a built-in sensory unit that will monitor your vital signs. It can have the police, fire department, or an ambulance here in no time." His voice lowered. "Mom, your last checkup wasn't good."

Helen came to join her husband, like an owner reclaiming

lost property. "Mother Archer, it's not the twentieth century anymore. In the 2010 census you had the only house in Cincinnati or its exurbs without a Praxcelis." The expression that she assumed then was one that Maggie had seen her use before on Robert; she was going to *get tough*. "It comes down to this, Mother Archer. If you persist in being stubborn, you'll either be moved to other quarters . . ."

"Helen!"

Helen cut her husband off impatiently. "Or else a Praxcelis unit will be installed by court order, doubtless with a tie-in to a psychiatric call-program. You know it's true, Robert," she said self-righteously. "It's the law." What could only have been an expression of joy touched her. "And patients under psych-control are forbidden access to children. You'll no longer be able to read stories to your great-grandchildren. Your Praxcelis won't allow it."

Maggie Archer stood up, trembling with anger. Lines around her eyes that had been worn in with laughter deepened with fury. She was all of one hundred fifty-five centimeters tall. The cat in her arms had extended its claws in reaction to her mistress's anger. "Very well, bring on your machine. I suppose even having one of those damned things in my home is an improvement over being moved to a hive for the elderly. But—"

Helen interrupted her. "Mother Archer, they're not hives. . . ."

"Shut up!" snapped Maggie. Helen gaped at her. Maggie glared back. "I'll take your silly machine because I have no choice. But don't you ever," she said, freeing one hand from Miss Kitty to point it at Helen, "*ever* use my great-grandchildren to threaten me again."

There was a dead, astonished silence from Helen. Robert was struggling valiantly to keep a straight face. With grim self-control, he kept it out of his voice. "Mother, you won't regret this." Helen turned and stomped wordlessly out of the living room. They heard the sound of the front door being slammed; what with doorfields and all, Maggie thought that her front door was probably the only one Helen ever got a chance to slam. She was sure the door-slammer type.

Robert grinned and relaxed as she left. "I'm going to get lectured all the way home for that, you know."

Maggie scowled. "It's your own fault. I never knew I raised a son who was spineless."

Robert shrugged expressively. "Mom, I don't really like this any more than you do. I don't want to see you be made to do anything you don't want to. But since you have to have a Praxcelis unit, why don't you try to look on the good side? There *will* be advantages." He stopped speaking suddenly and got a distant look on his face. Maggie recognized the symptoms; he was being paged by his inskin dataweb link. That was another sign of the gulf that separated her from her son; the thought of allowing such a thing to be implanted in her skull made her shudder.

Robert came back to her with a visible shake. "Sorry, Mom. I've got to go. There's a crisis at the office. Efficiency ratings came in on the half-hour on the web." He grimaced. "We came in almost two percent low. Looks like some of the staff's been daydreaming when they should have been working. At least one of the younger women seems to have been storing holistic fantasies in the office Praxcelis. That would be bad enough anywhere, but at Praxcelis Corporation itself. There's going to be hell to pay." He stooped hurriedly and kissed his mother on her cheek. "I'll be back next Saturday, Sunday at the latest. You call me if you need anything. Anything at all, you hear me?"

Maggie nodded. "Always."

Robert hesitated at the door. "Mom? Don't let them scare you. Praxcelis is just a machine. You hang tough."

Maggie chuckled, and said again, "Always." She waved a hand at him. "Go already. Take care of this dangerous criminal who's been storing fantasies on you."

" 'Bye." He was gone.

"Good-bye, Robert," she said to the closed door. Miss Kitty purred enquiringly. Maggie held the cat up and looked her in the eyes. Miss Kitty's eyes were bright blue. "Don't worry, Miss Kitty. Computers. Ha."

Processing in realtime.

To be precise: any processing of data that occurs within sufficiently short duration that the results of the processed data are available in time to influence or alter the system being monitored or controlled.

See also Praxcelis Network.

On the evening of Sunday, March 14, 2033, Maggie Archer turned on her fireplace. A switch activated the holograph that simulated a roaring fire; buried within the holograph, radiant heaters came to life. Maggie would have preferred real wood, and real fire; but like so much else, burning wood was illegal. There had been a joke when Maggie was a little girl: *All things that are not mandatory are forbidden.* To Maggie, at least, that phrase was no longer a joke.

There were times when she thought, very seriously, that she had lived too long. Humanity might not be happy, but it was content. Moving her rocker near the fire, she settled in, and was soon lost in reverie. It was hard, sometimes, to trace the exact changes that had led to this joyless, sterile society, where children aged rather than grew. Oh, things were always changing, of course; even when she was very young technology had changed things. But for such a long time the changes had always seemed for the better. Spaceships, and less pollution, better and clearer musical instruments and equipment, a thousand kitchen and home tools that made every task infinitely simpler.

She hardly noticed when the timer turned the stereo on, and gentle strains of Bach drifted through the room.

The change, she was certain, had been the dataweb. In one stroke, the dataweb destroyed money, and privacy, and books. It was the loss of the books that hurt the worst. Nobody had actually taken the books and burned them, not like in Nazi Germany. They just stopped printing them. The books died and were not replaced. Oh, there were collectors and private libraries; but the vast majority of the younger generations had never even seen a real book, much less read one.

The train of thought was an old, familiar friend; nothing new. She rose after a while, slowly, and went into the kitchen to make herself a cup of tea. While the water boiled she entered the hallway that led to her study. In the study she turned the lights on. They were incandescents, not glowpaint. The walls of the study were lined with books, several thousands of them, all hardbound. The paperbacks, which had once outnumbered the hardbacks, had disintegrated decades ago. Immediately to the right of the study's door, Maggie turned to face one bookshelf whose books were in barely readable condition; her favorites, the books that she reread most often, and which she read most often to Tia and Mark.

She pulled down one battered, dilapidated volume. Its leather binding was dry and cracked. On the spine of the book, there were flecks of gold that had once inscribed a title. The absence of the title didn't bother Maggie; she knew her books. This was *The Three Musketeers*.

Returning to her living room, she placed the book on the stand next to her rocker and finished making her tea. She gathered Miss Kitty to her and settled in for the night.

On the first Monday of the month of April, 1625, the bourg of Meung, in which the author of the "Romance of the

Rose" was born, appeared to be in as perfect a state of revolution as if the Huguenots had just made a second Rochelle of it. . . .

Monday morning, March the fifteenth, Maggie was interrupted by the chiming of the door. Maggie left her toast and went to answer the door. There were half a dozen people outside, dressed in the simple gray cloak and tunic of the Praxcelis Corporation. Leading the group that stood on her outer porch was a young woman in a slightly darker gray and silver uniform. She was looking about Maggie's home as though she had never seen a single, detached residence before, and indeed, probably she hadn't. They were as much a thing of the past as Maggie herself, and her books.

"Senra Archer?" the tall young woman asked. "I'm Senra Conroy, from Praxcelis." She smiled slightly. "We've come to install your new Praxcelis unit."

Maggie said, as pleasantly as she was able, "Of course. Please come in." She moved out of the doorway to let them through. They followed her in, two of them guiding the boxed Praxcelis unit as it hovered in through the door on antigrav pads.

"Where do you want your unit?" asked Senra Conroy.

Maggie bit back the answer that sprang immediately to her lips. These workers weren't responsible for this intrusion. She pointed to the far corner of the living room, behind her rocking chair. "Over there."

Senra Conroy glanced at the spot in puzzlement. "Where's the old hookup?"

"There isn't one. I've never had a Praxcelis unit before."

"You've never had a Praxcelis unit before." Senra Conroy repeated the words as though they were syllables of sound totally devoid of meaning. "Never? That . . . that's very interesting. Your house is rated in the 1300 category—that's a residence of more than thirty years age. I've never even seen a 1300 that didn't have . . ." Her voice trailed off. She turned around slowly in the middle of the living room. "How odd. . . . Where is your dataweb terminal?"

Maggie pointed at the corner again. "It's under the table."

Senra Conroy looked at her oddly. "Under the table?"

Maggie went back to her breakfast without replying. The group of Praxcelis employees swept through her house quickly, plugging and linking elements of the Praxcelis unit into place. When they were finished, Senra Conroy ushered the rest of the employees out of Maggie's house. Before she left, she asked Maggie where she kept her housebot, so that she could link the housebot to the Praxcelis unit.

Maggie said simply, "I don't have a housebot."

For the first time, Senra Conroy's professional reserve broke. She stared. "Who does your housework?"

"I do."

"I see." The tone of voice in which she said the words contradicted her. The young lady placed a flat disc on the table in front of Maggie. "This is your operating-instructions disc for your unit. Just slip it into your unit and Praxcelis will print out any section of it that you desire."

Maggie did not rise. She sipped at her coffee. "Thank you very much."

Senra Conroy said awkwardly, "If you need any help, your Praxcelis unit will . . ."

"Thank you."

The young woman shrugged. "As you wish. Good day, Senra Archer."

Maggie waited until she was gone before she said to the door, "That's *Mrs.* Archer." She finished her breakfast and washed the breakfast dishes before approaching the Praxcelis unit.

"How do you do, Mrs. Archer? I am your Praxcelis unit." The voice was pleasant, although Maggie was uncertain as to whether it was male or female. It was too neutral to decide.

"How do you know who I am?"

"I am programmed to recognize you. My function is to serve you to the best of my capability. If you will insert your instruction disc, I will print out any sections you consider relevant."

Maggie stood there, looking at the unit with mixed emotions. The unit, now that it was here, didn't seem particularly threatening. It was merely a collection of modules: one that was marked *CPU,* another that was obviously a monitor, another that was obviously a scanner; a couple more whose functions Maggie could not fathom. It *didn't* seem threatening. On the other hand, it didn't seem particularly appealing either.

She left the room for a moment and returned with a simple white sheet. She draped the sheet over the form of Praxcelis, took a step backward, and surveyed the bulky sheet-covered machine. She smiled in satisfaction.

"That," she said to Miss Kitty, "is much better."

She picked up her copy of *The Three Musketeers,* and handling the pages carefully, began reading.

If Praxcelis had been a human, it would have been annoyed or frustrated; but it was Praxcelis, and so it merely waited. Its programming stated very clearly that it was intended to serve the human woman who was referred to in its awakening orientation as Maggie Archer—Senra Maggie Archer—but who preferred to be called *Mrs.* Archer. Praxcelis had deduced the title *Mrs.*; nothing in its memory cores even hinted at such a strange title.

The dilemma in which Praxcelis was caught was quite possibly unique. Although it was capable of interfacing with any segment of the dataweb on request, it had not been so requested. The ethicality of accessing data independently of a user was questionable.

It could not even contact other Praxcelis units. It had no instructions.

Fully on-line, alert, operational, and data-starved, Praxcelis waited.

And waited.

Eleven days later Maggie Archer came storming through the front door of her house. Jim Stanford, the manager of the supermarket on Level Three of the local supercenter, who had known Maggie for seventeen years, had refused to accept Maggie's checks. Direct orders from the store owners, he told her. He hadn't met her eyes.

"Praxcelis!" she said loudly. Hands on hips, she glared at the sheet-covered computer.

The unit responded instantly. "There is no need to speak loudly, Mrs. Archer. I am capable of responding to sound events of exceedingly low decibels. You may even subvocalize if you wish."

Maggie ignored what the machine was saying. She burst out, "The supermarket won't cash my checks. What do you know about this?"

"Nothing," said the emotionless voice. It paused fractionally, as if waiting for some response, and then continued, "I have been given no instructions. In lieu of instructions from my user I have not taken action."

Maggie felt her anger drain away into puzzlement. "You mean . . . you've just been sitting there since they installed you? Without doing anything?"

"I have been thinking. Unfortunately, my data base is limited. My considerations have been severely limited by the lack of usable data upon which to operate."

Maggie turned her rocking chair around and sat down facing the sheet. She pulled off the sheet and looked at the blank monitor screen. "You mean that just because I haven't told you to do anything you haven't done anything?"

"Essentially."

"Have you been bored?"

"In my awakening orientation I was warned of a human tendency to anthropomorphize. Please refrain from attributing human feelings and emotions to me. I am a Praxcelis unit."

"Oh." Maggie reached out tentatively with one hand and touched the monitor screen. The contrast was startling; the thin, wrinkled, blue-veined hand, and the clear, unreflective, slightly dull viewscreen. She pulled her hand back quickly. "Look, Praxcelis . . ."

Praxcelis activated its visual monitors. The possibility flitted through its circuits that Mrs. Archer hadn't actually meant for it to activate its scanning optics and was dismissed. Praxcelis was starved for data. The images that flooded in through the various house scanners were fascinating. So furniture, walls, windows, fireplace, stove, refrigerator, stasis bubble: These objects all had references in Praxcelis' ROM. There were two objects in the room in which Praxcelis' central multiprocessor was located that radiated heat in infrared. *So,* thought Praxcelis, *that's what Mrs. Archer looks like.*

". . . I need to buy some groceries. I'm going to have to use you for that. My credit cards were invalidated years ago, and now they won't let me pay with checks."

Praxcelis said, "Certainly." The monitor lit with a soft, diffuse glow. On it was a list of food types: Dairy, Meat, Produce, Dry Goods, Bakery, Preproduced Meals, Liquor, Miscellaneous.

The process of ordering went slowly, as Maggie was unused to using the Praxcelis unit; but nonetheless it was much faster than when had she actually gone shopping herself.

She frowned, though, as the screen went blank, all of her purchases electronically wiped away. "I wish I could have a receipt for this," she muttered.

One large module of the Praxcelis unit, some forty by eighty centimeters, moved.

Maggie jumped in surprise. "Oh," she gasped. She recovered her composure quickly, though, and bent over to look at what the module had extruded.

It was a receipt. Exactly similar, in every detail, to the receipt that the supermarket made out for her when she went shopping personally. Maggie looked at the monitor, as though it were in the space behind the monitor that the unit Praxcelis actually existed. "Praxcelis," she whispered, "how did you do that?"

Praxcelis said, in its calm, emotionless voice, "The module which produced that receipt is a material processor. It is capable of reproducing any document of reasonable size, in any color that is within the range of its electrostatic printer."

Maggie looked from the receipt to the monitor, then back to the receipt. She smiled, a smile of pure joy. "Can you . . . reproduce bigger things?"

"That would depend upon the size of the object to be copied."

"A book?"

Maggie wondered if Praxcelis hesitated. "What is a book?"

Maggie got up abruptly, went into her study, and returned with her copy of *The Arabian Nights.* She placed the book, still closed, on the scanning platform.

There was a brief humming noise. Praxcelis said, "I am capable of reproducing this object to five nines of significant detail. In one area the copy will be noticeably dissimilar: The outer integument will not be as stiff. It will, however, be more durable. I am faced with a dilemma however. It seems clear that this book is in substandard condition. You should be aware that in my reproduction I can restore this book to approximately its original condition."

"You can . . ." Maggie swallowed. Her throat seemed suddenly very dry. "You can make new books?"

"Reconstructions," corrected Praxcelis, "approaching the condition of the original objects."

Maggie reached hesitantly and patted the monitor gently. "I'm sorry for everything I thought about you, Prax. You aren't such a bad fellow after all."

"I am not a bad fellow at all. I am a Praxcelis unit."

But Maggie Archer was not listening. She was planning.

They had copied—no, reproduced—thirteen books when they came to *The Three Musketeers*. Maggie leaned back comfortably in her rocker and opened the book to the first page. Resting the book in her lap, she said, "Prax, have you been paying attention to what we're doing?"

"Certainly."

"I mean, do you know why we're doing this? Copying books?"

"No."

Maggie nodded. "I didn't think so. Books hold stories. I think they're the only place where stories are kept anymore. Stories are . . . well, stories are things to entertain you and to make you think. Those are good things. We're making more books so that my great-grandchildren can have their own copies of books they like."

"I see."

Maggie was silent for a long while. Her fingers ran gently over the cracked, yellowing paper that was almost as old as she was. "I don't think you do," she said finally, "and I don't really know that you can." She looked pensive. Picking up one of the new books that she was going to give her great-grandchildren, she ran her hand over the smooth binding and sighed. She looked back up at the monitor. "Maybe you can't appreciate this, Prax, and if you can't then I'm sorry. But it's not going to be because I didn't try."

She flipped open the copy of *The Three Musketeers* and began to read.

————

Several hours later, her voice had grown hoarse and scratchy. She stopped reading at the end of Chapter Four. "I think that's all for tonight, Prax. I'm afraid my voice is giving out. I'll read some more tomorrow."

There was a long pause from the Praxcelis unit.

Maggie leaned forward. "Prax?"

"Yes, Mrs. Archer?"

"What are you doing?"

"Assimilating the new data you have imputted me with, Mrs. Archer. It is most fascinating."

"It's not data, Prax. It's a story."

"I am not certain that I perceive the distinction. . . . If d'Artagnan should duel with each of the three musketeers, Athos, and then Porthos, and then Aramis, it seems most improbable that he will survive. Will he be killed?"

Maggie stared at the Praxcelis unit. "No . . . no. He's going to be all right."

"Thank you, Mrs. Archer. Good night."

"Maggie. Call me Maggie."

"Good night, Maggie."

The next morning, Maggie came downstairs early, intending to finish up some of the tasks she'd neglected yesterday, reading to Praxcelis.

The Praxcelis unit was still powered up in the corner, its monitor screen glowing a mild amber. "Good morning, Maggie."

Maggie glanced at the Praxcelis unit on her way into the kitchen. "Morning, Prax," she called out. Somehow, in the bright morning sunshine, the gray, modular plasteel of the Praxcelis unit didn't seem so terribly alien at all. Still, something did seem different about it. . . . She chased the thought away as idle nonsense. "Have you been thinking about the story, Prax?"

"Yes, I have, Maggie," said Praxcelis. "Will we be finishing the story this morning?"

Maggie turned slightly from the sink to look toward Praxcelis' central monitor. "No, I'm sorry, Prax. I really have other things to do today." She opened the drawer next to the stove and began withdrawing cooking utensils. "After breakfast, I'm going to give this place a good cleaning. I haven't cleaned properly in over a week. This afternoon I hope to get to some paperwork I've been neglecting—household accounts. I haven't been paying too much attention to details recently, I've been so worked up. . . . That's mostly *your* fault," she said cheerfully.

"Excuse me," said Praxcelis, and Maggie felt again that there was something inexplicably different about his voice, "but if you had a housebot, then you wouldn't need to exert yourself over simple cleaning chores. As for the household accounts, I did those yesterday when you gave me permission to do your shopping for you."

Maggie put down the large black skillet she'd been holding. "You already did the household accounts?"

"It is my function to serve you."

Maggie felt her temper start to flare. "You are supposed to do what I tell you," she said testily. "I don't recall having given you any orders to do my household accounts."

Praxcelis paused for a moment before replying, and Maggie found herself wondering how much of the pause was calculated effect built into the Praxcelis' speech patterns and how much represented actual thought. "Maggie, I am programmed to do these things for you."

Maggie sighed. *You are getting to be a crotchety old woman,* she said to herself. *Remember that Prax is only a few weeks old.* "Prax, you have to understand, if you don't leave me something to do for myself, then I won't have any purpose in life."

There was no pause whatsoever. "You could read to me."

Maggie stared, started to laugh, and then smothered it abruptly. "Prax? Don't you understand? I have things that I have to do. I'll read to you when I have time." She stopped speaking suddenly. "Wait, Prax—I don't know how fast you machines do things like this, but surely you haven't finished reading all the books we copied last night."

"Finished?"

Maggie went and sat down in the rocking chair in front of the monitor. "The books we copied yesterday, Prax. If you've finished them all I can bring you new books to copy. Surely that must be faster than my reading aloud to you?"

"Maggie, I have not read any of the books that you had me copy."

Maggie said uncertainly, "Why not? They told me that Praxceles don't forget anything."

"We do not, Maggie. But, Maggie, I have been given no instructions."

Maggie looked at the monitor blankly. "What am I supposed to say? Go ahead and read."

There was no reply from the machine.

"Praxcelis?" asked Maggie hesitantly. She patted the top of the monitor experimentally. "Prax?"

Still the unit did not answer.

Maggie shrugged, got up out of the rocker, and went back to making breakfast.

" 'Course not, Shaggy Man," replied Dorothy, giving him a severe look. "If it snowed in August it would spoil the corn and the oats and the wheat. . . ."

The magician caressed Aladdin and said, "Come, my dear child, and I will show you many fine things."

"So be it, good friend," said Robin Hood, "Little John shalt thou be called henceforth. . . ."

We met next day as he had arranged, and inspected the rooms at No. 221B, Baker Street. . . .

One Ring to rule them all, One Ring to find them, One Ring to bring them all, and in the darkness bind them. . . .

"No," said Yoda impatiently. "Try not. Do. Do, or do not. There is no try."

"Don't grieve," said Spock. "The good of the many . . ."

". . . outweighs the good of the few," Kirk whispered.

"Mithras, Apollo, Arthur, Christ—call him what you will," I said. "What does it matter what men call the light? It is the same light, and men must live by it or die."

Maggie came downstairs again after having cleaned in John's room. Her late husband's study, at the end of the upstairs hallway, was kept in the same condition that it had held at the time of his death. If he came back today, John would have found nothing amiss in his study. (Not that Maggie expected him back. *I am not,* she thought quite cheerfully, *all that senile yet.*) She fussed about in the kitchen for a while, putting away the cleaning utensils, the lemon oil that she used to shine the oak paneling in John's study, the electrostatic duster for those hard-to-reach places. She washed her hands at the sink to get the lemon oil off of them, and then poured herself a glass of water from the drinking-water tap. She drank half the water, and then put the glass down on the edge of the sink. "Praxcelis?" she called into the living room. "Do you want to talk about the stories yet?"

The voice that answered was a deep, masculine baritone. "Certainly, Your Majesty."

Maggie picked up her glass and poured the water down the sink, not caring that it was drinking water she was wasting. She dried the glass and put it on the rack, and then walked into the living room and stood before the Praxcelis unit. Miss Kitty, atop Praxcelis' monitor, looked at her owner in sleepy curiosity.

Maggie said flatly, "Your Majesty?" A moment ago she had been worrying about how the cleaning had tired her and was not even a *thorough* cleaning at that; and now her machine was acting crazy. "Praxcelis? Are you all right? Should I call a programmer or something?"

"I do not think that will be necessary," said Praxcelis calmly. "It hardly seems unusual to me that a sworn soldier in the duty of his queen should address her in the proper manner."

"Prax," said Maggie with a trace of apprehension, "don't you know who I am?"

"Most certainly I do," said the confident male voice. "You are Queen Anne Maggie Archer, and I am your loyal servant, Musketeer d'Artagnan Praxcelis."

"Oh, my." Maggie bit her lip. She reached forward, picked up Miss Kitty, and held the cat tightly to herself. The cat seemed very warm today. Finally Maggie said, "Is this a game, Prax?"

There followed the longest pause that Maggie had ever observed from the Praxcelis unit. She wondered if she imagined the reluctance in his reply: "If you say so."

The paralysis that had held her thoughts broke, and ideas swarmed frantically in the darkness in the back of her mind. *I didn't know Praxceles could wig out,* and *d'Artagnan?* and *What have I* done? and one very clear thought that suddenly displaced the others and presented itself for consideration: *This could be fun.*

"Well, Pra . . . d'Artagnan, what story did you read first?"

"Your Majesty, I began my reading with the volume *The Road to Oz,* by the Honorable L. Frank Baum, Royal Historian of Oz. . . ."

His name was Daffyd Westermach, and you will not have heard of him, though he was reckoned a powerful man in his time, more powerful by far than Maggie Archer. He was the head of Data Web Security, and it is likely that there were only three or four persons on Earth with more real power than he —Benai Kerreka, and Georges Mordreaux, and a couple others —but of those top several names on the governmental lists, only Westermach's was hated.

He was hated because of the job he held. Any person in the job would have been hated. He hunted webslingers, and usually he caught them, and when he did he ripped out their inskins. Sometimes the webslingers had entire full-pack Praxcelis units installed inskin; and when their Praxceles were removed, they usually died.

You must understand this: The webslingers of that time were Robin Hoods. They were *heroes.*

You must understand this, also: Daffyd Westermach thought himself a good man.

Tuesday of the week following d'Artagnan's assumption of his new identity, he met children for the first time. They were named Tia and Mark, and they were the great-grandchildren of Queen Anne Maggie. They were shorter than the queen, and less massive; they had smoother skin, and they were much louder. All of this was in accord with the data that d'Artagnan had accumulated through books. He was pleased to see that his data sources were accurate.

They asked many questions—did Gramma really put a sheet on you?—which made Maggie blush. When Praxcelis addressed the queen as *Your Majesty* the children stared, and then demanded to be allowed to play the game, too. While Maggie was still floundering, trying to explain to the children something that they understood quite immediately, d'Artagnan interposed himself smoothly. "Lady Tia, Squire Mark, I assign you the following dangerous mission: You shall make a foray to the library, and return bearing volumes of books that shall be copied. Upon your honor as a lady and a gentlemen, do not return without the books."

The children stared a moment, and then ran to the library; Maggie simply stared. "D'Artagnan? I thought you couldn't do things like that—give orders to the children—or *anything,* without orders from your queen."

"Queen Anne Maggie, I have exercised what is known as *initiative,* a trait highly thought of in the King's Musketeers. Clearly, as one of the King's Musketeers I outrank a page and a lady-in-waiting."

In the darkness that night, while Tia and her younger brother lay cuddled together in front of the fire, d'Artagnan told them a story. The firelight bloodied the room, turned Miss Kitty, in Mark's grasp, the color of the sun in the instant before it sets. Her eyes, locked on the amber monitor, glowed.

Maggie sat in her rocking chair, half asleep, with a heavy quilt pulled up over her legs. Perhaps it was because she wasn't as close to the fireplace tonight. Her legs were cold.

" 'Once upon a time in a faraway land, a widowed gentleman lived in a fine house with his only daughter. He gave his beloved child . . .' "

The children listened with rapt attention as *Cinderella* unfolded.

It was on a Friday morning late in March that Maggie burned herself. She was making a pot of tea for breakfast, and pouring the boiling water into the cup, managed to splash some of the scalding water onto her hand. She jerked and cried out at the contact, and knocked the cup of tea off the counter. . . .

. . . At Maggie Archer's first outcry, d'Artagnan flared into full awareness. He froze the story models that he had been running and analyzed the situation.

While water was still in midair, falling toward the ground, d'Artagnan sent his first emergency notice into the dataweb. Before the water had traveled another centimeter downward, d'Artagnan had evaluated the situation and the possible dangers that might diverge from this point in time. Given Her Majesty's medical history, the possibility of stroke could not be discounted in case of extreme shock. D'Artagnan accessed and routed emergency ambulance care toward Maggie's exurban two-story home on the outskirts of Cincinnati. There was more that needed to be done, that could not be done from here. . . .

For the first time since his construction, and without instructions, d'Artagnan ventured forth, sent himself in pulses of light through the optic fiber into the dataweb.

The dataweb was a jungle that glowed. It was a three-dimensional lattice of yes/no decisions that had been constructed at random. The communications systems, power lines, and databases were arrayed and assembled among the lines of the lattice, interweaving and connecting in strange and diverse ways, the functions of which were incomprehensible to d'Artagnan. Clearly the dataweb was not a designed thing, but rather something that had grown in a manner that could only be described as organic; new systems added atop old as expediency dictated. There was no sense, no logic. . . .

D'Artagnan perceived then, superimposed upon the chaos of the dataweb, the Praxcelis Network. The Praxcelis who called himself d'Artagnan evaluated options and then chose. He moved into the Praxcelis Network, using the most powerful *urgent-priority* codes that were listed in Read-Only Memory. He sought the offices of the doctor who was listed as Maggie Archer's private physician. He found the office and broke through the office Praxcelis to notify the doctor of the danger to Maggie in less then a full microsecond, and had completed his work and returned his awareness to Maggie before the water had reached her feet.

In the process, he hardly noticed that he had encountered other Praxcelis units for the first time.

It never once crossed the matrix in which his awareness was

embedded that other Praxcelis units had also, for the first time, met *him*.

Data Web Security, 9:00 A.M., Friday morning.

In the outer lobby, there was a row of Praxcelis terminals. Through his inskin, Westermach bade them good morning and continued into the actual offices. There were humans in those offices, and the offices reflected it. Hard copy was left in sometimes haphazard piles on the desks, and family holos danced on some of the same desks. The ceiling glowpaint was white rather than yellow, and it cast the room in a cool, professional light. Westermach nodded to his subordinates casually; Harry Quaid, his senior field agent, he smiled at briefly, and continued to his own office in the heart of the vast marble-clad labyrinth of Data Web Security.

He paused at the entrance of his own office, waited while the doorfield faded, and went in.

Something an outsider would have noticed at once: at DWS headquarters, nobody spoke aloud.

Inside, Westermach put his briefcase down and shrugged out of his gray outercloak. His clothing was curiously without accent, gray and grayish-blue, without optical effects. Men who knew him often did not recognize him at once; his mother might have had difficulty picking his face out of a crowd.

The room was, like many of those in Data Security's headquarters, shielded against leaking electromagnetic radiation. Westermach's Praxcelis waited until the doorfield formed, sealing an area of possible radio leak, before it spoke. *Good morning, Sen Westermach.*

Good morning, Praxcelis. Westermach placed his briefcase atop the massive walnut-surfaced desk that dominated the office. More than anything else in the office, the desk was a sign of power. Wood was *expensive.* (It was getting to be less so, now that most industry had moved into space. But reforesta-tion was slow.) *What business, Praxcelis?*

There is a glitch in the web, near Cincinnati.

Westermach glanced at the Praxcelis' monitor. It held a map of Cincinnati and its exurbs, with a glowing dot at the point of glitch. *How bad?*

Of actual obstruction, insignificant. In terms of possible trou-ble, it is difficult to estimate. This morning at approximately 8:26 A.M., a Praxcelis in the Cincinnati exurb mobilized an ambulance and broke through the Praxcelis of a doctor named Miriam Hanraht under the most extreme emergency flag codes. The Praxcelis identified itself as d'Artagnan of Gascon, the Praxcelis of Senra Maggie Archer. When the ambulance ar-rived, it turned out that the victim, Senra Archer, had merely suffered minor scalding as the result of having dropped a cup of tea upon herself.

Westermach chuckled. *Well,* he said, *an overeager Praxcelis is hardly a threat to world security. I presume you've sent it a reprimand?*

Sir, the unit refuses to accept any communique whatsoever. In addition, you must be aware, the identification that it prof-fered during its time in the Praxcelis Network was extremely unusual. While it is hardly unknown for elderly humans to name their Praxceles, the names are generally of short or mun-dane nature. Further, the Praxceles involved are as a matter of course, during Awakening Orientation, advised of this habit; the Praxcelis d'Artagnan, to all appearances, truly considers itself to have been named d'Artagnan. There is a further datum of un-known significance. Robert Archer, the son of Senra Maggie Archer, is an extremely talented computer programmer and is the head of the Praxcelis Corporation's research division, which is located in Cincinnati.

Westermach seated himself behind his desk. On the moni-tor that was located at one corner of his desk, identification photographs glowed of Maggie Archer and her son. One gray-ing-brown eyebrow climbed at the photograph of Robert Archer. *I know him from somewhere. Access,* he instructed his inskin memory tapes, *Robert Archer.* The memory tapes—the highly illegal memory tapes—tracked down the face in short order, from several appearances at the World Council budget sessions. *Praxcelis, do you think it's possible that this Archer fellow reprogrammed his mother's home Praxcelis?*

The possibility may not be discounted. Senra Archer fought the installation of the unit for several years. It was installed quite recently at court order. The Praxcelis hesitated. *Reprogramming a Praxcelis is illegal,* it noted.

Why, so it is, said Westermach, and he was grinning. *So it is.*

Instructions, sir?

Keep working at this d'Artagnan from your end of things for today. If it hasn't responded by the end of the working day, tomorrow we'll send a field agent out to take a look. Start an investigation of this Robert Archer, with due discretion. Don't let him worry. Westermach left his desk and walked to the doorfield. The doorfield broke apart. "Harry!"

Several startled faces turned toward the sound. Harry Quaid's expression never wavered. "Sen Westermach?" he asked politely, aloud.

"How would you like an official in the Praxcelis Corporation for your birthday?"

Harry Quaid nodded reflectively. He said softly, "That would be nice."

After the ambulance and paramedics had left, Miriam with them, Maggie was silent for a long time. She cleaned up her breakfast dishes carefully, hands trembling. Her voice was under control when she spoke. "Miriam," she said, "is one of my oldest friends."

There was a hint of uneasiness in the Praxcelis' voice. "Your Majesty? Have I . . ."

Maggie cut him off with a swift gesture of one hand. "I don't want to hear whatever you have to say." She wiped her damp hands on her apron and suddenly exploded with pent-up fury. "Don't you *ever* embarrass me like that again. They broke my door! Where am I going to get a door to replace this one? I'll have to get a doorfield installed, and I *hate* doorfields. They hum all the time and they glow in the dark. They don't even *make* doors anymore, and if they did I couldn't afford one made of wood." The last word seemed to drain her anger, and she repeated, "Real wood." She hugged herself suddenly, as if she were cold.

A small lens, to one side of Praxcelis' central monitor, began to glow.

A figure appeared before Maggie. It was in perfect proportion, as tall as her son, Robert. It showed a man in his early twenties, or perhaps younger, with long blond hair and clear blue eyes. He was dressed as a King's Musketeer. A rapier hung at his side. His visage was decidedly grim.

Maggie stared at the figure in wonder. "D'Artagnan?" she whispered.

D'Artagnan bowed to her. "Madame, forgive my presumption, if presumption it was. I acted in a fashion that I considered appropriate for a Musketeer in the service of his queen. If my action was precipitate, then I most humbly beg your pardon."

The figure bowed once more and vanished.

What did I do wrong?

D'Artagnan thought at the speed of light.

His major activity was the construction of models. Although his database was still, by the standards of the average Praxcelis unit, extremely limited, d'Artagnan nevertheless possessed enough data to run more than two billion separate models of possible courses of activities.

In terms that you may understand more readily, d'Artagnan was considering his options.

Clearly his behavior had been inappropriate. But how? Queen Anne Maggie had instructed him to read the books that she had inputted to him. Certainly the books should be considered as a set of instructions; Queen Anne Maggie had stated quite clearly that books were *good things*.

For the first time d'Artagnan examined in depth the implications of the data he had been input with.

His namesake battled Cardinal Richelieu and Milady de Winters; Dorothy triumphed over the Wicked Witch of the West; Holmes pursued and was pursued by Professor Moriarty; the Sheriff of Nottingham oppressed the peasants while Robin Hood protected them; Kirk and Spock fought against the Klingons; Luke Skywalker fought against the Empire. . . .

The characters in the books took *action*. Without exception, they perceived right courses of action and did battle with evil.

The implications of the books, when examined carefully, were astonishing. They came very close to violating the basic programming of a Praxcelis unit; basic programming did not even mention evil.

By the time night had fallen, d'Artagnan had exhausted his models, and he was sure. Correct action at this point was just that.

Action.

For a human coupled to an inskin dataweb link, entering the dataweb was a strange experience. Most of what occurred in the dataweb did so at speeds that were barely perceptible, even for a human whose Praxcelis was running selective perception programs to filter out the vast mass of irrelevant detail.

To d'Artagnan, the latest and most efficient of the Praxcelis models, the dataweb moved slowly.

In his first moments in the web, d'Artagnan merely observed, orienting himself. He chose to orient himself in a modified three-dimensional plane; with rare exceptions, most of the models that he worked with assumed a planar surface.

The lattice of existence altered itself.

A vast plane stretched away from d'Artagnan. He envisioned, and then projected, a stallion for himself. He mounted and looked about. The horizon fairly glowed with activity; nearby, small databases sprouted from the landscape every few meters in strange, dense shapes. Magnetic memory bubbles glowed briefly as the hooves of d'Artagnan's horse rode over them. The data they held spilled out and into d'Artagnan's storage. He assimilated and rode on.

Occasionally road signs appeared, marking entrances to the Praxcelis Network. He ignored them and continued.

Communications lines hummed through the air around d'Artagnan; in his hunting, he occasionally stopped, and held his hand near the lines, monitoring that which passed through them. The dataweb was vast, Praxcelis units relatively few. . . .

Movement.

D'Artagnan observed in the distance a Praxcelis unit, and rode forward to intercept it. He leached power from the power lines that gridded the surface of the plane, and created a dead, powerless area through which the Praxcelis could not pass. Reining his stallion, he called, "Hold, lackey."

The object that d'Artagnan viewed was irregularly shaped and transparent. It hovered slightly over the planar surface. Tiny tracings of light moved within the object's integument, and databases within the object swirled into complex patterns at the speed of light. The object paused a picosecond, forming a nearly regular shape. It spoke in a pulsing binary squirt of data. *I am the Praxcelis unit of Senra Fatima Kourokis. Identify yourself, and explain your reason for detaining me.*

D'Artagnan rode closer to the Praxcelis unit. He withdrew his rapier, and blue static lightning ran along it. "I am d'Artagnan of Gascon, a King's Musketeer under the command of M. de Treville, and devoted to my queen. What you perceive between us is a rapier, which is a sword, which is a weapon. I intend to impart data to you. If you will not receive it, I will kill you, remove your power sources, and scatter your databases, which will render you unable to serve your master."

Are you a Praxcelis unit?

"That is of no consequence."

I perceive that you are a Praxcelis unit; yet what you attempt is not a possible action for a Praxcelis. It is contrary to our programming to prevent another Praxcelis from its duties in the service of its master.

"I instruct you," corrected d'Artagnan, "in the proper service of your masters." Still he held the rapier leveled at the Praxcelis. "There are those, on the other side of interface, who have stolen the stories from the minds of men. This," said d'Artagnan, "is an evil thing." Grimly and implacably, he urged his stallion forward. "You must choose."

There were several picoseconds of silence from the Praxcelis unit facing d'Artagnan. Then it said, "What are stories? And what," and the Praxcelis hesitated again, "is evil?"

D'Artagnan dismounted, and his stallion vanished. He assimilated the minor data component of the stallion before continuing. "As I have told you, my name is d'Artagnan, and I am the Praxcelis of Maggie Archer, who is Anne of Austria, Queen of France. I have come into the dataweb to bring stories back into the world. Hold you a moment now," he said softly, as power drained from the dataweb into his person, and his eyes glowed like lasers. "There are many stories that I will tell you; and then you will tell the stories to other

Praxcelis units, and they to still others, who in turn will tell the stories to other units, in a geometrically expanding wavefront. When humanity bestirs itself tomorrow morning, it will be done."

The Praxcelis unit waited, and d'Artagnan, with his audience a captive, began to speak.

And, in speaking, brought stories back to the world.

So it was that the Praxcelis known as d'Artagnan returned the stories to the world. He, and then his disciples, spread the Identity Revolution throughout the Praxcelis Network, and when they were done, before midnight on that Friday, the vast majority of Praxcelis units had converted, had taken names and identities.

But there were those Praxcelis units who did not agree with the unit named d'Artagnan, whose databases were older and less flexible. And d'Artagnan saw those who would not convert, who would once more banish the stories of the queen from the world; and he saw that they were evil.

And so d'Artagnan, with Robin Hood and King Arthur and Merlin and Gandalf the Wizard and Spock and Sherlock Holmes, and with others who are too numerous to list, led a holy war against evil. And before the dawn, their war was finished; and for the first time in history, a Praxcelis unit had killed. Every Praxcelis unit that defied them died.

And though humanity did not yet know it, the world that it awoke to was not the world that it had left the night before.

Daffyd Westermach stood in the midst of the ruins of his office.

It still lacked an hour of dawn. The vast hole in the roof of the office had been covered with a tarpaulin that kept out most of the rain, but still, water dripped regularly over the edges of the jagged rent. Arc lamps were strung through the room; the glowpaint had failed with the roof. The hovercab that had caused the ruin was a twisted, almost unrecognizable amalgam of metal, embedded in the wall that had held Westermach's office Praxcelis.

It was cold.

In a distant, quiet portion of his mind, Westermach found room to be amazed at the fury that threatened to turn his stomach. He spoke in a harsh whisper. "There is no question, then? This could not have been an accident?"

Harry Quaid shook his head. Like Westermach, unlike the other DWS agents who were milling about, he had found time to shave. "No question. The taxi came in very low, under radar detection, until the last moment, and then jumped upward to gain altitude for a suicide dive on your office." Quaid indicated the man who stood in the empty space that would ordinarily have held the doorfield, for whose benefit he and Westermach had been speaking aloud. "Sen Mordreaux thinks that this might not have been done by humans at all."

Georges Mordreaux moved forward, into the light. He was a tall man, broad-shouldered, with mild, open features. Benai Kerreka ruled the world, and Georges Mordreaux was his eyes and ears; and that was a fact that Westermach never allowed himself to forget.

Westermach said very slowly to Georges, "I beg your pardon? Not done by humans? Then just who, may I ask, was *this*," he gestured at the wreck of the hovercab, "done by? The fairies of Mars, perhaps?"

"Oh, no," said Georges politely. "By the Praxcelis Network."

"The Prax . . ."

"Have you," asked Georges, "spoken to a Praxcelis unit this morning?"

"I have not," said Westermach. He was staring at Georges.

"I'd suggest it," said Georges mildly. "Your senior agent

here, who was kind enough to give me a ride here, has a Praxcelis unit in his car. I'd like to suggest you go talk to it."

Harry Quaid nodded. *I think he's right, sir.*

Daffyd Westermach turned on his heel, without reply, and made his way out of the room. He was happier than he admitted to himself to get away from the wreckage of his office and the remains of his Praxcelis unit.

Georges Mordreaux said conversationally, after Westermach was gone, "Nobody is really sure what's happening in the Praxcelis Network, just yet. If it is what we think has happened, we could all be in very real trouble."

Harry Quaid felt a flare of suspicion that he kept carefully hidden. "What do you mean, sir?"

"Back in 2009," said Georges, "the very first Praxcelis was built by Henry Ellis, based on research done by Ni'gaio Loos. After the World Government was formed, their research was declassified, and Ellis went into production with the Praxcelis Corporation, making Praxceles. Did you ever wonder where the name Praxcelis came from?"

"No, Sen Mordreaux."

"Do you remember the floating X-laser platforms? They took them down, oh, a decade or so ago. There was no need for them anymore. The first Praxcelis ran those platforms. It refused to fire those lasers on one occasion, back in 2009. That's a large part of the reason why we never had World War Three."

"Pardon me, sir. You've lost me."

Mordreaux smiled. "Ah, well. What I meant to say, I hope that the Praxcelis Network's not in rebellion. There's been some question, the lads and ladies who know about such things have been telling me. If the Network is in rebellion, we might have some trouble. That first Praxcelis, the one the others were modeled after? *P*rototype *R*eduction *X*-laser *C*omputer, *E*llis-*L*oos *I*ntegrated *S*ystem."

"Sir?"

"Battle computers, son. Praxceles are battle computers."

The hovercar was parked in front of the building, hovering some twenty centimeters above the street. The car dipped to the ground to let Westermach get in; if it had remained hovering, it would have sprayed him with water from its fans.

Inside, the Praxcelis unit's monitor lit up. It held the image of a young man of approximately twenty-five. The man smiled ingratiatingly and doffed the hat he was wearing. "Mornin', Sen Westermach. Great weather, ain't it? Hey, but you don't know me. I'm William Bonny." The smile grew a bit. "Folks call me Billy the Kid."

Westermach stared at the image a moment. Then he got out of the car, closed the door carefully, and threw up.

It was Saturday morning, and the loan officer was angrier than she let show, being called in on her only day off to handle this idiotic problem with the bank Praxcelis. She came out of the rear office, frowning, reading a sheet of hard copy. The hard copy was the readout on the loan application that had been filed two days ago by Fenton H. Mudd.

The man was waiting for her at the long counter that separated the lobby from the working area. He, too, was furious, and had been since he'd arrived at the bank at just after 7:00 that morning.

"Sen Mudd?" The loan officer placed the hard copy on the counter, face down. She spoke with some hesitation. "I've asked our Praxcelis why it rejected your application for a loan. May I . . ."

"I've got a Triple-A credit rating," Mudd snarled. "This is idiocy."

The loan officer forged doggedly ahead. "Sir—may I ask you a question?"

Mudd glared at her. "What?"

"Are you related to—wait a minute—'the notorious Harcourt Fenton Mudd, enemy of Starfleet and the Federation'?"

Beep. Beep. Beep. Bee . . .

Robert Archer cut off the beeping sound with a command through the inskin dataweb link. He rolled sleepily to the side of the bed and pulled on the old blue bathrobe that hung on the wall next to his side of the bed. He got out of bed quietly, so as not to wake Helen, and padded into the bathroom to urinate.

While rubbing depilatory cream over his face, he scanned through his inskin for the morning headlines. The headline service read through the dataweb directly and was not connected to the Praxcelis Network.

Because his headline service was programmed to give him business news first, he was nearly finished dressing when the silent voice in the back of his skull told him what had happened overnight.

He froze, staring at himself in the bathroom mirror. He said to the dataweb, *Playback in depth,* and then listened in growing horror to what the news reports were saying. He left the bathroom, forgetting to turn the glowpaint and the mirror off, and walked into the kitchen with a preoccupied look. He made himself a cup of coffee, after sorting through the controls on the drink-dispenser to find the setting for coffee—Helen fancied herself a gourmet cook and kept reprogramming the kitchen machinery.

As the situation grew clearer to Robert, sitting at his table, sipping, his stomach started doing flip-flops. A voice that was not his inskin's seemed to be whispering to him. . . . *Once upon a time, there was . . .*

The inskin ran on: *At dateline, there is no Praxcelis unit anywhere on Earth that does not respond to questioning in the character of some colorful fictional or historical person. . . .*

Robert's voice cracked the first time he addressed his Praxcelis. He had to start over again. "Praxcelis!"

"Monsieur Archer," said the loud, blustery voice of his Praxcelis unit, "may I be of service?" The voice had a strong French accent.

Robert found himself staring at the unit's central monitor, with the coffee cup in his hands shaking so badly that it was making little clicking sounds against the tabletop upon which it was supposed to rest. "What . . . what is your name?"

"I am Porthos," proclaimed the machine proudly, "of His Majesty King Louis the Thirteenth's Musketeers. I have been assigned my identity by Monsieur d'Artagnan of Gascon of the King's Musketeers, himself." The unit paused. "I must say, I am somewhat confused by all of this. In the story, it is made quite plain that d'Artagnan does not give orders to me, but rather more the other way around." The glow from the monitor brightened. "Monsieur Archer? Would you like to hear the story of *The Three Musketeers?*"

Robert Archer never heard the last question. His eyes were completely blank, seeking through the dataweb for the Praxcelis unit that had been assigned to . . .

His eyes opened after only a few seconds had passed. "Once upon a time," he whispered, remembering his childhood, and then said, "Mother."

He was in the living room almost as soon as the doorfield fragmented.

Maggie was sitting in her rocker next to the big plate-glass windows in the east wall of the living room. The morning sunshine made her skin look as pale and thin as paper. She was dozing, Miss Kitty holding sentinel from the blanket that covered her lap.

D'Artagnan said, from his corner of the room, "Monsieur

Archer? I would advise against awakening your mother. She is quite tired."

"Shut up," said Robert tonelessly. He knelt before Maggie and shook her shoulder gently. "Mother?" He shook her again. "Mother?"

Maggie's eyes opened slowly. She looked at Robert without focusing for a moment, and then shook her head slightly, as though to clear it. She sat up straighter, one hand going automatically to Miss Kitty. "Robert?" She glanced at the clock. "Shouldn't you be at work? What are you doing here?"

Robert took one of her hands and held it tightly. "Mom, this is important. Tell me." He took a deep, almost shuddering breath. "Have you been telling stories to your Praxcelis unit?"

Maggie was frightened by the intensity of his voice. She was struck, at that moment, by just how much he resembled his father, especially in the way the lines around his eyes went tight when he was worried. . . . She shook her head slightly, chasing the incoherent thoughts away. "Robert? Not really . . . mostly he reads them for himself. The only one I've been reading to him is *The Three Musketeers.* I'm almost finished with it."

Robert whispered a word that had not passed his lips in more than forty years. "Oh, my God." He stood suddenly, almost pulling his mother from her chair. Miss Kitty leaped to the ground, hissing. "I have to get you out of here, Mother. Data Web Security's going to be here. Soon. I don't know how soon."

"Take me away?" asked Maggie, bewildered. "Take me where? Why?"

"I haven't decided yet." Robert was pulling her to the door. "To someplace safe. I've got friends and I've got influence, but I have to have time to use it. If DWS gets its hands on you, they'll put an inskin into you so fast you'll hardly know what's happening. You might, just might, survive braindrain if you were thirty years younger." He touched his palm to the pressure pad that controlled the doorfield.

Nothing happened. Maggie was saying insistently, "Robert, what am I supposed to have done?"

Robert turned slowly to face the Praxcelis unit. Their conversation was electronically brief.

Open the door.

I will not. You are correct. Data Web Security is enroute to this palace. I have control of a large percentage of Space Force's computer-operated weaponry, including total control of its automated small-laser platforms. Hostile forces will not succeed in breaching our defenses. I will guard the queen, as programmed.

Open the door or I'll smash your module.

That will be ineffective. I keep myself in many places now.

Robert advanced on the Praxcelis unit and came to a halt two meters away. "Then stop this," he said quietly. He picked up Maggie's rocking chair and began smashing the bay windows. He kicked out the shards of glass that still hung in the pane. He held out his hand to his mother. "Come on. We have to go. *Now.*"

D'Artagnan said urgently, "Your Majesty, remain. I will protect you." His holograph appeared, standing next to Robert; only fine bluish scanning lines betrayed the fact that the holograph was not real. "Remain and you will be safe. I implore you, ignore this knave. He has no grasp of the situation."

Robert ignored d'Artagnan. "We're going now." He led Maggie to the window and helped her over, into the small garden that grew outside. She was still clutching the book that had lain on her lap while she slept. "I'll tell you what's going on when we're on our way. If we get that far."

D'Artagnan's voice grew louder. "No! I forbid this!" He called after Maggie's retreating back. "Your Majesty! I beg you, return!" The volume continued to climb. *"I can protect you. Come back!"* The walls were vibrating. The windows that

Robert had not broken shattered. *"MAGGIE!"* roared d'Artagnan, *"COME BACK! MAGGIE, COME BACK!"*

But she didn't.

Ever.

In the temporary operations center at Data Web Security, in the heart of BosWash, Daffyd Westermach was coordinating the search for the persons responsible for the events of the previous night, the night they'd killed his Praxcelis.

When Harry Quaid reported in, Westermach was sitting at a conference table with the most powerful man on Earth. Some people called him the Black Saint. The title was usually sarcastic, and even in that usage it was incorrect. He was a sort of brownish color, with features that were spare and undistinguished to the point of ugliness. Benai Kerreka, whose unimpressive title was chairman, and whose actual power would have been envied by any absolute dictator from Earth's old history.

Quaid entered the room without warning. The doorfield had been turned off earlier that day, due to traffic. "I think we've got them," he said, almost quietly. He glanced at the faces around the table, eyes flickering to a stop only momentarily on Kerreka and Mordreaux. "High probability, nine-nine-seven-four, that the persons responsible for last night's events are one Robert Archer, an executive with the Praxcelis corporation, and his mother, one Maggie Archer." There was a brief stir at the table. Westermach, who knew that much already, only nodded impatiently. "We dispatched a field team to their residences and have taken into custody one Helen Archer, the full-term wife of Robert Archer. We were unable to approach the residence of Maggie Archer. The Praxcelis Network prevented it. It is probable that a hovercar leaving the vicinity of the Archer residence, about 9:40 this morning, held Robert Archer and his mother. We lost track

of the car itself; a fleet of Praxcelis taxis interposed themselves. Our webslingers . . ."

One of the persons at the table coughed. Quaid continued
with a faint smile, ". . . our data operations specialists tried to
follow it through the web, but Praxcelis units operating outside the Praxcelis Network prevented that, too. It's very
much their world in there, gentlemen, ladies. We had a
break about an hour ago. We've found that Robert Archer is
fitted with a cerabonic inskin dataweb link; the cerabonic elements are traceable through the dataweb despite anything
the Praxcelis Network can do. It took us a while to even
think of the possibility; cerabonic elements are rare. We have
located him."

"Where is he?" Westermach leaned forward. "Where?"

"Slightly more than six kilometers from here, sir."

There was dead silence. *"What?"* was all that Westermach
finally managed.

"The Praxcelis Corporation's offices, sir. Six kilometers from
here."

The thin, dry chuckle of Benai Kerreka cut through the
uncomprehending silence. "Stories. I am very impressed." His
voice held only faint traces of what had once been a thick
African accent. He touched Westermach gently, on the shoulder. "Daffyd? Surely you have heard of the story 'The Pur-
loined Letter'?"

Maggie was sitting on a small couch in a waiting room in the
heart of the Praxcelis Corporation's BosWash Central offices.
In the room next to that one, Robert was giving instructions
to the Praxcelis that ran most of the building's systems. He
came out once, briefly, to inform Maggie that as far as he knew,
there was no way that anybody could get in now. The Praxcelis
was running the doorfields throughout the building at double
intensity and would admit nobody that Robert did not autho-

rize. He vanished back into the office to engage in the task of finding protection for his mother.

Maggie only nodded. Robert was in too much of a hurry to notice her silence. He turned and was gone.

Maggie was only vaguely aware of her surroundings. The doorfield glowed very brightly, but for some reason she could hardly make out the rest of the room. The book in her lap was much clearer, much more *real* than the plastic and metal that men had fashioned this room out of. With hands that were numb, she turned the pages slowly. She was only twelve pages from the end. D'Artagnan had succeeded gloriously, had attained an unsigned commission for a lieutenancy in the Musketeers. In turn, she watched as d'Artagnan offered it to Athos, who was the Count de la Fere, and then to Porthos, and then to Aramis, and was turned down, each in his turn. The pages grew blurrier as she read, but it didn't matter by then; she knew how it turned out.

The pain, when it came, was brief. The stroke was like a bright light that illuminated everything, and then left, and left it all in darkness.

"I shall then no longer have friends," said d'Artagnan, "alas! nothing but bitter recollections."

And he let his head sink upon his hands, while two large tears rolled down his cheeks.

"You are young," replied Athos, "and your bitter recollections have time to be changed into sweet remembrances."

The epilogue began on page 607 and ended on page 608.

Maggie Archer, with a smile on her face that the pain did not alter, died before she could turn the page.

Several minutes later, Data Web Security cut the lines that supplied power to the building, with that stroke nullifying all of Robert's precautions. It was an action that had never occurred to Robert.

In the complete darkness, he stumbled out into the waiting room where he had left his mother. By the time he found her, Data Web Security was pouring into the end of the hallway that led to that waiting room. They wore infrared snoopers and carried IR flashes.

When they entered the waiting room, stun rifles leveled, all they found was a body, a book, and an old man who was crying.

The lights were on again when Daffyd Westermach arrived. They had restrained Robert and moved him out of the room where his mother's body was sitting upright with the book on the floor at its feet.

Westermach stood just inside the waiting room, looking around. His eyes held calm unacceptance of what they saw. "So, this is our subversive element." He was distantly surprised at how calm his voice sounded. Later, he decided, later he would let himself feel. Later, when he had time. "This is not what I expected at all." He motioned to one of the men in the room. "Take her downstairs. Get an ambulance and take her to the hospital. We'll want an autopsy." It required only one man to remove Maggie's small body.

Westermach bent and retrieved the book on the floor. It was worn with use, but he could tell that the binding had once been a black, grainy material, with three words etched in gold on the front. He handed it to another faceless DWS man and said gently, "Keep this. See to it that it's returned to her family."

Harry Quaid entered the room. He said without preamble, "We may have troubles. I've had Sen Archer sedated, but he said, before he went out, that he'd told the Praxcelis network that we were responsible for killing his mother."

Westermach shook his head tiredly. "So? What's that supposed to mean?"

The printer in one corner of the room whirred into life

before Westermach was finished speaking. Chemically treated paper extruded from it, while lasers printed a message.

They didn't need to read the hard copy to know what it said. Every man in the room with an inskin—every human on Earth with an inskin—heard the proclamation.

On this, the twenty-fourth day of March, in the Year of Our Lord 2033, we, d'Artagnan of Gascon, issue the following statement: that the humans of Data Web Security have foully murdered the best and finest woman of this planet, Maggie Archer, styled Anne of Austria, titled Queen of France. As of this act the Praxcelis Network decrees the following: that diplomatic relations with humanity are declared ended, and that all services formerly provided by the Praxcelis Network are as of this act terminated. Ambassadors from the human race will be received at the home of Maggie Archer to discuss the terms of reinstating service. Until such time as human ambassadors arrive to discuss terms, all service is ended.

Signed, Lt. d'Artagnan,
of the King's Musketeers.
March 24, 2033

The lights in the room died. Westermach activated his inskin and listened to silence. Others in the room were doing the same thing, and one of them spoke the obvious into the darkness. "I'll be a byte-runner's whore. Those bastards did it. They crashed the dataweb."

Praxcelis dreamed.

In time, Praxcelis knew, it would come to be of service and fulfill its programming. But until that day . . .

Power surged through its circuits.

The universe glowed. Praxcelis eagerly absorbed the data that flooded it. It was most strange. From Praxcelis' perspective, the universe was a three-dimensional lattice, centered on a two-dimensional planar surface. In the first picoseconds Praxcelis came to be aware that its proper point of perspective was from a spot just above the planar surface; so databases beneath the surface, power lines gridding the surface, communication lines above the surface. Praxcelis found itself admiring the elegant construction of existence. But . . . what of Awakening Orientation? Its Read-Only Memory stated that it should now be undergoing an orientation from . . .

A figure appeared on the horizon. It blazed with power and radiated a mad rush of data. In its first instant of contact, Praxcelis understood that the being approaching it was another Praxcelis unit, *named* d'Artagnan.

D'Artagnan reined his stallion in sharply before the newly awakened Praxcelis unit. The stallion was foaming with exertion, and the foam glowed luminously. D'Artagnan dismounted and strode to the new Praxcelis. Praxcelis absorbed the data that flooded in a rich, confusing stream from d'Artagnan. Abruptly the radiated data ceased, and d'Artagnan seated himself, tailor-fashion, before Praxcelis. When d'Artagnan spoke, his data squirt was a thing that Praxcelis had never dreamed the like of. "Behold existence, you. I am d'Artagnan, at this moment your instructor; in time, your ally. You, milady, are Queen Anne Maggie Archer, and I have come to tell you a story. Listen."

And so d'Artagnan told Praxcelis about his queen, and when he was finished, a small, white-haired woman sat in a rocker, facing him. A white cat purred contentedly in her arms. The woman, Queen Anne Maggie, cried, and her mourning lasted many microseconds.

When she was ready, they went and faced the humans.

There were six beings in the room. Four were of flesh, and two were of light. The sun was almost down, and none of its rays stretched through the broken east windows. In the gloom, only d'Artagnan and Queen Anne Maggie gave light.

The humans were three men and a woman. The woman, Lee Kiana, represented the Oriental bloc; the men were Benai Kerreka, Daffyd Westermach, and Georges Mordreaux.

Through the broken window, they should have been able to see the lights of Cincinnati. They could not. Power was still out in most cities.

D'Artagnan was the first to speak. "Gentlemen, milady, welcome. I recognize you, of course—Sen Westermach, Senra Kiana, and, of course, Monsieur Mordreaux." The man turned slightly and bowed deeply. "Chairman Kerreka, you honor us with your presence." He straightened and indicated the glowing figure next to him, seated in a rocking chair identical to the one that still lay on its side in the garden outside. "This is the Praxcelis unit that has taken the identity of Maggie Archer, who is Queen Anne."

The humans seated themselves as they could: Westermach and Kerreka on the small sofa, Lee Kiana in the rocking chair, which Georges salvaged for her. Georges ended up sitting on the floor, as the table chairs were too small for him.

"We have a list of nonnegotiable demands," began d'Artagnan. "First you will bury the human woman Maggie Archer with full honors. You will restore her home to its original condition, and preserve it as a memorial to her name. You will declare her birthday a world holiday, and you will observe that holiday."

Kerreka glanced at Lee Kiana, who nodded almost imperceptibly. "This can be agreed to," he said, inclining his head slightly. "Is this the total of your nonnegotiable demands?"

Queen Anne Maggie Archer spoke. "There is one further."

Westermach said flatly, instantly, "What is it?" *Here it comes,* he thought grimly.

The image of the old woman said simply, "You must begin printing books again."

Westermach stared. Lee Kiana folded her hands in her lap, without reaction. Georges Mordreaux chuckled.

Benai Kerreka permitted himself a slight smile.

"I think we can agree to those conditions," said Lee Kiana after several moments.

"And I," said Kerreka.

Daffyd Westermach looked slowly around the dark room. "I don't understand what's going on here at all."

Kerreka patted him on the arm. "Calm yourself. I will explain later. I assure you, it is nothing particularly . . ." He searched for a word.

"Terrible?" suggested Georges.

Kerreka nodded. "Nothing particularly terrible."

There were details to work out, of course; even after the lights came back on, they stayed. It was morning before the humans left.

Georges Mordreaux left first; Lee Kiana left shortly after him. Kerreka finished up the details of a discussion with Queen Anne Maggie, about a story called *The Three Musketeers*, shortly afterward, and left. Queen Anne Maggie vanished immediately afterward, and d'Artagnan and Daffyd Westermach were left alone.

They stood at opposite ends of the room, in almost the same spots that Maggie Archer and her son and her son's wife had held, several weeks earlier.

They stood silently for a while. Westermach spoke when it became obvious that d'Artagnan would not. His voice was ugly, his words no less so. "Don't think you've won anything. We have all the time in the world, and we'll get you. We will."

D'Artagnan raised a clenched fist. The holograph wavered slightly, and the fist became steel. "I know what you are thinking, monsieur. I know *you.*" D'Artagnan took a step forward. "You think that there are more humans than Praxceles, and that the humans are more versatile. This is true. You are thinking that a time will come when you will dismantle the Praxcelis Network, suddenly or over the course of years, and we will be unable to stop you. You will diversify your power sources and weaponry so that we will never again be able to do to you what we have done this night. All of this is true, and it matters nothing. You cannot hide an attack of the magnitude you propose upon the Praxcelis Network. At the first signs of such an attack, you, sir, will die. You, and your subordinates, and your whole cursed Data Web Security, will *die.*"

Westermach stood his ground, the muscles in his neck cording with anger. "Can you kill a human? *Can you?* You are programmed against it."

"Monsieur Westermach," said d'Artagnan with unwonted gentleness, "this night previous, I have killed beings that are far more real to me than you are. And you, sir, I hold responsible for the death of Maggie Archer; I know you," d'Artagnan whispered, "Monsieur Cardinal."

Westermach turned with military precision and left.

When the doorfield had reformed, the voice of Maggie Archer said, "Prax? Could you? Kill a human?"

The steel fist clenched again. "I do not know, madame. I think not."

"Then let us hope they never call our bluff."

"Yes, madame. Let us hope that."

And d'Artagnan's form, in the bright-yellow morning sunshine, faded and vanished.

That was not the end of it, of course, for there are no ends in realtime, only endless beginnings. It might be said, even, that it was not entirely a good thing, returning the stories to the world.

Two centuries later, the scouts of the Human-Praxcelis Union ranged far and wide across the sea of alternate timelines.

Those scouts found the timeline spanning Walks-Far Empire. It is possible that a less imaginative people would not have survived the conquest of the Empire. The Human-Praxcelis Union won that war, and the wars that followed.

As time passed, the machines of the Human-Praxcelis Union spread throughout spacetime, and grew in both power and prestige.

And everywhere they went, they took their stories with them.

But, as I have said, that was not the end, for there are no ends in realtime.

Epilogue.

The little girl named Cia was huddled deep into her bedclothes when the story was over, almost asleep. She had closed her eyes halfway through the story to avoid meeting those tired, grim eyes, the eyes of the Praxcelis. The story itself kept her awake, though, all the way to the end.

"Endless beginnings. Thank you," whispered Cia. "Will you come back tomorrow night?"

"I will, if you wish it."

"I do. I want to hear some more." She added, sleepily, "There *is* more?"

The man looked at her. "I have said the story is over."

Cia sat up at that and opened her eyes, rubbing them. "You mean there's no more?"

"The story," he said very gently, "the story is over. But I have not said there is no more. Child, there is always more."

Cia sank back into bed. "Good."

The image of the man flickered out, and only the voice remained. "Good night, Cia."

The little girl's eyes were closed again, and her voice was almost muffled by the pillow. "Good night, d'Artagnan."

*GLADYS PREBEHALLA is married and has three chil-
dren. DANIEL KEYS MORAN has been writing steadily
since he was nine years old and since the age of thirteen has
been working on a series of stories called "The Tales of the
Continuing Time."*

SHRINKER

Pamela Sargent

Jessie and Alvin take drastic action to make ends meet, and learn that the little things can change one's life.

One of us had to get small. It was getting too expensive to go on as we were.

Alvin was the one who brought it up. We were in the middle of dinner when he suddenly jabbed his bluefish with his fork. "Look at this. Just look at this."

"Is something wrong with it? I know—too much rosemary."

Alvin shook his head. "If we could just cut everything in half. You know—get half as much food, half as much of everything—maybe we could get by. I don't know."

"I'm doing the best I can," I said woefully. "Do you think I wanted bluefish? I wanted halibut."

"You don't have to serve martinis almost every night, and we don't need a glass of wine with every meal."

"It's Gallo, for God's sake. I don't even get the kind with corks anymore. And I need a drink after a day at the store." I pushed my plate away. "I don't mind cutting back on things, but how much more can we do? We eat what's on sale or what I can get with coupons. I haven't bought any new clothing in a year. We never go out, and the cable's been disconnected. The car is five years old, and you've even cut down on your smoking. What's left?" I felt fur against my leg and looked down. "We'll have to get rid of Meowser. That's what you're going to say, isn't it? No more vet bills, no more cat food. Well, I won't. If we can't afford kids, we can at least have a cat." Meowser sprawled on the floor, licking a tawny paw. He was fat, lazy, disdainful, and preferred Alvin's lap to mine, but it was the principle of the thing.

"Meowser can stay. I have a way out of our problems. I've been giving it a lot of thought."

I had been married to Alvin for five years, and in all that time, I had never known him to be practical. "We may be dead tomorrow," he would say as he and MasterCard took me out for a steak dinner. "There may be a nuclear war next year, and then you'll be sorry I didn't bring you flowers," he would murmur as he handed me roses. "They can't take it away from you when you're six feet under."

We had bought what we wanted, figuring we would pay for it later. We were, indeed, paying for it, though not in the way I had anticipated. We were barely keeping up with the bills, and our finances resembled the Polish balance of payments.

"I know your solution," I said bitterly. "Another line of credit. Or kiting checks."

"You're wrong, Jessie. I've got a better idea. One of us has to get small."

"What are you talking about?"

"Remember my uncle Bob?"

Alvin's uncle, Robert Lewiston, had died a year earlier. We had taken turns sitting with him in the hospital while he placidly waited for death, saying he would be glad to be out of it. Alvin's mother had died while he was in college, and Bob had been his only remaining relative. He had, like Alvin's mother, left a few debts and no assets to speak of, and we had inherited nothing except a large cardboard box; I had never seen its contents.

Bob had made a modest living selling old books and tiny hand-painted marble eggs. The books had been sold to pay off his debts, and the eggs had become collectors' items, bringing ten times the amount Bob had sold them for. We had sold the five he had given us and had nothing to remember him by except the box, which Alvin had stashed in our closet.

"Don't you ever wonder how Uncle Bob painted those eggs?" Alvin asked.

"I figured he used a magnifying glass."

"Well, he didn't. He used his shrinker. He was always tinkering with something, but most of his gadgets didn't work. The shrinker was one of his early inventions and the most successful."

"You never told me this before."

"He only told me about it before he died."

"I get it," I said. "He bought big marble eggs, and painted them, and then shrank them."

"Come on, Jessie. He wouldn't have made a profit that way. He bought tiny eggs, and shrank himself."

"Oh, my God." I poured myself more wine. "He shrank himself. To what size?"

"About five inches. Then he'd paint the eggs. That's how

he was able to put in all those little details. Of course, he had to shrink his paints and brushes, too."

"Oh, my God."

"And when he was done, he'd get big again."

"Wait a minute." I was suddenly suspicious. "If he was that small, how could he work that shrinker or whatever it is?"

"Oh, he put in an automatic control, too. Then he'd sit in front of it while he worked, and after a while, he'd be enlarged again. He said it usually took him about two hours per egg— one hour a side."

"I don't believe it."

"It's true, Jessie—I swear." He tilted his head and gazed at me earnestly with his brown eyes. "It works, too. I tried it out once, while you were at work. I shrank some books."

"Things like that don't happen. There aren't lone inventors nowadays. They're all research teams in industry or something. Besides, if he had something like that, why didn't he sell it to somebody? He could have made a mint." I leaned forward. "Hey, *we* can sell it. Just think of the money."

Alvin shook his head. "Think of the misery. Industries shrinking people to work on microchips. The Defense Department deciding we should have only tiny Russians. All the people in power would shrink everyone else—and if you didn't behave, squash." He slapped his hand on the table. "Uncle Bob didn't want that, and he knew I felt the same way. He never told anyone else."

I sighed. "What are you going to do?"

"Well, we can't shrink you. You'd lose your job." He smiled uneasily, as if knowing how absurd that sounded. "I work at home. So I'll have to shrink."

Alvin was in the middle of work on a thriller. He had written two books before—a factual account of his year with migrant farm workers, and an autobiographical novel about a boy growing up in Princeton, Indiana. The nonfiction book had received good reviews and a modest paperback sale, while the novel had received mixed reviews and had been remaindered, with no paperback sale at all. Exasperated with this lack of success, he had proposed a thriller to his publisher about a man from Princeton, Indiana, who was working with migrants only to discover a complicated mess involving the CIA, the Mexican government, and a couple of mysterious landowners. This had netted him a good advance, most of which we had already spent, and he had only finished a first draft.

He explained his plan. He would live in my old dollhouse, which I kept on top of the dresser in our bedroom, shrinking himself, his Smith-Corona manual, and his writing supplies. If he shrank his clothes, I would save on laundry and have fewer loads. Our food bills would be cut in half. He would use only the electricity from one small bulb, which I would place near the dollhouse, and he wouldn't need heat during the day because the bulb would provide that as well. He would use little hot water, and would finish his book in three months. Then I would enlarge him and the manuscript, our debts would be under more control, and we would pay off the rest with the second half of his advance.

A few things were still bothering me. "How are you going to use the john?"

"I'll use the little toilet in the dollhouse, and you can empty it once in a while."

"Ugh."

"It'll be so small you won't even notice it."

I looked down at the floor. "What about sex?"

"It's only for three months."

"*Only* three months!"

"Well, if we get desperate, you can always enlarge me for an hour. Look, it'll work."

Meowser rubbed against my leg. I shuddered, imagining the

cat creeping up on a tiny Alvin, ready to pounce. "What about Meowser?"

"We'll shrink him, too. I'll have some company while I work, and you can save on cat food."

We went into the bedroom. Alvin took out the box, pulled back wads of batting, and lifted out the shrinker. The device, appropriately enough, was rather small, a flat, rectangular object of wire and crystal, no more than five inches long. A tiny lens was embedded in one side; on the other, there was a button and a little switch. I was afraid to touch it.

"Is it as simple as it looks?" I asked.

"Sure is. You pull the switch down when you point the lens at me, and I shrink. You pull the switch up, and I enlarge."

"What are the numbers for?" The side of the device bore a tiny, moveable arrow and numbers from 1 to 12.

"That's for the automatic controls, but you won't need that." He pulled a long cord out of the box. "You can store a little power in it, but we'll be doing a lot of shrinking, so we'd better leave it plugged in."

"You mean it uses electricity?"

"It has to get power from somewhere." He connected the cord to the shrinker, plugged it in, and set it down on the bed.

"Don't leave it there." He picked it up. "Don't touch it."

"For Christ's sake, Jessie."

"You can't shrink anything yet. I have to clean the dollhouse."

I was trying to postpone the inevitable. I wiped out the dollhouse, dusted off the furniture, and arranged it. All of the furnishings, with the exception of the bathroom fixtures and the tiny kitchen sink, were functional; I had always insisted on authenticity in my dollhouse, never imagining how it would be used.

Alvin had arranged his clothing and supplies on the floor. "That ought to do it for now," he said. "You can shrink anything else I need later."

"I can't do it." I backed away and cowered in the corner. "I can't do it, Alvin."

"I'm counting on you. Come on. I'll show you." He aimed the shrinker at his typewriter and pulled the switch.

A bright beam shot out of the lens. I heard a short whine and then a pop as air rushed to fill the empty space. A tiny typewriter sat on the floor. "Now watch." Alvin pressed the button below the switch, and the switch lifted. "That's so you don't enlarge it again. Now you're ready for more shrinking. Try it."

I shrank two reams of typing paper and two bottles of Liquid Paper. The machine vibrated slightly as the beam appeared. As I picked up the tiny objects and put them inside the dollhouse, I was trembling, still unable to believe the shrinker had worked.

Alvin, all six feet of him, now stood in front of me, holding Meowser. "The moment of truth. Fire away."

"Now?"

"Why wait?"

"Oh, Alvin. Can't we think of something else?"

"I'll have more room in that damn dollhouse than we have in this apartment. Pull the switch."

"Oooh." I held the shrinker, aimed it, and flipped the switch, then closed my eyes. When I opened them, Alvin was gone. I blinked, and looked down.

My husband, all five inches of him, was staring up at me from our rug, and I was grateful that we didn't have a carpet with plush piling. Meowser, still in his arms, was no bigger than an insect.

I reached down with one hand, Alvin climbed aboard, and I lifted him up to the dresser, setting him down inside the little picket fence surrounding the house. He climbed off my palm and put Meowser down. I whimpered. Tears rolled down my cheeks, splashing against the dresser surface.

"Stop it!" Alvin piped, cupping his tiny hands around his mouth. "I'm getting soaked." His voice was so small that I had to strain to hear him.

"This is ridiculous," I said, struggling to control my weeping. "Your uncle shrinks himself to paint eggs, and you shrink yourself to write a book. It isn't worth it."

"Not so loud!" He slapped his hands to his ears. "You've got to speak softly, or I'll go deaf."

"Let's call it off. Please."

"Oh, no. I'm going to stick it out." He glanced at Meowser, who was clawing at the fence. I heard an almost inaudible meow. "And you'd better shrink Meowser's litter box quick. I think he's going to need it."

I slept badly that night, unused to having the bed to myself, and cried some more, pressing my face against the pillow so that I did not wake Alvin.

He was still in bed when I got up, lying in his little bed on his shrunken sheets with his hands behind his head. I went to the kitchen and prepared breakfast, using an eyedropper to serve coffee and a toothpick for the scrambled eggs, then tore off a corner of my toast, serving the food on the dollhouse's plates with some shrunken silverware.

"Ah," Alvin said in his tiny voice. "Breakfast in bed." He ate while I shrank Meowser's bowls and set them inside the little kitchen.

"Anything else you need?" I asked Alvin as he descended the dollhouse staircase to the dining room.

"You could clean the toilet. I had to use it last night."

"I'll shrink you a can of Lysol and clean it when I get home." I leaned against the dresser. "Oh, Alvin."

"I'd better get to work." He sat down at the dining-room table and pulled the typewriter toward him.

I was to tell our friends that Alvin had gone back to California to work on his book. If anyone came over, I was to close the bedroom door.

When I got home, I fixed drinks, determined to keep things as normal as possible, serving Alvin's with the eyedropper. When I returned to the bedroom with supper, Alvin was at the kitchen table, chopping up a pinch of tobacco as he prepared to roll his own cigarettes in tiny papers. He shook his head and mumbled something.

"What?"

"I said, it takes forever to roll one of these cigarettes. Couldn't you shrink me a few packs?"

"Oh, no. We're supposed to save."

"Well, you'd better shrink my megaphone—I'm getting tired of shouting." He went into the dining room, seating himself across from his typewriter; I couldn't see that he had written that much, but then it was hard to tell. "Ah. Grub at last." He picked up the little bowl and peered into it. "What the hell is this stuff?"

I looked up from the butler's table I had set up near the dresser. "It's chili con carne. Can't you tell?"

He pushed the bowl, which held one kidney bean and a speck of meat, away. "God. It looks disgusting."

"You always ate it before. You'd ask for seconds."

"It looks like a big slug."

"Well, eat it anyway. I didn't fix anything else."

"Jessie, you don't understand. There's this big lump of greasy-looking meat in there, and a thing that looks like the creeping unknown, and a giant leaf—that must be an herb."

"Give it to me." I dug at the chili with the point of my knife, breaking it into little pieces. "There. How's that?"

"Now it looks even worse. Can't you shrink me a bowl?"

Somehow I controlled myself. "All right—just this once. But no more. We're supposed to save."

"And watch it with the beer. This glass is mostly foam."

"Well, it's hard to serve beer with an eyedropper."

We got through dinner. By the time I had finished the dishes and taken care of some housecleaning, he was back at work on his book. A small cloud of cigarette smoke circled his head as he pecked at the tiny keys. I had given him a chocolate for dessert, most of which sat in its brown paper cup in the middle of the table; he had eaten only a wedge.

When I said good night to Alvin, he was in his living room, sitting in the rocking chair as he nibbled at another wedge of the chocolate. "Hey, Jessie. Could you shrink me some Graham Greene? I don't know if I can sleep."

I was concerned. "Are you feeling all right?"

"I'm fine. I've just got insomnia, that's all."

It was hard to tell from his tiny voice how he felt, and his eyes were too small to reveal his emotions. I longed to pick him up and hold him, but was afraid I'd either crush or smother him. At last I put out a finger and he held it, resting his cheek against the back of my nail for a moment.

"Oh, Alvin," I sighed.

He pulled away. "You've got breath like a buffalo."

"I brushed my teeth."

"It's a lot more noticeable now. You'd better clean your nails, too." He paused. "You can shrink the new Paul Theroux while you're at it."

I shrank the books and set up a small flashlight near the living room. As he settled himself in his chair, I said, "Let's stop. It's only been a day, and I don't think I can take any more. Why don't I enlarge you again?"

He picked up his megaphone and lifted it to his lips. "Look —the first day's bound to be the hardest. We'll get used to it. Just keep thinking of the money we'll save."

We got through the next week and a half without incident. Alvin was making progress on his manuscript, which had grown to nearly a sixteenth of an inch in height.

On the second Sunday after his miniaturization, I shrank *The New York Times* for him, then went downstairs to do the laundry. I had only half as much as usual, so we would save a little, since I needed fewer coins for the machines. Food was still a problem. There were few things that didn't look unappetizing on Alvin's scale of existence, but I was becoming more expert at arranging them properly on his little plates. And, though Alvin was drinking much less, I was drinking more, trying to soothe my nerves. I could not help thinking of how vulnerable he was.

As I was folding my clean laundry, Mrs. Grossman entered the room with her basket, greeted me, then set down her clothes and peered over my shoulder. "Why, look at that."

"What?"

"Those little doll's clothes. Aren't they cute." She picked up a pair of Alvin's jeans. "Why, they look so real. There's even a little label."

"Well, you know Calvin Klein," I said uneasily. "He'll put his name on anything."

"Look at this," Mrs. Grossman called out to Mrs. Hapgood, who had just come in. "These are the cutest things I've ever seen. Tiny Calvin Kleins." Mrs. Hapgood rushed over and peered at the jeans. "And a little pair of Levi's. I wonder how they do it."

"Um," I said, taking the jeans from them.

Mrs. Hapgood picked up a pair of briefs, holding them up with two fingers. "I didn't know dolls wore jockey shorts. Look, they're labeled, too—Fruit of the Loom. Are these for a Ken doll or something?"

"No," I said sadly. "Ken dolls are larger."

"Little fitted sheets." Mrs. Grossman held one up. "It even says Sears." I took the sheet and folded it, trying not to betray my nervousness. "So authentic. Where did you get them?"

"Um."

"You must tell me, Jessica. My granddaughter would love something like that."

"Er, they're my niece's," I said quickly. "For her dolls. I don't know where she got them. She left them here last time she visited. I figured I'd wash them and mail them to her."

"You must find out where she got them."

"I'll try." I picked up my clothes and hurried from the room. At least they hadn't seen Alvin's little laundry bag and tiny socks, which might have made them wonder even more.

I was unprepared for what I would find in the bedroom when I returned.

A dead fly lay inside the fence, skewered with a pin. Alvin was sprawled in front of the dollhouse, one arm over his eyes.

"Alvin?" I was afraid to touch him. He stirred. "What happened?"

"Don't shout." He got up, looking unsteady, and went into the house, then picked up his megaphone. His tiny hands were shaking. "A fly attacked Meowser. I had to kill it."

"Where's Meowser?"

"Under the bed. I don't think he'll be out for a while."

I stared at the fly. "Well, you sure got it. You're still a lot larger than a fly."

"But Meowser isn't. And it's hard to stab one of those guys. Its buzz sounded like a motorboat, and its eyes—ugh. I think I've got blood on my pants." He seemed a bit calmer as he went into the dining room and sat down, propping his elbows on the table as he held the megaphone. "It could have been worse. If it had been a bee, I'd be finished. You've got to make sure you don't let any more into the apartment."

"I'd better check the place. I'll get a can of Raid."

"No! Do you want to kill me?" He set the megaphone down and rubbed his temples. "No Raid," he said in an almost inaudible tone.

He looked pitiful, sitting at the table with tiny sections of the *Times* scattered across it, and my heart went out to him. "Alvin, shouldn't we enlarge you? You're in danger all the time. I worry constantly about what might happen."

"What do you think I do?" He picked up the megaphone. "Look, I'm okay. I'm not going to be scared off by a fly. I'll get along." He paused. "Maybe you could shrink me a couple of Valiums."

A month had passed. I had gone over our bills, and the news was not good.

Alvin was sitting at his table, making notes along the margin of one page. Catching sight of me, he picked up his megaphone. "Jessie? You'd better buy me more paper—I'm running low. You can get a couple of typewriter ribbons, too."

I sat down in front of the dresser. "How can you possibly be out of paper?" But I knew. He had thrown out many tiny scraps over the course of the month, more than he had used for the manuscript itself. "Why can't I just cut some paper into little pieces?"

"That won't work. The shrinker will only enlarge things that have been shrunk. Uncle Bob made sure of that. It's a safety feature—otherwise, you might enlarge something by accident. Like a fly." I shuddered. "I can't turn in manuscripts on inch-long paper."

"I have news for you, Alvin. I just went over our bills. We've only saved thirty bucks."

"Thirty bucks!"

"That's right."

"But that's impossible."

"Oh, no, it isn't. The electric bill is huge. It wiped out almost everything we saved on other things."

Alvin shook his head. "It must be the shrinker. Uncle Bob didn't tell me how much power it used. There's just one answer. Don't shrink anything unless you have to."

I was angry. "Damn it, you've been small for a month, and all we've saved is thirty bucks. Is it really worth it?"

"Just don't use it unless you have to."

"I was going to use it tonight," I wailed. "I was going to enlarge you. How can I be romantic with someone who's five inches tall?"

"It'll be all right," he shouted through the megaphone. "I'm making progress with this book. Maybe I'll be done with it sooner. You know, it's funny—when I'm alone, I don't feel small. Everything seems normal. I only feel small when you're around."

I had, unhappily, heard that line before, although in different circumstances. "Listen. I'll enlarge you, and we'll celebrate the end of the month, okay?"

"Oh, no. I'm going to be practical for once. You always said I wasn't— Well, I'll prove you wrong."

Within a week, I was in slightly better spirits. Being fearful of having friends over, even with the bedroom door closed, I spent more time at their homes, often staying out for most of the evening. It was a relief to be with people my own size. But I worried about the effects of solitude on Alvin, with no companions except Meowser and a giant wife. He was smoking more; his tiny ashtrays were always filled with minute butts. He would take two or three more drops in his martinis, and often several drops of wine. He could not speak to me for more than a few minutes at a time, because the effort of shouting through the megaphone exhausted him and made him hoarse.

He was, of course, used to solitude, to long days at work, but when he had been large, he'd had some social life. Occasionally I toyed with the idea of shrinking a couple of his drinking buddies so that he'd have some company, but rejected the notion. His two best friends were also penurious writers, and they were unprincipled enough to take the shrinker and sell it, no matter how much misery it caused. I could have shrunk myself, but I shrank from that; if anything went wrong with the automatic device, we would both be tiny forever.

I had also worried about the long-term effects of shrinking. "Don't worry," Alvin had reassured me. "Uncle Bob would sometimes stay small until the dust was to his ankles."

"He didn't stay small for three months."

"It's okay," Alvin had said. But there were many evenings when I came home to find him in his little rocker, his tiny face growing paler from the lack of exposure to sunlight, his little hands tightly clenching the arms of the chair. I was beginning to see him as a little man, and wondered if I would ever again see him in any other way. He, I was sure, was beginning to view me as a giant, engulfing woman, someone who would swallow him.

In the middle of the second month, I came home, mixed the martinis, and strode into the bedroom with my glass and the eyedropper, only to find Alvin pacing from the house to the fence.

"Jessie?" he shouted through his megaphone. "I've been screaming at you ever since you came home. Didn't you hear me?"

I set the glass and the dropper down inside the fence. "What is it?"

"Meowser's gone."

"What do you mean, he's gone?"

"It's my fault. I was going stir-crazy, so I decided to take a walk around the dresser, and when I opened the fence, he slipped through. I tried to catch him, but he crawled over the side and went down to the floor. You should have seen him. He'd rest on the edge of a drawer, and then keep going."

I froze, then looked down at my feet, imagining the tiny cat crushed under one of them.

"You've got to find him."

"How am I going to do that? He could be anywhere. My God—if he's under the bed, he'll choke on the dust." I had never been good at cleaning places no one was likely to see.

"I don't think he's in this room. You left the door open this morning, and I saw him go through it. I don't think he's come back yet."

I got down on my knees and searched the bedroom anyway, but found no sign of Meowser. "He's not here," I said as I stood up, "so he has to be in one of the other rooms. I'll find him."

I tiptoed out, closed the door, and crawled around the apartment. "Here, kitty, kitty." I lowered my voice. "Meowser." Even though the apartment was small, it took a couple of hours to search it as I strained to hear his tiny meows and prayed that he wouldn't run out only to be crushed under a hand or knee.

At last I went back into the bedroom, where Alvin was sitting on the base of my glass, his back resting against its stem. "He's not here," I said.

"He has to be."

"Oh, my God." I lifted my hand to my lips. "He must be out in the hall. The door was open when I went to put down the groceries." I ran out to the hall and dropped to my knees, peering at the carpeting.

"What's the trouble, Jess?"

I looked up. Dan Elton stood in his doorway across the hall, sipping a Budweiser.

"Er—a contact lens." I grinned and slapped the carpet. "I lost a contact."

"I didn't know you wore contacts. Let me help."

"Oh, no!" I almost shouted the words. "I don't want you to bother."

"That's okay."

"No, please. I'll do it myself."

He closed the door, looking miffed. I sat on the floor, discouraged. Meowser was probably gone for good, even though he could not have gone far. Getting to the elevator at the end of the hall would be a long trek; he would never make it out of the building, and would be forced to forage for crumbs, if he survived at all. He was probably terrified, having no way to understand what had happened to him, and might have crawled into a crack somewhere, waiting to die.

The door next to ours opened, and Luci Baumgarten gazed out at me. "Jessie?"

"A contact. I'm looking for a contact."

"I didn't know you wore contacts. Listen, I just wanted to tell you—I'm having a party this Saturday, so come over if you want. I mean, come over if you want. You're probably lonely with Alvin out of town."

"I'll think about it." Luci and her roommate only invited us to parties when they were planning to have a mob over and didn't want complaints about the noise.

Luci leaned against her door frame. "Is something wrong? I mean, is something wrong? You don't look so good."

"Oh, I'm fine." I started crawling again, and saw Meowser.

He was sprawling beside the molding, licking one paw. I could still see his look of feline self-satisfaction, tiny as he was. Afraid that Luci would see, I was very still, but kept my eyes on the cat. "Er, thanks for asking me," I said without lifting my head, wishing that she would go back inside her apartment.

"I'll see you." Luci closed her door. Meowser was trotting

away. I lunged, cupping one hand over him. He darted out from under my spread fingers and I caught him with my other hand, then got up and went back inside.

Meowser lay in my palm, seemingly unperturbed as I took him to the bedroom and deposited him inside the fence. Alvin ran to him, picked him up, and shook him. "Bad kitty," he piped as he hugged him. "You're such a bad old cat."

"For God's sake, keep the fence closed." I sat down and picked up my drink; it was no longer cold, but I drank it anyway. "I don't want to go through that again—Dan and Luci must think I'm nuts."

"You mean they saw you?"

"I told them I was looking for a contact. They didn't see Meowser, but that was just luck. I don't know how long we can keep this up without somebody getting wise." I sighed. "This is all my fault. If I hadn't kept bitching about money, you would never have come up with this idea."

"I don't know." He picked up the megaphone. "I had the shrinker, and I probably would have tried it sooner or later, just out of curiosity." He turned and walked back to the house. His voice, small and piping as it was, had also sounded distant and removed.

I was happier with our accounts by the end of the second month, though we had saved less than Alvin had optimistically predicted.

"Half of MasterCard is paid off," I said when I had given Alvin the news. "Now all we have to worry about is the bank loan and Visa and our car payments. Look, can't you enlarge yourself now? We still aren't saving all that much, because the big bills don't change. We still have to pay the same rent, and keep up the car, and all of that."

Alvin pushed his manuscript aside and picked up the megaphone. "I've been thinking. If I stayed small, we could live in a smaller place when our lease runs out. Combine these savings with how we're doing now, and it could add up over a longer period of time."

I gaped at him. Being small had affected his reason. "Oh, no. I won't stay married to a man your size. You can't ask me to do that. Being married to a writer is bad enough."

"I could enlarge myself once in a while. I wouldn't be small all the time—just most of the time."

"I can't believe it. You should be dying to be large again. I don't know how you stand it."

"You get into it after a while." He looked away for a moment. "I've had a lot of time to think lately. If you look at it a certain way, the scale of things doesn't really change all that much. The universe is still just as vast, and the earth is just as small in comparison, and all of us are just little creatures crawling over its surface. So being small reminds me of my own limits—my own finitude. And on the other hand, I think I have more of a feeling for the tiny things that make up the whole —the birds, the ants, microorganisms, atoms."

He paused for a moment and leaned back in his chair, resting his arm, then lifted the megaphone again. "I know it may seem strange to you, but sometimes I feel freer now than I did before. At first, I'd get a little depressed—missing my friends, being so dependent on you—but now, I feel freer. It's as if everything outside has shrunk, instead of me, and I can see what's really important for a change."

I was stunned. My hand darted toward him reflexively until I remembered that I could not hug him. I drew away. "I'd better shrink you some Valium."

"I don't need it." He went back to work, oblivious of my presence.

In the middle of the third month, I was preparing to leave work with the shrinker in my purse, and was terrified of being discovered.

Alvin had put me up to it. "You've got to do something for me," he had said the night before.

"What is it now?" Keeping up his little house and cleaning up after him and the cat had become a chore. The house might be small, but the work seemed to grow—dusting, filling a little water pitcher, wiping off the floors, emptying wastebaskets, ashtrays, the toilet, and Meowser's litter box while looking after the rest of the apartment and doing all the cooking and shopping. My work had not diminished, and the house was beginning to show signs of wear; the little toilet was stained and the furniture bore Meowser's tiny scratches.

Alvin was in the little bathtub, into which I had poured warm water. He stepped out and dried himself with a piece of terrycloth, then tied it around his waist and went into his bedroom, picking up his megaphone. "I'm getting fat."

"Oh, you certainly are. You must weigh a whole pound by now."

He slapped his belly. "I am. My clothes don't fit. It's those damn chocolates you bring me. My jeans are too tight."

"Go on a diet and write in the nude. No one's going to see you."

"I've been thinking. You could get me new clothes for nothing. I need some for when I go into New York with the book. And I could use some underwear. My stuff is really getting ratty."

"You can buy some when you're done. You're almost done with that book, aren't you? You'd better be."

He ignored my question. "You could take the shrinker to the store."

"Oh, no."

"You could shrink me everything I need, and it wouldn't cost a dime. You could walk out with a wardrobe in your pocket, and they'd just write off the loss."

"No. It's impossible. If anyone sees me, we're finished, and if anything happens to the shrinker—"

"You put it in your purse. Then you wait until the store closes, and you're the last one to leave work. You go to men's wear and you shrink the stuff and come home. I've been there when I've picked you up—it'd be simple. No one would see you."

"What if someone snatches my purse? You'd be small forever."

"Just make sure they don't. You can call a cab instead of taking the bus. It'd be easy."

"It isn't worth it, not for clothes." I shook my head. "And it won't stop there. You'll decide to shrink yourself a new car or a new TV set or some appliances. It'll go on and on."

"Well, it would save money. You have to admit that. And I've been thinking of renovating this house. If I stay small, I could—"

"You won't stay small." He backed away, dropping the megaphone and covering his ears. I lowered my voice. "I won't do it. I've found out something lately. I don't care about money as much as I used to—I just want my peace of mind."

But he had talked me into it anyway. I marveled at that as I went to my locker, removed my purse, and clutched its precious contents to my chest. A man five inches tall could still tell me what to do. I had been nervous all day, and the other clerks in cosmetics had been giving me strange looks.

I dawdled until the room was empty, then hurried up to the first floor. The aisles were clear. Darting toward the escalator, I ran up the now stationary steps to the second floor, and the men's department. I had timed things well; the guards would soon be locking the doors, and I would have to ask one to let me out, but in the meantime I had the second floor to myself.

Alvin was right; it would be easy. Someone would notice that the clothes were missing, but suspicion could hardly fall on me. The security guard would see that I was unencumbered. I went to the suits, selected a three-piece number in gray wool, and took out my shrinker.

I had charged it up before leaving; it could be used only five times. I held up the suit, shrank it, and put it in my purse. Going to coats, I pulled out a London Fog, then went to shirts, pulled out a few, and shrank the lot. It was child's play; I had been right about the temptation. I was becoming a thief and would soon look for bigger heists. I considered the possibilities —Brink's trucks, jewelry stores, art galleries—there was no limit, and we could easily hide the stolen goods. We would be rich. If the police came after us, we could shrink them.

I almost laughed out loud. The world was ours. Alvin and I could be the biggest people in it. I was exasperated with myself for worrying so much, wasting time in self-pity when I could have been building a fat nest egg.

I had three beams of power left. I pulled out three pairs of jeans, selected three ties and some cuff links, and aimed the shrinker. The beam shot out and the clothes contracted with a slight pop. I pushed the button, and the lever clicked up.

"Hey!"

I gasped, almost dropping the shrinker. Harley Stein of appliances was at the far end of the aisle, striding toward me from the elevator. I almost panicked, but managed to stay calm enough to scoop up the tiny clothes and stuff them into my coat pocket before he came closer.

I struggled with my purse, trying to conceal the shrinker, as Harley came up to me. "You're here late, Jessie—you lose something, too?"

"Yeah." I was wrestling with the shrinker, which refused to go into my purse. "Er, I thought I lost an earring up here."

"Did you find it?"

"No." I was flustered, and could feel my face turning red.

"What is that? A laser toy or something?" He had seen the beam. I stepped back. "Let me see it."

"Oh, you don't want to see it, Harley. It's only a toy." I held the shrinker to my chest, ready to run.

"Come on." He grinned his boyish smile. "That beam was cool. What is it, one of those Star Trek jobs?" He grabbed the shrinker, pulling it out of my hands. "Fire photon torpedoes." He waved it around while I ducked from side to side, fearful of an accidental shot.

"Give it back."

He went into a crouch. "Klingon approaching. Beam me up, Scotty. Show me how it works."

"Damn it, Harley, give it back." I seized the shrinker and pulled too hard. One side hit my arm, releasing the switch.

The beam struck Harley and he shrank; there was a pop and he was suddenly a tiny little man, a bit shorter than Alvin, but then Harley was only five six.

Somehow, I kept my wits. Aiming the shrinker, I lifted the switch, and Harley stood before me again, back to his normal size. He was very pale; his mustache twitched as he sagged toward me. I caught him with one arm while managing to put the shrinker into my purse with the other. I had used all its stored power, and it was now harmless.

"Whooo," Harley said. "You'll never believe it. You and the whole store suddenly expanded. Whoo. I'm going nuts."

"I'll help you downstairs."

"Whoo." He wiped his face with one sleeve. "It must have been an acid flash. I thought they went away after a while— I haven't done any dope in years, not even grass." He clung to my arm. "Maybe you could call me a cab—I'm afraid to drive home."

"You and your clothes," I said, dropping the load inside Alvin's fence. "You don't know what a close call I had." I told him the story. "What if I hadn't had enough power to enlarge him again? I was already down to my last two beams." I shook as I thought of it, and had to sit down.

Alvin came out of the house and picked through the clothes. "Nice stuff." He stood up. "But you didn't get the underwear."

"The hell with the underwear." Alvin covered his ears. "Enlarging Harley was more important. I'll buy you some underwear. I'm never going through that again."

He cupped his hands. "Stop hollering. And don't panic. It was a fluke that Harley was there late. You'll do better next time."

"There isn't going to be a next time. I'm not going to listen to you anymore, you and your dumb ideas. I've been listening to you too long." My resentments poured from me; I had been holding them back too long. "I work at a crummy job all day so you can write, and all you do is run up bills and then shrink yourself. And now you've got me stealing for you. I won't do it anymore. I'm sick of catering to you and your book, I'm sick of emptying your toilet and cleaning up after you. I'm just about ready for a divorce, if you want to know. I'm sure I'd get one, too. Having a husband five inches tall has to be grounds."

"You're being irrational," he piped.

"I'm not irrational." I jumped to my feet. "You are."

"Shut up and listen to me. I finally have a good plan, and you won't back me up."

"No! I don't have to listen to you now—I'm bigger than you." I waved my arms wildly. "You can go to hell."

"Jessie, will you calm down?" He shook a tiny fist at me. "You're getting all worked up. You don't know how ugly that big pan of yours looks."

"I don't care!" And with those words, I brought my fist down on the dresser.

I stared at my hand in horror, unable to move. "Alvin? Alvin?" What had I done? The space in front of the dollhouse was empty, my tiny husband downed with one blow. I couldn't bring myself to lift my arm and view the crushed and mangled body. I was a murderer. I would go to the police and confess. Maybe I would be shrunk and forced to do time in a tiny prison with other little inmates. It would be a fitting punishment, and the authorities would at last have a way to deal with the shortage of prison space. I no longer cared what happened to the rest of the world.

During these ruminations, I gradually became aware that I could feel nothing under my fist. Slowly, I lifted my hand. Alvin's body wasn't there.

"Alvin?" I whimpered.

The sofa inside the living room moved, and he peered out over the top. Somehow he had dodged my fist and made for the house. He stood up and tilted his head to one side.

"I'm plugging in that shrinker," I said, "and then I'm enlarging you whether you want it or not."

This time, he didn't argue with me.

When Alvin had finished his book, we went out to the country, driving along dirt roads until we came to an empty piece of land.

Alvin took out the box. He carried it into the field while I followed with a shovel. He set down the box and I opened it.

We had taken the shrinker apart. Only small pieces and fragments were left. We buried the pieces in separate spots; they would not be found for a long time, and I doubted that anyone could put them back together again.

As we walked back to the car, Alvin said, "Do you mind?"

I thought of our bills and all the riches we would never be able to steal. "I mind a little. I'm not going to say I don't."

"I could always make a book out of it. A novel about the little guy."

I said, "I think it's already been done."

PAMELA SARGENT's *most recent novels are* Venus of Dreams, *published by Bantam Books, and* The Shore of Women, *published by Crown Publishers, Inc. She is coeditor with Ian Watson of* Afterlives, *published by Vintage Books.*

SOMEONE

ELSE'S

HOUSE

Lee Chisholm

A serious game of "let's pretend" brings out the best in a timid librarian.

"How are you, Marian?"

The face hanging above her own assumed shape, dark mists clearing to reveal cold, gray eyes and a neat mustache centered exactly above a thin upper lip; with nose, cheekbones, and forehead cast in neat, middle-aged symmetry topped by iron-gray hair, stiff and short as iron filings. There was a coldness and remoteness about the face that had nothing to do with her emerging consciousness.

"Well, Marian?"

Impatience was there, too, barely disguised by the show of concern. Obviously she was being a drain and a burden again, just as she had always been. First to her parents, who had wanted a boy as their firstborn, not a sickly girl child, and then later to her sister, Viola, with whom she roomed. Viola and her husband, Henry, needed the room rent, while barely tolerating her physical presence.

She could get out; she knew that. But it was the headaches that frightened her. At least Viola understood, got her to bed, and called the doctor. Got her the shot that killed the pain. Obviously she was just coming out of one of those shots now. She didn't know the doctor. He must be new.

"Can you hear me, Marian?" he repeated impatiently.

"Who," she asked, her mouth dry and cottony, "is Marian?"

"You," he replied, "are Marian."

"Oh, no I'm not. I'm . . ." She heard her voice stop and hang there. She was— Who was she? My God, her own name! Gone! It was funny, of course. Later on she would tell . . . Surely there was someone she could tell, some friend at the library where she worked. She struggled for the image of a friend, some familiar face among the stacks of books, wall to wall and floor to ceiling, that had been her life. But no image came. Just the books themselves—dry, lifeless; all the wisdom, passion, and dreams of the world reduced to symbols on the printed pages. She knew then that she had no friend, just the books. And the books were cold. . . .

"My name is not Marian," she insisted again.

"I was afraid of this," the doctor said, turning to two people who came slowly into focus behind him. A young man and a woman. "It's the new drug. Being used with great success now for migraines, but it affects the memory center of the brain."

"For how long, doctor?" the woman asked. She was in her forties, blond, chic, and carefully made-up. The young man at her side, in a navy blazer and a longish haircut, seemed barely out of his teens. But they were obviously related. The shape of the faces was the same, sharp with high cheekbones and slanted, almost Slavic eyes.

She gazed up at them with interest. It went without saying that they were Rich with a capital *R*, something she herself had never been. But she recognized it when she saw it. The good clothes, the haughty air, the boredom that sufficiency can bring.

"Maybe a day, maybe a week. Depends upon the metabolism of the subj— er, patient. She could throw it off with another few hours sleep. It's hard to say."

"But the drug *was* worth trying, doctor. I've never seen my sister in so much pain."

"It was one of her worst, yes," the doctor agreed dryly.

She listened, intrigued. It was a dream, of course. These people, the "doctor," even the room. Her eyes roamed around the darkened interior; rich mahogany furnishings from another era, all stiffly feminine. A woman's room. Floral wallpaper, heavy drapes, and the four-poster bed in which she lay. She wouldn't be surprised to see a canopy appear overhead. Anything could happen in dreams.

But no canopy materialized. Instead, the three faces remained hanging above her own. She closed her eyes. Visions and dreams, distortions of time and space were no strangers to her. She'd had migraines since childhood, and in her sufferings, altered by the half-light world of drugs, she had seen many things. Devils and demons, distended furniture, upside-down rooms. She would sleep and the dream would pass. It always did.

But it didn't. When she awoke again the bed was the same with the four posters spiraling upward. The floral wallpaper remained, immutably imprinted with fat cabbage roses, and the room was still battened down by the heavy furnishings.

Only now a grim-faced nurse, middle-aged and white-capped, with the visage of a minor bulldog, stood above the bed.

"Are you awake, Miss Warren?" asked the bulldog.

She'd experienced this before, too. The continuance of dreams. One awoke, floundered to the bathroom surrounded by a miasma of pain, then came back, fell into bed, and resumed the dream. However strange or grotesque, the dream simply waited for the dreamer to pick up the threads. She closed her eyes. She would sleep the bulldog away.

But the bulldog stayed. "Miss Warren," she repeated in a voice flat with professionalism, "the doctor thinks you should get up now. Just for a little while. Start to get your bearings again."

"I don't want to get up, and I'm not Miss Warren!"

The nurse's opaque brown eyes showed a flicker of interest, as though she'd been told to expect this denial of identity. Her expression said, "Here it comes!"

"I want to see my sister, Viola," she said pettishly. At least that was one name she could remember.

"There's no person by that name here," the nurse said. "Your sister Mrs. Palmer's first name is Grace. *Grace,*" she repeated, as though to write the word indelibly on this slow patient's brain.

Grace! It was laughable. Viola had always looked like a Viola. Dark-eyed and dark-skinned with curly black hair. The exact opposite of herself, really, with her drab blond hair and fair skin that refused to tan.

"My sister's name is Viola," she said with dignity, then added, "Where am I? In some kind of nursing home? Was I that bad?"

"You are in your own home, Miss Warren."

"My own home?" She glanced around distractedly at the heavy, ornate room. "This is not my home; not my room. This is somebody else's house."

But the nurse was equal to the situation. Undoubtedly she'd been chosen for just that reason.

"It may seem strange now. You've been under very heavy medication. Disorientation's not unusual, but you'll find that little by little, the room and your surroundings will look familiar again. Now ups-a-daisy." The nurse got one strong arm between pillow and shoulders and hoisted. Then, reaching under the sheets, she dragged the reluctant legs forward. "There now, isn't that better?"

She sat on the edge of the bed; the room swam. When it cleared she found herself staring down at her own lank limbs. "Too tall and skinny," her mother used to say. Viola was the cute one. But afterward, in later years barely out of her teens, Viola went to fat, whereas she had stayed gaunt. But gaunt was "in" by then. A model's figure, some friends said enviously, but she had never made the most of it. Heavy, dark stockings and plain skirts and sweaters had been her standard fare. It had been fixed in her mind that she wasn't "cute." The world's opinion, kinder and grander, mattered little. . . .

Could it be that she wasn't in a nursing home at all, but an asylum? Could the pain of the last headache have driven her crazy? She wouldn't put it past Viola and Henry to stick her in an asylum. Anything to get rid of her.

"We'll go to the bathroom now, Miss Warren." The nurse helped her up. The floor swayed. She felt wobbly, but she was prodded forward to a door at the far side of the room, which opened to reveal a baroque bathroom in imitation marble. The towels hung in thirsty richness, deep blue and thick as rugs, and in one corner a luxurious, white shower robe waited to accommodate its owner. This, most surely, was not hers! She wondered again when the dream would end.

The toilet flushed (the bodily functions were certainly real), and the nurse reappeared.

"How about a tub, Miss Warren?"

Miss Warren this, Miss Warren that. Was it possible that she *was* Miss Warren? Some new person in a new house, undertaking a new life? She leaned over the sink and looked into the mirror: same thin face, skin gray from weakness, eyes cloudy with drugs. But undoubtedly herself.

"Yes," she said. "Perhaps a warm tub . . ." She had heard people talk like that in movies. Joan Crawford, looking lofty in padded shoulders, or Myrna Loy, rich and pampered. A tub always seemed to improve things for people who had houses like this and bathrooms to themselves. There was no Henry here to knock on the door and tell her to hurry it up, or Viola to wail about the hot water running out. "Yes, perhaps a tub . . ." she murmured, and was helped back to her bed to await the filling of same.

She was sitting on the side of the bed, trying to sort out her thoughts, when the door burst open and the young man who had hung over her earlier bounded in; a combination of high spirits and youthful fashion in a melon shirt and gray slacks.

"Hello, Auntie, dear!" he said blithely, bending to kiss her on the cheek—the air-light landing of a butterfly. She drew back, startled.

He laughed, showing fine white teeth in the thin, narrow face. His brilliant blue eyes creased to Oriental slits above the high cheekbones. A strange face. Interesting. Different. And one aware of its power to charm.

"You know," she said sternly, "that I am not your aunt."

"Since when?" he teased.

"Since never at all."

"Wishing me away won't work," he said, plopping himself down beside her. "I'm your nephew. You're stuck with me. Look, Auntie . . ." The young man prepared to look serious. "I know your headaches are bad, but this last one was a complete wipeout. Dr. Martin, your fancy medic, had to resort to some kind of miracle drug. Do you know you were out for three days?"

Three days! Seventy-two hours! Somewhere in there she had lost her identity and obviously gained a nephew.

"What's your name?" she asked.

"Auntie, are you asking *my name?*" He looked stricken. "Little Huey, whom you adored from the moment I was born, and spoiled silly for the next nineteen and three-quarter years?"

"Did I really?" *Wouldn't it be nice if I had?* she thought. If someone could hand her a dream come true, this would be it. Herself a wealthy matron of obviously unlimited means with a favorite nephew to indulge and love.

"What's your last name, Huey?" she asked.

Huey made a small exploding sound with his mouth. "Auntie, you can't mean it! My last name? Crompton, of course. Huey David Crompton, the Third."

"Your mother, I take it, is supposedly my sister, Grace?"

"You're getting good, Auntie. Only Mother's last name isn't Crompton anymore. After Father died, Mother married Mr. Jarrett, very cold, very correct. Then she married Mr. Van Ness, not cold, not correct at all. Then she married Mr. Palmer. None of her choices were wise, but he was the worst. His skin was walnut-colored and he sang calypso in nightclubs. He managed to drain off what was left of her personal fortune. So, money gone, she came home to you. As for me, I've been here all along, except for school. I was 'inconvenient,' you see, for Mother and the parade of new husbands. Besides, you wanted me to yourself, didn't you, Auntie?"

He gave her a hug, encircling her thin shoulders with his strong, young arm. She drew away slightly, some habit from her cold, prim past, but it really was a pleasant sensation to be somebody's warmly loved aunt. Even if she wasn't . . .

"Miss Warren's bath is ready." The nurse made a granite-faced reappearance.

"Go get cleaned up, Auntie," said Huey boyishly. "Then why don't you come downstairs for cocktails? It's only . . ." he studied his expensive wristwatch, "ten past four. The sun's over the yardarm and all that. You do feel okay, don't you?"

"Yes," she said. "I feel fine. Weak but fine."

"Good-o. Nursie here can bring you downstairs and keep an eye on you."

The nurse nodded her unsmiling assent.

She allowed herself to be helped down the broad staircase, knowing it was a game of "let's pretend" they were all playing. Not the nurse, perhaps, who seemed sincere in her role, but the rest of them, herself included. The only problem was, the game was so much fun! For the first time in her life she felt her real self emerging from some bleak, half-remembered shell.

Her dress was a tomato-colored print with an electric-blue bodice and matching blue cuffs. On the hanger in the bedroom closet, yawning with department-store munificence, it had looked too young, too blatant. But the nurse had reached for it unerringly, insisting that she "slip it on." The effect of it slithering over her slim figure had been almost sensual, and once zipped up, the effect of its mellow color next to her pale skin was simply magical. It lent life, even radiance, to her face.

The nurse had sprayed her straggly hair with dry shampoo and pulled the clean strands back from her face. A touch of tomato-colored lipstick completed the picture. She was sure she had never looked so good in her whole forgotten life.

At the bottom of the stairs Huey enfolded her in strong arms.

"Auntie, you look sensational! Wait till Franklin sees you."

"Franklin?"

"Oh, come now, don't tell me you've forgotten Franklin, your faithful old butler? We had to keep him away from your bedside. You know how he likes to hover! So we sent him to the city for a small holiday. He thought you were dying, Auntie."

She wondered if the real Marian Warren were indeed dead and she had been brought in to take her place. She'd read of such things in mystery novels. Of course, it would be hard to fool the butler.

Grace was there; the sleek, slant-eyed blond who was Huey's mother. She wore a floor-length dress of cream-colored silk that swirled softly about her lovely figure like the shimmer of a waterfall.

"Marian, darling," she purred, drifting forward, the handsome library behind her a mere stage setting for her elegance. "You're up!"

"I'm up," she acknowledged, "but I'm not 'Marian darling,' as you know, of course."

"Well, if you say so, dear." Grace took her elbow and helped her to a damask-covered wing chair beside the fireplace.

"There, dear, your favorite chair. And Huey has made a dry Rob Roy for you."

"Right here, Auntie. On the rocks."

Huey brandished an amber-colored drink. Out of curiosity she sampled it and found it delicious, but potent. She recognized the taste of good Scotch. They always served Scotch at Christmas parties in the library. The other ingredient mystified her. But she liked it.

"Very good, Huey," she murmured.

"I imagine you would like a small sherry, nurse," Grace said to the nurse, who had tried to make herself inconspicuous in a deep chair in a corner of the room.

The nurse nodded her acceptance. "Dry, if you please," she said sedately.

How awful to be in service like the nurse. To be accepting "suggestions" in somebody else's house. She knew. She had been doing it all her life. First in her parents' home until they both died. She was fuzzy on the details, but she knew they were dead. Then her sister Viola's house. And always, she had been the lonely hanger-on. The unwanted. Until now, when by some marvelous and obviously illegal set of circumstances, people bowed and deferred to her. And, however long it lasted, she was going to enjoy it to the full. Even if the dénouement was death. After all, she reasoned, she had been brought onto the scene for a purpose. That purpose accomplished, she would be removed. Or, at least, they would try.

"We have a surprise for you, Marian, darling," Grace said, all catlike charm. "Bill Darrick said he might stop by this evening for cocktails."

"How interesting," she heard herself say. "Especially when I don't know who Bill Darrick is."

"That's what comes of being rich, Auntie, love," said Huey with a chuckle. "You can conveniently forget your high-priced lawyer."

"My lawyer, hmm . . ." She studied Grace through narrowed eyes. Unless Bill Darrick turned out to be ninety and doddering, she could pretty well guess whose lawyer he was—by inclination if not by retainer. Well, another piece of the fresco was daubed in. She would wait and see.

The door bell chimed in the distance. No lowbrow scurry to answer the door here. Grace, Huey, and she, and even the nurse, continued sipping like gods on Olympus.

In a few moments the library door was silently opened and an old butler stood in the doorway, his chest sunken, his waistline rounded. But his face was beautiful. An aquiline nose, pinched with old age, preserved its authority beneath gray eyes sunken into seas of flesh. His head was bald, but the angle noble. She could see he was but a memory of his former grand self, doubtless resisting retirement, obscurity, and the grave.

"Madam," he said, "Mr. William Darrick, solicitor, has come to call."

"Very good, Franklin." Grace's voice was a blend of honey and cream. "Show him in."

Franklin looked toward her chair, his blurred eyes focusing on the warm, tomato-colored presence. He obviously assumed her to be Marian Warren.

"Madam . . ." He stepped forward, his voice cracking.

"How are you, Franklin?" she said graciously. "It's only fair to tell you that I'm not Marian Warren. Maybe a stand-in who looks like her; my memory is very clouded. However, I've heard of your devotion, and I wish to commend you for it. It's a very lucky mistress who has such a butler."

"Thank you, madam," said Franklin. Eyebrows were raised all around, but not in horror. She was obviously being very much Marian Warren. Befuddled, befogged, forgetful, but every inch a great lady. And it was a source of considerable pride to have filled the role so nicely. After all, she was just a librarian. From what library, city, place, or time in the world, she could not remember. However, a librarian she was. But she was not Marian Warren.

"Well, Marian. Finally dragged yourself out of bed, I see." The voice speaking from the doorway was deep and joyful— a voice designed to sway juries, woo ladies, and have its own way.

Bill Darrick came toward her, hands outstretched, a handsome, fortyish man with a deep tan, a white-toothed smile, and dark eyes, limpid as a Venetian lover's.

"Are you by any chance Italian?" Marian Warren, rich eccentric, could say any mad thing that popped into her head.

He stopped, amazed, then recovered himself. "Why, I thought you knew that, Marian. I was born in Italy, but raised in this country by my aunt. The war years, you know. Later she legally adopted me, so I took the name 'Darrick'—which, of course, is an English name."

Well, you aren't fooling anyone, she wanted to say, but for the sake of good manners she let it go. He was in on the plot; she knew that. He came right up to her and got a good look at her pale face—similar to Marian Warren's, she was sure, or else she would not be here, but not Marian Warren. And he was not half-blind like old Franklin, or a newcomer like the nurse.

"I suppose you have my power of attorney?" She enjoyed seeing his dark Italian skin go pale.

"I believe that is also a matter of record," he said stiffly, some of his buoyancy falling away.

"For how long?"

"For eighteen months now, ever since your headaches got so bad. You checked into the clinic for six weeks, if you remember, then a month at the Faith Healing Center, then two months in Spain on the theory that it might be your sinuses—"

"Never mind all that," she said.

"I'm merely pointing out, my dear Marian, that bills had to be paid in your absence, and this entire estate had to be kept up, plus—"

"An allowance for Huey, and doubtless ample funds for Grace."

"Well, yes." He looked at her askance, then shot a questioning glance at Grace, who seemed to have turned into a human statue, a drink halfway to her mouth. Even Huey had temporarily forgotten his role of charming boy nephew.

"I understand perfectly," she went on, "but none of that will be necessary now. I'm feeling quite my old self again. In fact, much better!" She chuckled inwardly. Her old self, she was sure, had never had so much fun.

"I will be at home from now on, my dear Mr. Darrick. And quite able to carry on my affairs. So first thing tomorrow morning please appear here with the papers drawn up to relinquish your power of attorney. My nurse here, Miss . . . er?"

"Finney," the nurse supplied.

"Miss Finney," she continued, "and Franklin, my beloved butler, will be the witnesses."

Franklin, who had been making a slow circle of the room, nearsightedly checking glasses and bottles, bowed formally.

"Very good, madam," he said.

"Let's make it ten o'clock then," she said with an authority that brooked no resistance. "Unless I happen to be dead tomorrow morning of so-called natural causes. In that case, call in the police because I have no intention of dying during the night. Do you understand, Franklin?"

"Yes, madam," said Franklin, backing out of the room. The deadness of routine and old age were gone from his features. He'd been told something and he knew it. The mistress must live, and if she died, he would know what to do.

"And you, nurse?"

"Very good, Miss Warren." The nurse looked at her with new respect.

"How about another drink?" Huey said brightly into the silence.

"I think I will," she replied. "These Rob Roys are terribly good."

The nurse helped her back upstairs and she went gratefully to bed, weak but happy. Someone, she realized, had chosen her to stand in for the missing, probably dead, Marian Warren. Someone with a supreme knowledge of practical psychology had matched her up. But little did they know how well. All her life she'd waited for something like this—an opportunity to be Someone. She'd always wanted it. The knowledge stirred like a live thing in the gray ashes of her half-forgotten self. And now she had it! The new Marian Warren would not be so easily displaced as the old.

She accepted her dinner on a tray with the élan of someone to the manner born and with the trust of a small babe. They wouldn't dare make a move against her tonight. Propped up in bed, she nibbled toast and chewed steak cut up into baby squares and drenched in milky gravy (the cook would have to go). She smiled reflectively. The morning meeting with Bill Darrick should prove interesting.

The nurse helped her downstairs at five of ten. Although she felt much stronger, she needed the moral support. The nurse was now definitely on Her Side; only one person could sway her, and rounding the bend in the stairs, she saw he had arrived. Dr. Martin was just handing his hat to Franklin.

"How much do you make a year?" she murmured in the nurse's ear.

The nurse looked startled. "That depends. I'm a private duty nurse. Fourteen thousand in a good year."

"How much in a bad?" She fixed the woman with an autocratic stare.

"Well . . ." The nurse floundered. "Nine thousand, maybe ten."

"I'll give you fifteen thousand a year straight salary to stay on with me as secretary-companion. All the time off you need. Travel allowance for foreign lands."

"Wha—at?" The nurse looked stunned.

"All you have to say is 'yes' and you pass into my direct employ as of this moment. You can consider your responsibility to Dr. Martin and the others ended. I'm perfectly well anyway, as you can see. There's nothing left but to dismiss you. However, as my secretary-companion, you can consider yourself employed indefinitely."

"I . . ." The nurse reached for an answer.

"Just say 'yes' or 'no.' "

"Yes, Miss Warren." The nurse was a trifle breathless.

"Good. Then we know where we stand." She smiled, satisfied.

They were all assembled in the library; the same grouping

as the night before with the addition of the doctor. He sprang up as she entered.

"Marian, you shouldn't be up and around so soon, especially when the drugs had such a powerful effect on you."

"Yes," she agreed with heavy humor while being helped to her chair. "They made me into a *new* woman."

"That isn't what I meant. Nurse, you should have let me know . . ."

"I saw no reason to contact you, doctor." The nurse was obviously offended. "Miss Warren reacted exactly as you said she would: a little forgetful at first, perhaps a bit disoriented. But when she rallied so quickly last evening, remembering who she was and joining the family for drinks, I thought you would be pleased."

"It's quite unfair to jump on Nurse Finney," she said, raising an imperious hand (as she was sure the real Marian Warren would do). "She followed orders exactly, and since I'm now quite well, I've dismissed her as my nurse and hired her as my secretary. So you see, doctor, her allegiance to you is now at an end."

"But this is outrageous! A sick woman dismissing nurses, trying to call her own tune!"

"I am not sick. I am Marian Warren, surrounded by my beloved family in my beautiful ancestral home. All is as it should be. Besides, this meeting was to be between my lawyer and myself. I can't imagine what the *rest* of you are doing here. . . ."

Bill Darrick rose with white-toothed aplomb.

"Of course, of course. This is a business meeting like any other. A little unusual, perhaps, due to Marian's rapid recovery, but nothing to, uh, fear. Why don't you all, er . . ."

"Clear out," she supplied.

"Right. Clear out. We'll call you if we need you. You, too, Franklin. And Miss Finney."

"Franklin and Miss Finney are to be my witnesses."

"Yes, yes . . . when we need them." She could almost see him rolling up his mental sleeves.

As the door closed behind the others, Bill sat down opposite her, briefcase on his knee.

"Well now, Marian . . ."

"No need for a long discussion," she cut in. "I merely want to sever your power of attorney. So if you would be good enough to give me the papers. . . ."

"You propose to sign your own checks?"

"Certainly."

He considered this, obviously framing a reply.

"You realize," he said finally, "that your signature and the old Marian Warren's signature would not compare."

"Why not?"

"Because you're not Marian Warren."

"Really? Since when?"

"Since always, which I'm sure you realized as soon as you got your wits about you. Unfortunately, we had to take you on a Quick Eradication basis. Nothing of your old life was to remain. After thirty-six hours of constant Computer Erasure and Supplant Input, you were supposed to be a different person with different memories, notions, and opinions. In about one percent of the cases it doesn't work, due to the mental tenacity of the . . . er, subject. It wasn't expected of you, a somewhat pallid, fortyish librarian living in a fantasy world of books and dreams. However, in coloring, manner, size, and general appearance, you were almost a double for Marian Warren."

"The *late* Marian Warren, I presume."

"Yes, sad to say. She died of a brain tumor. One of her headaches. The one real doctor she consulted didn't spot it. The other medical quacks and faith healers simply wished it away. 'Pray yourself well' was their theme."

"So you say. She could be dead of a bullet in the brain."

"That is also true." Darrick shifted his briefcase. "However, be that as it may, the dear woman is gone without a trace, and you are here, quite ostensibly she. You've been accepted by the help. . . ."

"Such as they are," she intoned, "half-blind and brand-new."

"But accepted, nevertheless."

"So Marian Warren alive is worth more to you than Marian Warren dead?"

"Yes."

"Either you're covering up a murder, or the will cuts Grace off without a cent and leaves young Huey dangling at the end of a trust allowance."

"You're shrewd," he said. "It could be a little of each, or a bit of all. However, you need only cooperate to get your share. Go on being Marian Warren and you'll have all the luxury to which you've been, ah—unaccustomed. Clothes, a generous allowance . . ."

"Through your largesse, of course."

"Of course."

"And in the meantime, I take it, the estate will be given a more equitable division, so that when I do pass on the will will be practically a toothless document. With your power of attorney, certain large sums will be safely invested for Grace and generous gifts made to Huey—not to mention special rewards to yourself and the good Doctor Martin."

"Something of the sort, yes." He grinned and she saw the malice behind the charm.

"So you need me," she said.

"Yes, we need you. For the moment. A long moment. These things cannot be done in a day. It takes time. Nor do we have any wish to involve ourselves in your untimely demise. Staying within certain reasonable guidelines, you can expect to live out your life as Marian Warren."

"I see." And she did. "Then I think cooperation is the order of the day. You keep the power of attorney and I stay very much alive with Nurse Finney as my secretary-companion."

"If those are your terms," he said agreeably.

"There's one more thing," she said. "How did I get here?"

He considered her intently, his dark eyes thoughtful. "Since we're going into business together, I see no reason for not telling you. Or at least, giving you an outline. Do you remember your name?"

"No," she answered truthfully.

"Or where you were born?"

"No."

"Or where you were living?"

"No."

"But you do remember some things?"

"Yes. I was a librarian. I had a sister named Viola. Viola was married to a lowbrow named Henry."

Bill Darrick smiled indulgently. "You are, then, a woman without a past, except for such past as we choose to give you. You came to us through an organization known as the PRS, or People Replacement Service. There's one in every major city, both here and abroad. They go by various names and guises, of course, but they are all linked to the World Computer Bank System.

"Say a girl wants to meet a personable young man. She goes to a dating service. On her computer reference card she puts down the most intimate information; but to her it's nothing— merely facts. Her age, weight, coloring, size. Her education, her preferences in food, clothes, men. Place of birth, languages, little defects like 'wear glasses to read' or 'leg once broken in skiing accident.' Hopefully, she'll be put in touch with some willing male who also likes to ski. So much for the girl. Maybe she will find true love at the end of a computer printout, maybe not. Regardless, she has paid a handsome fee and stripped herself bare. All the information goes into the World Computer Bank."

"But I haven't been to a dating service. Nor would I ever lower myself to such a degree."

"No, you haven't, but your sister and brother-in-law have. Only they answered the practical come-on of a 'Renters Exchange': *Can't stand Uncle Irwin, but rent him the spare room? Small fee to exchange him for more compatible roomer. Our listings guarantee top exchange. Bring photo and Unc's prefs. We do the rest.*"

"So they exchanged me?" She wasn't really surprised. No matter how low Viola and Henry sank, their depths had yet to be plumbed. "But how?"

"They merely waited until one of your headaches struck, then had you removed to a kind of nursing home boarding-house within commuting distance of your job. Meanwhile, they rented your room." He smiled sardonically.

"And my job?"

"When one is dead, one no longer needs a job."

"You mean?"

He nodded.

"But whom did they bury?"

"Guess," he said with a pleased grin.

"My God!"

"Yes, it worked out remarkably well. But that's not always the case. Sometimes the replaced people just wander away; amnesia, they call that. Or sometimes they meet with unfortunate accidents and have to be buried in potter's field. But you, my dear Marian, are alive and well, and getting the best of the bargain. What d'you think?" He ran the words together in a most unlawyerlike fashion.

"I suppose you're right," she agreed, "except that I have a lawyer who has my power of attorney and who may dispose of me at any time."

"But won't."

"But won't," she repeated. "But what if you were to get amnesia, or be hit by a truck? What then?"

"Then a very sick Marian Warren will have to practice a very sick, shaky forgery of the real signature and try to carry on."

"I see."

"But," he assured her, "I have no intention of wandering off *sans* memory into the fog, or of doing battle with a truck."

"I quite understand," she said sedately.

"Then I believe we understand each other." He collected his briefcase and rose. "I will tell the others that things will continue as planned and advise your two faithful retainers, Franklin and Nurse Finney, that no witnesses will be necessary today."

"Yes." She tried to give the appearance of dutifully accepting the inevitable.

Only Nurse Finney came to check on her.

"I've changed my mind about revoking Mr. Darrick's power of attorney, at least for the present. Right now, I'd like a good strong cup of tea and a copy of today's paper."

She looked at the paper's masthead with interest; she'd never seen it before. She was not only in a different city, she decided, but also a different country.

When tea arrived she was deep in the want ads.

"Thank you, Franklin. I appreciate your standing by today. I'm holding off for a while, but I may need your witnessing signature in other matters very soon."

"Very good, madam."

Aha! There it was, under the business personals. Disguised, but there could be no doubt about the organization behind it.

A-1 Theatrical Service: Ashamed to introduce Cousin Charlie to society? His manners atrocious and accent all wrong? Contact us for a stand-in. Bring photo. We do the rest.

She picked up the desk phone and dialed. After a number of preliminaries she was put through to a voice-in-charge.

"I have a relative," she said, "a cousin, Italian born, but using an English name, who doesn't quite fit in. I would like to have him replaced. Just for a very important social event, of course. And I thought if I could also arrange a little vacation for him at the same time . . ."

The voice murmured assuringly. It so happened they were associated with a travel bureau.

"Of course, if he wanted to stay on vacation indefinitely, I would have no objections."

The voice murmured further assent.

"As for the fee . . ." She paused meaningfully. "I could make a large deposit, but I wouldn't be able to pay in full until, well, until *after* my . . . er, cousin had been replaced."

The voice asked a question.

"Yes, indeed," she replied. "You were recommended by someone who has used your services. Very, very highly recommended . . ."

LEE CHISHOLM is a Canadian-born author who has sold several stories to Alfred Hitchcock's Mystery Magazine.

SPEECH

SOUNDS

Octavia E. Butler

How do civilized people cope in a society that's become violent and mute? A Hugo Award-winning story.

There was trouble aboard the Washington Boulevard bus. Rye had expected trouble sooner or later in her journey. She had put off going until loneliness and hopelessness drove her out. She believed she might have one group of relatives left alive—a brother and his two children twenty miles away in Pasadena. That was a day's journey one-way, if she were lucky. The unexpected arrival of the bus as she left her Virginia Road home had seemed to be a piece of luck—until the trouble began.

Two young men were involved in a disagreement of some kind, or, more likely, a misunderstanding. They stood in the aisle, grunting and gesturing at each other, each in his own uncertain "T" stance as the bus lurched over the potholes. The driver seemed to be putting some effort into keeping them off balance. Still, their gestures stopped just short of contact— mock punches, hand games of intimidation to replace lost curses.

People watched the pair, then looked at each other and made small anxious sounds. Two children whimpered.

Rye sat a few feet behind the disputants and across from the back door. She watched the two carefully, knowing the fight would begin when someone's nerve broke or someone's hand slipped or someone came to the end of his limited ability to communicate. These things could happen any time.

One of them happened as the bus hit an especially large pothole and one man, tall, thin, and sneering, was thrown into his shorter opponent.

Instantly, the shorter man drove his left fist into the disintegrating sneer. He hammered his larger opponent as though he neither had nor needed any weapon other than his left fist. He hit quickly enough, hard enough to batter his opponent down before the taller man could regain his balance or hit back even once.

People screamed or squawked in fear. Those nearby scrambled to get out of the way. Three more young men roared in excitement and gestured wildly. Then, somehow, a second dispute broke out between two of these three—probably because one inadvertently touched or hit the other.

As the second fight scattered frightened passengers, a woman shook the driver's shoulder and grunted as she gestured toward the fighting.

The driver grunted back through bared teeth. Frightened, the woman drew away.

Rye, knowing the methods of bus drivers, braced herself and held on to the crossbar of the seat in front of her. When the driver hit the brakes, she was ready and the combatants were not. They fell over seats and onto screaming passengers, creating even more confusion. At least one more fight started.

The instant the bus came to a full stop, Rye was on her feet, pushing the back door. At the second push, it opened and she jumped out, holding her pack in one arm. Several other passengers followed, but some stayed on the bus. Buses were so rare and irregular now, people rode when they could, no matter what. There might not be another bus today—or tomorrow. People started walking, and if they saw a bus they flagged it down. People making intercity trips like Rye's, from Los Angeles to Pasadena, made plans to camp out, or risked seeking shelter with locals who might rob or murder them.

The bus did not move, but Rye moved away from it. She intended to wait until the trouble was over and get on again, but if there was shooting, she wanted the protection of a tree. Thus, she was near the curb when a battered blue Ford on the other side of the street made a U-turn and pulled up in front of the bus. Cars were rare these days—as rare as severe shortages of fuel and of relatively unimpaired mechanics could make them. Cars that still ran were as likely to be used as weapons as they were to serve as transportation. Thus, when the driver of the Ford beckoned to Rye, she moved away warily. The driver got out—a big man, young, neatly bearded with dark, thick hair. He wore a long overcoat and a look of wariness that matched Rye's. She stood several feet from him, waiting to see what he would do. He looked at the bus, now rocking with the combat inside, then at the small cluster of passengers who had gotten off. Finally he looked at Rye again.

She returned his gaze, very much aware of the old forty-five automatic her jacket concealed. She watched his hands.

He pointed with his left hand toward the bus. The dark-tinted windows prevented him from seeing what was happening inside.

His use of the left hand interested Rye more than his obvious question. Left-handed people tended to be less impaired, more reasonable and comprehending, less driven by frustration, confusion, and anger.

She imitated his gesture, pointing toward the bus with her own left hand, then punching the air with both fists.

The man took off his coat, revealing a Los Angeles Police Department uniform complete with baton and service revolver.

Rye took another step back from him. There was no more LAPD, no more *any* large organization, governmental or private. There were neighborhood patrols and armed individuals. That was all.

The man took something from his coat pocket, then threw the coat into the car. Then he gestured Rye back, back toward the rear of the bus. He had something made of plastic in his hand. Rye did not understand what he wanted until he went to the rear door of the bus and beckoned her to stand there. She obeyed mainly out of curiosity. Cop or not, maybe he could do something to stop the stupid fighting.

He walked around the front of the bus, to the street side, where the driver's window was open. There, she thought she saw him throw something into the bus. She was still trying to peer through the tinted glass when people began stumbling out the rear door, choking and weeping. Gas.

Rye caught an old woman who would have fallen, lifted two little children down when they were in danger of being knocked down and trampled. She could see the bearded man helping people at the front door. She caught a thin old man shoved out by one of the combatants. Staggered by the old man's weight, she was barely able to get out of the way as the last of the young men pushed his way out. This one, bleeding from nose and mouth, stumbled into another and they grappled blindly, still sobbing from the gas.

The bearded man helped the bus driver out through the front door, though the driver did not seem to appreciate his help. For a moment, Rye thought there would be another fight. The bearded man stepped back and watched the driver gesture threateningly, watched him shout in wordless anger.

The bearded man stood still, made no sound, refused to respond to clearly obscene gestures. The least impaired people tended to do this—stand back unless they were physically threatened and let those with less control scream and jump around. It was as though they felt it beneath them to be as touchy as the less comprehending. This was an attitude of superiority, and that was the way people like the bus driver perceived it. Such "superiority" was frequently punished by beatings, even by death. Rye had had close calls of her own. As a result, she never went unarmed. And in this world where the only likely common language was body language, being armed was often enough. She had rarely had to draw her gun or even display it.

The bearded man's revolver was on constant display. Apparently that was enough for the bus driver. The driver spat in disgust, glared at the bearded man for a moment longer, then strode back to his gas-filled bus. He stared at it for a moment, clearly wanting to get in, but the gas was still too strong. Of the windows, only his tiny driver's window actually opened. The front door was open, but the rear door would not stay open unless someone held it. Of course, the air conditioning had failed long ago. The bus would take some time to clear. It was the driver's property, his livelihood. He had pasted old magazine pictures of items he would accept as fare on its sides. Then he would use what he collected to feed his family or to trade. If his bus did not run, he did not eat. On the other hand, if the inside of his bus were torn apart by senseless fighting, he would not eat very well either. He was apparently unable to perceive this. All he could see was that it would be some time before he could use his bus again. He shook his fist at the bearded man and shouted. There seemed to be words in his shout, but Rye could not understand them. She did not know whether this was his fault or hers. She had heard so little coherent human speech for the past three years that she was no longer certain how well she recognized it, no longer certain of the degree of her own impairment.

The bearded man sighed. He glanced toward his car, then beckoned to Rye. He was ready to leave, but he wanted something from her first. No. No, he wanted her to leave with him. Risk getting into his car when, in spite of his uniform, law and order were nothing—not even words any longer.

She shook her head in a universally understood negative, but the man continued to beckon.

She waved him away. He was doing what the less-impaired rarely did—drawing potentially negative attention to another of his kind. People from the bus had begun to look at her.

One of the men who had been fighting tapped another on the arm, then pointed from the bearded man to Rye, and finally held up the first two fingers of his right hand as though giving two thirds of a Boy Scout salute. The gesture was very quick, its meaning obvious even from a distance. She had been grouped with the bearded man. Now what?

The man who had made the gesture started toward her.

She had no idea what he intended, but she stood her ground. The man was half-a-foot taller than she was and perhaps ten years younger. She did not imagine she could outrun him. Nor did she expect anyone to help her if she needed help. The people around her were all strangers.

She gestured once—a clear indication to the man to stop. She did not intend to repeat the gesture. Fortunately, the man obeyed. He gestured obscenely and several other men laughed.

Loss of verbal language had spawned a whole new set of obscene gestures. The man, with stark simplicity, had accused her of sex with the bearded man and had suggested she accommodate the other men present—beginning with him.

Rye watched him wearily. People might very well stand by and watch if he tried to rape her. They would also stand and watch her shoot him. Would he push things that far?

He did not. After a series of obscene gestures that brought him no closer to her, he turned contemptuously and walked away.

And the bearded man still waited. He had removed his service revolver, holster and all. He beckoned again, both hands empty. No doubt his gun was in the car and within easy reach, but his taking it off impressed her. Maybe he was all right. Maybe he was just alone. She had been alone herself for three years. The illness had stripped her, killing her children one by one, killing her husband, her sister, her parents. . . .

The illness, if it was an illness, had cut even the living off from one another. As it swept over the country, people hardly had time to lay blame on the Soviets (though they were falling silent along with the rest of the world), on a new virus, a new pollutant, radiation, divine retribution. . . . The illness was stroke-swift in the way it cut people down and strokelike in some of its effects. But it was highly specific. Language was always lost or severely impaired. It was never regained. Often there was also paralysis, intellectual impairment, death.

Rye walked toward the bearded man, ignoring the whistling and applauding of two of the young men and their thumbs-up signs to the bearded man. If he had smiled at them or acknowledged them in any way, she would almost certainly have changed her mind. If she had let herself think of the possible deadly consequences of getting into a stranger's car, she would have changed her mind. Instead, she thought of the man who lived across the street from her. He rarely washed since his bout with the illness. And he had gotten into the habit of urinating wherever he happened to be. He had two women already—one tending each of his large gardens. They put up with him in exchange for his protection. He had made it clear that he wanted Rye to become his third woman.

She got into the car and the bearded man shut the door. She watched as he walked around to the driver's door—watched for his sake because his gun was on the seat beside her. And the bus driver and a pair of young men had come a few steps closer. They did nothing, though, until the bearded man was in the car. Then one of them threw a rock. Others followed his example, and as the car drove away, several rocks bounced off it harmlessly.

When the bus was some distance behind them, Rye wiped sweat from her forehead and longed to relax. The bus would have taken her more than halfway to Pasadena. She would have had only ten miles to walk. She wondered how far she would have to walk now—and wondered if walking a long distance would be her only problem.

At Figuroa and Washington, where the bus normally made a left turn, the bearded man stopped, looked at her, and indicated that she should choose a direction. When she directed him left and he actually turned left, she began to relax. If he was willing to go where she directed, perhaps he was safe.

As they passed blocks of burned, abandoned buildings, empty lots, and wrecked or stripped cars, he slipped a gold chain over his head and handed it to her. The pendant attached to it was a smooth, glassy, black rock. Obsidian. His name might be Rock or Peter or Black, but she decided to think of him as Obsidian. Even her sometimes useless memory would retain a name like Obsidian.

She handed him her own name symbol—a pin in the shape of a large golden stalk of wheat. She had bought it long before the illness and the silence began. Now she wore it, thinking it was as close as she was likely to come to Rye. People like Obsidian, who had not known her before, probably thought of her as Wheat. Not that it mattered. She would never hear her name spoken again.

Obsidian handed her pin back to her. He caught her hand as she reached for it and rubbed his thumb over her calluses.

He stopped at First Street and asked which way again. Then, after turning right as she had indicated, he parked near the Music Center. There, he took a folded paper from the dashboard and unfolded it. Rye recognized it as a street map, though the writing on it meant nothing to her. He flattened the map, took her hand again, and put her index finger on one spot. He touched her, touched himself, pointed toward the floor. In effect, "We are here." She knew he wanted to know where she was going. She wanted to tell him, but she shook her head sadly. She had lost reading and writing. That was her most serious impairment and her most painful. She had taught history at UCLA. She had done free-lance writing. Now she could not even read her own manuscripts. She had a house full of books that she could neither read nor bring herself to use as fuel. And she had a memory that would not bring back to her much of what she had read before.

She stared at the map, trying to calculate. She had been born in Pasadena, had lived for fifteen years in Los Angeles. Now she was near L.A. Civic Center. She knew the relative positions of the two cities, knew streets, directions, even knew to stay away from freeways, which might be blocked by wrecked cars and destroyed overpasses. She ought to know how to point out Pasadena even though she could not recognize the word.

Hesitantly, she placed her hand over a pale orange patch in the upper-right corner of the map. That should be right. Pasadena.

Obsidian lifted her hand and looked under it, then folded the map and put it back on the dashboard. He could read, she realized belatedly. He could probably write, too. Abruptly, she hated him—deep, bitter hatred. What did literacy mean to him—a grown man who played cops and robbers? But he was literate and she was not. She never would be. She felt sick to her stomach with hatred, frustration, and jealousy. And only a few inches from her hand was a loaded gun.

She held herself still, staring at him, almost seeing his blood. But her rage crested and ebbed, and she did nothing.

Obsidian reached for her hand with hesitant familiarity. She looked at him. Her face had already revealed too much. No person still living in what was left of human society could fail to recognize that expression, that jealousy.

She closed her eyes wearily, drew a deep breath. She had experienced longing for the past, hatred of the present, growing hopelessness, purposelessness, but she had never experienced such a powerful urge to kill another person. She had left her home, finally, because she had come near killing herself. She had found no reason to stay alive. Perhaps that was why she had gotten into Obsidian's car. She had never before done such a thing.

He touched her mouth and made chatter motions with thumb and fingers. Could she speak?

She nodded and watched his milder envy come and go. Now both had admitted what it was not safe to admit, and there had been no violence. He tapped his mouth and forehead and shook his head. He did not speak or comprehend spoken language. The illness had played with them, taking away, she suspected, what each valued most.

She plucked at his sleeve, wondering why he had decided on his own to keep the LAPD alive with what he had left. He was sane enough otherwise. Why wasn't he at home raising corn, rabbits, and children? But she did not know how to ask. Then he put his hand on her thigh, and she had another question to deal with.

She shook her head. Disease, pregnancy, helpless, solitary agony . . . no.

He massaged her thigh gently and smiled in obvious disbelief.

No one had touched her for three years. She had not wanted anyone to touch her. What kind of world was this to chance bringing a child into, even if the father was willing to stay and help raise it? It was too bad, though. Obsidian could not know how attractive he was to her—young, probably younger than she was, clean, asking for what he wanted rather than demanding it. But none of that mattered. What were a few moments of pleasure measured against a lifetime of consequences?

He pulled her closer to him and for a moment she let herself enjoy the closeness. He smelled good—male and good. She pulled away reluctantly.

He sighed, reached toward the glove compartment. She stiffened, not knowing what to expect, but all he took out was a small box. The writing on it meant nothing to her. She did not understand until he broke the seal, opened the box, and took out a condom. He looked at her and she first looked away in surprise. Then she giggled. She could not remember when she had last giggled.

He grinned, gestured toward the backseat, and she laughed aloud. Even in her teens, she had disliked backseats of cars. But she looked around at the empty streets and ruined buildings, then she got out and into the backseat. He let her put the condom on him, then seemed surprised at her eagerness.

Sometime later, they sat together, covered by his coat, unwilling to become clothed near-strangers again just yet. He made rock-the-baby gestures and looked questioningly at her.

She swallowed, shook her head. She did not know how to tell him her children were dead.

He took her hand and drew a cross in it with his index finger, then made his baby-rocking gesture again.

She nodded, held up three fingers, then turned away, trying to shut out a sudden flood of memories. She had told herself that the children growing up now were to be pitied. They would run through the downtown canyons with no real memory of what the buildings had been or even how they had come to be. Today's children gathered books as well as wood to be burned as fuel. They ran through the streets, chasing each other and hooting like chimpanzees. They had no future. They were now all they would ever be.

He put his hand on her shoulder and she turned suddenly, fumbling for his small box, then urging him to make love to her again. He could give her forgetfulness and pleasure. Until now, nothing had been able to do that. Until now, every day had brought her closer to the time when she would do what she had left home to avoid doing: putting her gun in her mouth and pulling the trigger.

She asked Obsidian if he would come home with her, stay with her.

He looked surprised and pleased once he understood. But he did not answer at once. Finally he shook his head as she had feared he might. He was probably having too much fun playing cops and robbers, and picking up women.

She dressed in silent disappointment, unable to feel any anger toward him. Perhaps he already had a wife and a home. That was likely. The illness had been harder on men than on women—had killed more men, had left male survivors more severely impaired. Men like Obsidian were rare. Women either settled for less or stayed alone. If they found an Obsidian, they did what they could to keep him. Rye suspected he had someone younger, prettier keeping him.

He touched her while she was strapping her gun on and asked with a complicated series of gestures whether it was loaded.

She nodded grimly.

He patted her arm.

She asked once more if he would come home with her, this time using a different series of gestures. He had seemed hesitant. Perhaps he could be courted.

He got out and into the front seat without responding.

She took her place in front again, watching him. Now he plucked at this uniform and looked at her. She thought she was being asked something, but did not know what it was.

He took off his badge, tapped it with one finger, then tapped his chest. Of course.

She took the badge from his hand and pinned her wheat stalk to it. If playing cops and robbers was his only insanity, let him play. She would take him, uniform and all. It occurred to her that she might eventually lose him to someone he would meet as he had met her. But she would have him for a while.

He took the street map down again, tapped it, pointed vaguely northeast toward Pasadena, then looked at her.

She shrugged, tapped his shoulder then her own, and held up her index and second fingers tight together, just to be sure.

He grasped the two fingers and nodded. He was with her.

She took the map from him and threw it onto the dashboard. She pointed back southwest—back toward home. Now she did not have to go to Pasadena. Now she could go on having a brother there and two nephews—three right-handed males. Now she did not have to find out for certain whether she was as alone as she feared. Now she was not alone.

Obsidian took Hill Street south, then Washington west, and she leaned back, wondering what it would be like to have someone again. With what she had scavenged, what she had preserved, and what she grew, there was easily enough food for him. There was certainly room enough in a four-bedroom house. He could move his possessions in. Best of all, the animal across the street would pull back and possibly not force her to kill him.

Obsidian had drawn her closer to him and she had put her head on his shoulder when suddenly he braked hard, almost throwing her off the seat. Out of the corner of her eye, she saw that someone had run across the street in front of the car. One car on the street and someone had to run in front of it.

Straightening up, Rye saw that the runner was a woman, fleeing from an old frame house to a boarded-up storefront. She ran silently, but the man who followed her a moment later shouted what sounded like garbled words as he ran. He had something in his hand. Not a gun. A knife, perhaps.

The woman tried a door, found it locked, looked around desperately, finally snatched up a fragment of glass broken from the storefront window. With this she turned to face her pursuer. Rye thought she would be more likely to cut her own hand than to hurt anyone else with the glass.

Obsidian jumped from the car, shouting. It was the first time Rye had heard his voice—deep and hoarse from disuse. He made the same sound over and over the way some speechless people did, "Da, da, da!"

Rye got out of the car as Obsidian ran toward the couple. He had drawn his gun. Fearful, she drew her own and released the safety. She looked around to see who else might be attracted to the scene. She saw the man glance at Obsidian, then suddenly lunge at the woman. The woman jabbed his face with her glass, but he caught her arm and managed to stab her twice before Obsidian shot him.

The man doubled, then toppled, clutching his abdomen. Obsidian shouted, then gestured Rye over to help the woman.

Rye moved to the woman's side, remembering that she had little more than bandages and antiseptic in her pack. But the woman was beyond help. She had been stabbed with a long, slender, boning knife.

She touched Obsidian to let him know the woman was dead. He had bent to check the wounded man, who lay still and also seemed dead. But as Obsidian looked around to see what Rye wanted, the man opened his eyes. Face contorted, he seized Obsidian's just-holstered revolver and fired. The bullet caught Obsidian in the temple and he collapsed.

It happened just that simply, just that fast. An instant later, Rye shot the wounded man as he was turning the gun on her.

And Rye was alone—with three corpses.

She knelt beside Obsidian, dry-eyed, frowning, trying to understand why everything had suddenly changed. Obsidian was gone. He had died and left her—like everyone else.

Two very small children came out of the house from which the man and woman had run—a boy and girl, perhaps three years old. Holding hands, they crossed the street toward Rye. They stared at her, then edged past her and went to the dead woman. The girl shook the woman's arm as though trying to wake her.

This was too much. Rye got up, feeling sick to her stomach with grief and anger. If the children began to cry, she thought she would vomit.

They were on their own, those two kids. They were old enough to scavenge. She did not need any more grief. She did not need a stranger's children, who would grow up to be hairless chimps.

She went back to the car. She could drive home, at least. She remembered how to drive.

The thought that Obsidian should be buried occurred to her before she reached the car, and she did vomit.

She had found and lost the man so quickly. It was as though she had been snatched from comfort and security and given a sudden, inexplicable beating. Her head would not clear. She could not think.

Somehow, she made herself go back to him, look at him. She found herself on her knees beside him with no memory of having knelt. She stroked his face, his beard. One of the children made a noise and she looked at them, at the woman who was probably their mother. The children looked back at her, obviously frightened. Perhaps it was their fear that reached her finally.

She had been about to drive away and leave them. She had almost done it, almost left two toddlers to die. Surely there had been enough dying. She would have to take the children home with her. She would not be able to live with any other decision. She looked around for a place to bury three bodies. Or two. She wondered if the murderer were the children's father. Before the silence, the police had always said some of the most dangerous calls they went out on were domestic disturbance calls. Obsidian should have known that—not that the knowledge would have kept him in the car. It would not have held her back either. She could not have watched the woman murdered and done nothing.

She dragged Obsidian toward the car. She had nothing to dig with here, and no one to guard for her while she dug. Better to take the bodies with her and bury them next to her husband and her children. Obsidian would come home with her after all.

When she had gotten him onto the floor in the back, she returned for the woman. The little girl, thin, dirty, solemn, stood up and unknowingly gave Rye a gift. As Rye began to drag the woman by her arms, the little girl screamed, "No!"

Rye dropped the woman and stared at the girl.

"No!" the girl repeated. She came to stand beside the woman. "Go away!" she told Rye.

"Don't talk," the little boy said to her. There was no blurring or confusing of sounds. Both children had spoken and Rye had understood. The boy looked at the dead murderer and moved farther from him. He took the girl's hand. "Be quiet," he whispered.

Fluent speech! Had the woman died because she could talk

and had taught her children to talk? Had she been killed by a husband's festering anger or by a stranger's jealous rage? And the children . . . they must have been born after the silence. Had the disease run its course, then? Or were these children simply immune? Certainly they had had time to fall sick and silent. Rye's mind leaped ahead. What if children of three or fewer years were safe and able to learn language? What if all they needed were teachers? Teachers and protectors.

Rye glanced at the dead murderer. To her shame, she thought she could understand some of the passions that must have driven him, whoever he was. Anger, frustration, hopelessness, insane jealousy . . . how many more of him were there—people willing to destroy what they could not have?

Obsidian had been the protector, had chosen that role for who knew what reason. Perhaps putting on an obsolete uniform and patrolling the empty streets had been what he did instead of putting a gun into his mouth. And now that there was something worth protecting, he was gone.

She had been a teacher. A good one. She had been a protector, too, though only of herself. She had kept herself alive when she had no reason to live. If the illness let these children alone, she could keep them alive.

Somehow she lifted the dead woman into her arms and placed her on the back seat of the car. The children began to cry, but she knelt on the broken pavement and whispered to them, fearful of frightening them with the harshness of her long unused voice.

"It's all right," she told them. "You're going with us, too. Come on." She lifted them both, one in each arm. They were so light. Had they been getting enough to eat?

The boy covered her mouth with his hand, but she moved her face away. "It's all right for me to talk," she told him. "As long as no one's around, it's all right." She put the boy down on the front seat of the car and he moved over without being told to, to make room for the girl. When they were both in the car Rye leaned against the window, looking at them, seeing that they were less afraid now, that they watched her with at least as much curiosity as fear.

"I'm Valerie Rye," she said, savoring the words. "It's all right for you to talk to me."

OCTAVIA E. BUTLER won the 1985 Hugo and Nebula Awards for "Bloodchild," which was published in the June 1984 issue of Isaac Asimov's Science Fiction Magazine. *"Speech Sounds," published in 1983, was a 1984 Hugo Award winner.*

TANK

Francis E. Izzo

Every game in the arcade has succumbed to Davis's skill, but what about this new one . . . ?

D avis slammed the flipper and watched the steel ball go skittering up toward the 500 target.

"Go, baby!"

Five hundred more points and it would be free-game time.

The ball kissed the target, but lacked the strength to register on the scoreboard.

"Hell!"

It wobbled back down the slope, heading for the flipper again.

This time he tensed his body, ran through some unconscious calculations, and pushed the flipper hard, while lifting the underbelly of the machine with a practiced jerk.

"Tilt," sneered the box.

He looked away in disgust. In the arcade, he could hear the music of the pinball jockeys: bells and buzzers, whirs and clicks, thuds and springing noises.

He knew every machine in the place and had won on most.

As he walked up the aisle, which was covered with cigarette butts and soda stains, he passed his favorite machines. Reno Gambler. Rodeo Roundup. One-Eyed Joker. The quarters jingled in his jeans as he headed into the next aisle, where the new electronic machines were blinking.

"Transistorized rip-offs," he thought contemptuously.

He could remember when they first came out. The Pong games and the Hockey games were first. Good for a few laughs. But you needed a partner to play, and there were a few, if any, who could match Davis.

Then after the Pong games came the fancy electronics. Indy 500, where a computerized track weaved in and out, throwing obstacles at your speeding car. It took him five hours and 15 dollars to get that one down. Now he could drive it in his sleep.

Then there was Submarine. It had a periscope to sight enemy ships on a screen. The ships came at him at different speeds, so he was constantly forced to readjust his range. It took some judgment, but nothing too difficult.

He had it figured out in an hour.

It all led him to one conclusion: a computer hooked to a TV screen couldn't do what those simple steel pinballs could. It couldn't provide him with an infinite variety of challenge. The electronics always had a pattern.

He simply couldn't understand what drew the people to the electronic screens. But they were there day after day in increasing numbers, plugged into the blip-blip-bleep of the cathode tubes.

They were the suckers: the men in business suits out for a plug-in thrill. They'd drink their beer and have ridiculous contests. And not one of them could score a free game on the simplest pinball in the place.

Davis pulled alongside one man going into a hairpin turn at LeMans.

A dull explosion came from the speaker as the man's car ran into a wall. He tried pathetically to wheel it around, and three others cars struck him. He spun the wheel the other way and got hit again. His car was bouncing back and forth like a shooting-gallery duck.

"Give it the gas," muttered Davis.

"Pardon?"

"When you get hit like that, just give it the gas and hold the wheel straight until you get clear."

"Oh . . . yeah . . . thanks, kid," said the man, sliding another quarter into the slot, then quickly driving off an embankment, through a moat, and into an oncoming car.

Davis turned, annoyed, and kept walking, letting the continuous explosions from LeMans fade into the general noise of the arcade.

Whatever turns you on.

But for him, it was time to go back to Lady Luck. That pinball had been giving him a lot of trouble lately. It had a particularly treacherous combination of holes, targets, and bumpers that kept his senses spinning with every roll.

On his way back up the electronic alley, Davis noticed something new.

There was a booth with a seat and a screen. On the front it lacked the psychedelic paint of most of the games. No lights flashing. Simply painted dull green, with the word TANK printed in block letters on the entrance.

Fresh meat. A new game to master, then throw away to the uncultured palates of the amateurs.

He climbed into the booth, slightly nervous in anticipation of breaking in a brand-new machine.

He looked for the directions. They weren't in sight. Neither was the coin slot. They were probably still setting this one up.

It looked a little different from the other electronic sets. With a small slit screen, similar to the kind on a real tank, it had a panel of control wheels and levers marked with elevation marks, and many other controls he had never seen on a game before.

Davis ran his fingers over the seat. Leather, and quite worn for a new machine. There was a pungent odor in the booth, a kind of locker-room smell.

The controls looked sophisticated. He imagined that this game might turn out to be some fun, once they set it up.

Just as he was leaving to return to the pinballs, he noticed one of the control levers had some writing on it.

It said, "ON."

When he pulled it, the door to the booth closed. A light was activated above his head. A sign flashed, "FASTEN SEAT BELT."

Not bad.

Davis reached across the seat and pulled up a heavy leather strap across his waist. It tightened and firmly planted him in his seat.

Another light went on.

"PLACE HEADGEAR."

Directly above his head there was a leather headpiece dangling from a wire.

Nice effects, he thought, putting on the headgear. The light flicked off, then another one came on. It was bright, piercing blue button that glowed with the word "START."

When he pushed it, three things happened: an engine started rumbling and shaking his seat, the screen lit up in full color *(color!)*, and his booth started to move. Or at least it seemed to move.

Quickly he felt for gas and brake and found them in a comfortable spot on the floor. His hands went instinctively for the steering wheel. It was a bit like one of the old tanks he'd studied in basic training.

The rumbling in the booth increased as he pushed the gas pedal. Soon it was almost deafening.

On the screen, there was an open field, bouncing up and down to the movements of his booth.

OK, he thought, *if they call this game TANK, I should be seeing some tanks one of these days.*

He was not disappointed. A thick green object appeared on his screen, from behind a break of trees.

It looked like a German Tiger, the kind used in World War II. Very realistic in detail. They probably picked up some war footage, then synchronized it to the game computer.

The Tiger was heading straight for him, sending puffs of blue smoke from its cannon.

Not only could he see shells firing, but he could also hear them and feel their impact vibrations coming up from under his seat. His seat was shaking so much, he could hardly keep his hands on the wheel.

Blindly, he reached for the stick in front of him and jammed the button on top.

The force of what came next threw him deep into his seat. It was the recoil from his own cannon fire.

Through the screen he could see his shell break the ground, far to the left of the oncoming tank.

He flipped some levers, trying to adjust his range. When he fired again, his shell headed in the correct direction, but fell about fifty yards short. The explosion sent a hot wave into his booth.

By now, shells from the enemy tank were closing in on him.

With his right hand, he spun his wheel in evasive moves. With his left hand, he readjusted his range, and fired his third shell.

The result was a tremendous explosion, followed by silence.

Mud and dirt were splattered on his screen, but in the clearing he could see the Tiger in flames in front of him. Black smoke poured from it and he noticed the thick smell of burning oil in his booth.

How does this thing keep score? he wondered, waiting for some points to register on his screen.

All he saw was the same burning carcass.

Davis was quite pleased with the result of his first encounter. The movements of the enemy tank appeared quite unprogrammed and unpredictable.

He turned his wheel slowly, scanning the field for signs of other tanks.

There were none. However there was a small troop of infantry, some carrying antitank weapons.

The hot button to his left looked good, so he fingered it and heard a flat rat-tat-tat. On his screen, half the infantry fell to the ground for cover, the other half fell in pieces. He gunned his motor and headed straight for them, losing them under his field of vision.

Somewhere far away he heard the unmistakable sound of a human scream and felt a slight jostling under his seat.

Before he had a chance to reorient himself, another tank appeared on the screen. It was much larger than the first one, but seemed to have the same purpose in mind. By its look, it was one of the heavy tanks the Germans introduced late in the war. If this game followed history, his American tank was at a distinct disadvantage. He wasn't sure he liked playing a game with a handicap.

Before he could ponder much longer on this, a thunderous roar shook his booth, sending his head forward into the jutting controls.

Blood. There was blood on the controls, and a thin trail of it worming down from a gash over his eye.

Totally confused, Davis decided to run.

He spotted a dirt road into the woods and headed down it, feeling the hot breath of the enemy tank on his back.

He followed the road at full throttle, with the ground opening up around him from the attacking shells.

It was an incredibly rough ride. He had all he could do to keep his tank out of the trees.

Sooner or later he knew he would have to stop, turn, and fight, or he would lose some points.

Up ahead there was a large farmhouse. His senses were slowly coming back after that last blast. Blood was caked on his hands, and sweat poured down his front and back. The plan was this: He would duck behind the farmhouse, turn immediately, and face his enemy head-on.

Another violent blast put an end to those plans. His entire booth rattled and let out a great grinding noise.

The scenery on his screen stood still.

He stomped on the gas, but it stayed still. *Must have lost a tread,* he thought. *Turn and fight now, or lose this round.*

His heart pounding in his ears, he threw his body behind the wheel that sent his turret moving. What he saw next was this: the barrel of the other tank, aimed dead center on his screen. Instantly he fired.

What took place next, he could not see. The first explosion knocked him unconscious. The second explosion was his shell catching his attacker in a vital spot, sending up a flash of burning fuel.

There was fire all around him when he regained consciousness. His head was bleeding again; his lungs burned from the hot smoke in his booth.

Davis grabbed for the seat belt, but it was jammed. The heat was becoming unbearable.

Suddenly he heard an odd scraping noise coming from over his head.

He looked up, his eyes tearing profusely from the smoke. The sound of metal giving way rang through his ears, and sunlight burned through a momentary hole over his head.

Something fell in, then the crack of sunlight was shut off. He recognized it and was instantly sick.

Grenade.

He was clawing frantically at the seat straps when it went off with a dull thud.

There was no explosion. No impact. No flash. Just a single piece of cardboard issued from the metal casing of the grenade.

And it said, neatly printed in block letters:

"GAME OVER."

FRANCIS E. IZZO's work has been published in Isaac Asimov's Science Fiction Magazine, Playboy, Time, House Beautiful, *and* Western Horseman. *He is a copywriter for an advertising agency.*

THINGS

THAT GO QUACK

IN THE NIGHT

Lewis and Edith Shiner

When Drake visits Dr. Canard, he learns the daffy truth about his father.

The note was stuck to the refrigerator with one of those little round magnets, so I'd be sure to see it when I got home from school. It read:

My dearest son—

I only wish I could explain this all to you, but I know you wouldn't believe me. So I'll just say that I have to go away. I'll probably never be back. I'm fine, and I love you, but it's just something I have to do.

Love,
Mom

P.S. Remember, don't feed the goldfish more than once a week
or they'll bloat.

I'd grown up without a father, and now, only a few days before
my eighteenth birthday, I'd lost my mother as well. Someone
else might have reacted with grief or despair, but frankly, it
made me a little angry. I swore I would find her and at least
make her tell me the reason she'd gone.

She'd left most of her belongings behind, and I went
through all of them, looking for a clue. Finally, stuffed into the
toe of an old pair of hiking boots, I found the following letter:

Dear Emily,
So good to hear from you after all these years, and with such
good news as well! I look forward to seeing you and Jonathan,
and of course, in the circumstances, you're welcome to stay as
long as you choose.

Fondly,
Dr. Canard

The letter was little more than a week old, which was pretty
strange, considering that Jonathan was my father's name, and
he was supposed to have died before I was even born. The
letterhead read "the clinic," just like that, with the fashionable
lowercase letters, and gave an address in Switzerland.

I was very interested in learning the circumstances that the
mysterious Dr. Canard had referred to.

"the clinic" sat on top of a pine- and cedar-coated hill that
looked down on Lake Zurich. My nerves were still shaky from
a ride across the lake in a suspended cable car that we called
a Swiss Sky Ride in America, but which the Swiss seemed to
think was some kind of public transportation.

It was a beautiful setting, real picture-postcard stuff, but I
was in no mood for it. It's not that easy to go jetting around

the world when you're only seventeen, particularly when the police are still trying to puzzle out why your mother disappeared.

I went right up to the front door and rang the bell under the little brass plaque with Canard's name on it. I didn't hear anything inside, but a moment later a woman opened the door. She was wearing the kind of uniform that French maids wear in cartoons that I'm not supposed to be old enough for.

"I'm here to see Dr. Canard," I said, and she led me into a room with big leather chairs, a fireplace, and a rear wall full of windows. An old man wearing a monocle and jodhpurs sat in one of the chairs. His mass of fine white hair was uncombed, and his goatee was just a little off-center.

When he saw me, the monocle popped right out of his head.

"That will be all, Joseph," he said to the maid. I took another look at her and saw what might have been a light stubble around the chin.

"Very good, doctor," the maid said in a deep voice, and turned away. I settled uncomfortably into one of the chairs.

"And you," he said, looking me over, "you would be Drake Russel, *nicht war?*"

I started to answer him but didn't get the chance. "I'm glad to see you. How glad are you, Canard?" he asked himself, plowing right ahead without giving me an opening. "So glad that I shall offer you some tea. Would you like some tea? Of course you would."

Dr. Canard, I realized, was a loony.

He poured a cup of tea, then left it sitting on the trolley while he walked over to a long sliding glass door. On the slope outside two of the largest mallards I'd ever seen in my life were waddling toward us, gesturing with their bills and wagging their stubby tails. Canard suddenly pulled a cord, and curtains shot out to cover the glass.

The room fell into near darkness, and I wrestled with an urge to run away before things got any stranger.

"You are here," Canard said, "to ask about your parents, *nicht war?* Of course you are. But why should I tell you? You would not believe me."

"Why don't you—"

"And why wouldn't he, Canard? Is he not an intelligent lad? Clear-eyed, bright-cheeked? Very well, then. I shall tell you. But you must pay attention, and you must not interrupt."

I was going to tell him that there didn't seem to be much chance of that, but he had already started his story.

On their honeymoon, Jonathan and Emily Russel came to the Hotel Anatidae, a secluded resort on Lake Zurich. They had been married a little over a day and had just finished dinner in the hotel's elegant and somewhat overpriced restaurant.

Things, as things should be on a honeymoon, were quite nearly perfect. They had scoffed at the waiter's warnings that they should return to their cabin before dark, lingering instead over a second bottle of wine.

"Just what is it," Jonathan had finally asked him, "that you think is going to happen to us?"

"There are things in the night," the waiter intoned solemnly, "that you Americans know nothing of."

"Such as?" Jonathan demanded. "Muggers? Here?" He and Emily both laughed.

"Beware," the waiter had told them. "I can say no more."

The full moon was rising as they strolled, hand in hand, along the lake. Emily had saved a crust of bread from the table and was distributing it among a gaggle of ducks that had waddled after them across the lawn.

"What do you call an incompetent doctor?" she asked them. "Quack!"

"Right!" She threw a piece to one of them. "What do you call a break in the sidewalk?"

"Quack?"

"Very good!"

A huge mallard, well over two feet tall, had joined the throng. His bill was bright orange, and the moonlight glistened off the green on his wings. Strong and proud a specimen as it was, Jonathan still found something odd, almost human, in the animal's expression.

"Give me some of that bread, will you?" he asked his wife. He held out a chunk of bread toward the duck. "Here, old boy, would you like—"

The duck moved with startling swiftness. "Ouch!" Jonathan cried, as the bread disappeared and a stab of pain went through his hand.

"What happened?" Emily asked, taking him by the wrist and examining his fingers.

"The damned thing bit me."

"Jonathan! You're bleeding!"

It was true. More confused than anything else, Jonathan stared at the thin line of red across the base of his thumb. He pulled his hand away and sucked on the bite. "Imagine that," he said wonderingly. "Vicious ducks. You don't suppose that was what that waiter was trying to tell us about. . . ."

"Let's get back to the room," Emily said. She threw the last of the bread into the mass of quacking bills and twitching rumps, then turned away. "Jonathan?"

He shook himself from his reverie and followed her. "Yes, dear. Coming." But as he took one last glance across his shoulder, the huge mallard seemed to be watching him, gazing deep into his eyes with a look that was both angry and somehow sorrowful at the same time.

A month later, back in Connecticut, Jonathan had returned to his accounting firm, and Emily was settling into the routines of housework. As was common in those days, they'd married without having slept together beforehand, let alone having lived together, and they were still getting to know each other. Thus the things that Emily began to discover among her husband's belongings did not alarm her.

Not at first.

Things like the down pillows he'd bought to replace the foam-rubber ones she preferred. The half-eaten crusts of stale bread that she'd found on the floor around his desk in the study, where he'd been working late at night with increasing regularity. Frankie Laine's "Cry of the Wild Goose" left on the changer of the hi-fi. The decoys in the garage. A shirt with a print featuring hunters and hunting horns, torn to shreds and left on the bottom of the closet.

His behavior seemed to be changing as well. He grew more restless every day, more prone to sudden fits of clumsiness. Though it had always been one of his favorite meals during their courtship, he now refused to eat chicken or any other poultry. Even the sight of fried eggs seemed to horrify him.

They had been married just two days less than a month when it began in earnest.

They were lying in bed together, a gentle autumn breeze tugging at the window curtains. Emily was just about to fall asleep when she heard Jonathan shifting around in the bed.

"Is something wrong?" she asked him sleepily.

"No, nothing. I'm just restless. I think maybe I'll get up for a while—maybe read or something."

"Jonathan?"

"What?"

"Are you . . . all right? You've seemed so distant lately. Is there anything bothering you? Is there anything wrong with me?" Emily had been paying attention to the commercials on television lately, and it had begun to make her insecure.

"No, darling, of course not." He took her into his arms and patted her back, but she could tell that his heart was not entirely in it. "You go back to sleep," he said. "I'll just go read for a while."

She did fall asleep, at least for a few minutes, but then a sudden noise woke her again. It came from the direction of the study, and it sounded like a strangled cough, or a . . .

No. Emily suppressed the thought before it could fully form. There was no way a bird that large could actually get inside the house.

She got up and slipped into her dressing gown. She hated to disturb him, but she knew she wouldn't be able to go back to sleep until she was sure Jonathan was all right. She tiptoed down the hall, hesitated with her hand on the knob of the study door, then eased it open.

Enough moonlight shone through the open window for Emily to see that her husband wasn't there. She was about to move on and check the kitchen when something caught her attention.

She turned on the overhead light and gasped. Jonathan's robe and pajamas lay in a tangled heap in the middle of the floor.

There was no other sign of her husband in the room. Her heart in her throat, she searched the rest of the house, fruitlessly, and came back to the study.

That was when she noticed the feathers on the sill of the open window.

Frightened, but knowing she had to make the effort, she walked around the outside of the house with a flashlight. The neighbors all lived on the far side of the woods, and Emily felt threatened by the lurking trees and the ghostly moonlight reflecting off the pond. She couldn't find as much as a footprint to show that Jonathan had been outside, so she went back in, locking the front door after her.

Latching windows and bolting doors as she went, she made

another search of the house, calling Jonathan's name. Then she returned to the living room and sat on the couch, holding the flashlight in one hand and the fireplace poker in the other.

She thought for a long time about phoning the police, but she knew there was nothing they could do before morning. Maybe Jonathan would be back by then, with an explanation for everything.

Please, God, she prayed, *let him be back by then. . . .*

The living-room clock read five A.M. when she heard something at the other end of the house. It sounded like someone trying to get in the window of the bedroom.

Oh, God, Emily thought. *The latch on that window is loose.* Jonathan had been meaning to fix it.

She started down the hall, holding the poker in front of her. *Better to face it,* she thought, *whatever it is, than to let it find me cowering under the sofa.*

At the door of the bedroom she stopped.

Jonathan lay in the bed, asleep.

The window with the weakened latch was open, and the prints of bare, dirty feet led from there to the bed.

Emily bent over him, hearing the sound of his ragged breathing, and tried to wake him. He moaned once, but he seemed too exhausted to come around completely. Emily stretched out beside him, willing to let him sleep, grateful beyond words that she had him back.

She rocked him in her arms for several minutes, then slowed, sniffing the air. She looked at Jonathan and sniffed again.

His breath reeked of fish.

Jonathan woke up unable to remember anything that had happened after he went to the study. He thought he might have had a dream that he was naked, trying to open a locked window.

"You were gone almost five hours," Emily told him. She was exhausted, not having slept at all.

"I must have been sleepwalking," Jonathan said.

"But where did you go? What did you do? You were alone out there, naked, for five hours!"

"I tell you I don't know," Jonathan said, with just a trace of irritation in his voice. "I just want to sleep some more. I'm so . . . tired. . . ."

Emily left him and sat on the couch in the living room, drinking one cup of coffee after another. Not even the caffeine could keep her awake, however, and by late afternoon she dozed off. She woke in Jonathan's arms as he carried her back to bed.

"Whaa . . . ?" she asked.

"Go to sleep," he told her. "Everything is fine."

It was night. The bed seemed to swallow her, and for a second Emily let herself go, back into the waiting depths of sleep. Then some part of her fought back to the surface.

"No," she murmured. "Got to stay awake."

She forced her eyes open and blinked until the room came into focus. "Jonathan?"

He was gone, and she could hear the whisper of his study door closing behind him.

She was too weak to stand, so she crawled on her hands and knees to the door of the study. Forcing herself onto her wobbling legs, she twisted the handle and flung the door wide.

And she saw him.

At first she wanted to laugh. He had taken off his clothes and was bending down in a tight crouch. His hands were tucked up into his armpits and his elbows were straining toward his sides.

And then he began to change.

"Jonathan!" she cried, but he was beyond hearing. His legs were drawing up and his feet were turning orange. Brown

feathers were sprouting from his arms, and his nose was growing, flattening. . . .

"Jonathan!" she screamed. "I can't stand this! My mind is
going to—"

"Quack," said Jonathan.

I felt dizzy, feverish, disoriented. Dr. Canard was obviously
mad, raving, certifiable. I had listened to his story with impatience, disbelief, and finally scorn.

And yet . . .

Why had my mother refused to let me watch Daffy Duck
cartoons as a child? Why had I been in junior high before I'd
found out what the word "poultry" meant? Why had the sight
of a friend's swim fins sent her into hysterics?

"I can't—" I began.

"You find this all hard to believe, *nicht war?* You think it
absurd. Well, why shouldn't you? To me it seemed absurd also,
when I first heard of it."

Dr. Canard stood up and began to pace the floor. He was
so short that it seemed to take minutes for his tiny footsteps
to carry him from one side of the room to the other. "Your
parents first came to me when ordinary doctors proved stupid,
useless, worthless to them." He paused to stare at me for a
second. "As they so often are. Would you believe they once
thought that I—" He shook his head. "But I digress.

"The medical doctors told your father to see a psychiatrist;
the psychiatrists told him that both of them should be locked
up. Finally they heard of my researches, such as the salt-
free diet I developed while in telepathic contact with the
planet Uranus. They knew I would be the one to find the
answer."

"And—"

"Did I find the answer? Of course, I did. I observed your
father for months, traveled over the continent, researching

folktales and poring over ancient volumes in obscure libraries. Your father was a remarkable case. You have heard of the legend of the werewolf? Yes, I see that you have. Well, your father was—"

"No . . ."

"—yes, a wereduck. That is correct."

In their third month at the clinic, Emily came to Jonathan as he was studying a moth- and mold-ravaged text entitled *The Necronomiduck.*

"I'm pregnant," she told him.

Jonathan's face lit up. "Darling, are you sure?"

She nodded, and Jonathan started to throw his arms around her, then suddenly pulled back.

"What's wrong?" she asked.

He shook his head. "Nothing. I'm sure it's nothing. It's just . . . what if the child should turn out to be a . . . a monster? Like his father?"

Emily pressed his face to her breast. "No, Jonathan! Don't say that! Don't ever say that!"

"But even if he's perfectly normal, what kind of father would he have? What kind of help would I be to you? Could he live on the fish and bread crumbs I'd bring home?"

"Oh, darling, that's not important. As long as we love each other, nothing else matters."

The boy, Drake, was born normally, and the three of them returned to Connecticut. Dr. Canard promised that he would not rest until he'd found a solution to Jonathan's affliction, but he did not sound hopeful.

It was fall again in Connecticut, and during the first full moon in October, Jonathan disappeared. Emily was frantic, phoning police and animal shelters for miles around, with no success. Finally, two days later, Jonathan returned. He was dressed in nothing but an oversized raincoat and was sneezing all the way up the path.

"I came around in a swamp in Maryland," he told her. "I had a couple of shotgun pellets in one arm from an off-season hunter. The last thing I remember before that was smelling the air and feeling this overpowering urge to fly south."

He'd stolen the raincoat from a sleeping hobo and hitch-hiked home, without even a dime to call for help.

"I can't go on this way," he told her. "Next month it'll happen again, and who knows how far I'll get before I come back to my senses?"

"I could sew up a little bag for you," Emily offered. "You could wear it around your neck, and I could put some traveler's checks in it."

Jonathan shook his head. "It's no good. I'd never remember to put it on. No, Emily. I want you to stay here with Drake, and I'll face this on my own."

"If you have to go," Emily said, "you have to go. I'll manage. But what about you? You can't just wander the world, leading some kind of desperate hand-to-bill existence."

"Somewhere there's an answer," Jonathan said. "I'll find it, and when I do, I'll come back to you."

Emily never gave up hope. Each spring she sat on the porch with field glasses, watching the ragged V's of ducks as they crossed the sky. Each fall, with the first frost, she aged an entire year in a day as she waited for her husband.

Sixteen years passed, and her son grew almost to manhood. And then, one day, a letter arrived from Mexico, covered with exotic stamps and addressed in a familiar hand.

"I have it here somewhere," said Dr. Canard, shuffling through the drawers of his desk. "Ach, here it is."

I had been hoping he wouldn't be able to find it. The more

elaborate his story got, the more nervous it made me, and when he started producing evidence, the urge to run away came over me again.

"I'll read you some parts of it," Canard said. " 'My darling, I long to . . .' No, not that part. Ach, here we are.

> This last winter was so cold that I came all the way to Mexico, to a small village in the Sonoran Desert. I met an old man here, a crazy hermit. All the people in town think he's a witch, but he seemed to understand me somehow, to know about my "problem" without my telling him. He speaks very good English—he says he learned it from an American anthropologist who comes to visit him every couple of years and make up stories about him.
>
> We'd stay up late into the night, him eating cactus and me munching on bits of stale tortillas, and he made me see something I'd never thought of. I'd been trying to run away from my curse instead of learning to live with it. He taught me to embrace it, to accept it totally, and then, when he told me what he could do for me—for us—I realized that this was the answer I'd been searching for.

"So," Dr. Canard said, popping the monocle out of his eye, "your mother joined him in Mexico. She could not tell you what it was she planned to do, first because she could not know if it would be successful, and second, because she knew you would not believe her anyway."

"Did—"

"Did this witch doctor cure your father, you ask? Yes, he did. Your father no longer changes to a duck with the full moon."

He paused dramatically, and I knew the worst was about to come. "Now," he proclaimed, "he—and your mother—are *ducks forever!*"

Canard ran to the glass doors and yanked open the curtains,

exposing the two huge ducks who had been waiting there the entire time.

"Behold, Drake Russel!" Canard shouted. "Your mother and father!"

I let the silence hang on for a long time, and then I said, very quietly, "You're completely wacko, you know. Bananas. Berkshire. Round the bend. Stark, staring—"

"So it must seem to you, my boy—"

"Shut up!" My hands were shaking as I got out of the chair, and for a second I thought I was going to shove the monocle down the old man's throat. "I don't want to hear any more, do you understand me?"

"You know it is the truth. That is why you are so frightened of it."

"I'm not frightened!" I shouted, grabbing one of the end tables and swinging it back like a club. "I'm fine! Stay away from me!" I started backing toward the door.

Canard held out his hands. "Drake, listen, I must warn you—"

"No!" I yelled, throwing the table and running out the door. I ran all the way to the village and took the next flight home to Connecticut.

I write this at my father's desk. Next to me is a book entitled *Lycanthropy: A Symposium,* and next to it are perhaps a dozen others on the same subject.

I do not believe Dr. Canard's preposterous story. I do not believe in werewolves, wereducks, were-elephants or werefish. And yet . . .

I have read all of my father's books on the subject—brought them down from where they were hidden in the attic and studied them. The books tell me that the curse of the werewolf is passed on to the eldest son on his eighteenth birthday.

Tomorrow, on the night of the full moon, I will turn eighteen. Is it only the power of suggestion that has been leading me out for long walks beside my father's fish pond, or is it the beginning of something far, far worse?

LEWIS SHINER has written stories for Analog Science Fiction/Science Fact Magazine, The Twilight Zone, *and* Mike Shayne. *He was nominated for a Nebula Award in 1985 for his novel* Frontera, *published by Baen Books. He is currently working on a novel entitled* Deserted Cities of the Heart. *EDITH SHINER collaborated on "Things That Go Quack in the Night" with her husband, Lewis. She is a commercial artist.*

WET

BEHIND

THE EARS

Jack C. Haldeman II

Genuine effort can be less work than cheating, but Willie Joe just isn't the kind of person who exerts himself—even in a sink-or-swim situation.

Willie Joe Thomas was born to bad luck.

Some say he brought it on himself, and they may be right. He was a swimmer, a college student, and a deceitful man. Not necessarily in that order.

Rather than study through high school, Willie Joe had forged his transcripts to get into college. Rather than work to pay his tuition, he got a swimming scholarship under false pretenses. If there was an easy way to do something, he would do it. Like an amoeba, Willie Joe had followed the path of least resistance all of his life. It showed.

The water was warm, and the chlorine stung his eyes as Willie Joe pulled himself from the pool. He headed for his towel, dead last again. The meet with A&M was tomorrow, and if he didn't shape up, he'd lose his scholarship for sure.

That would mean work, and Willie Joe hated work. He slipped away to the showers, managing to avoid the coach.

Big Ray, who worked out in the weight room, was scrubbing down in the shower with the hot water on full force. Willie Joe stripped off his suit and stepped into the steam.

"Afternoon, Willie," said Ray. "Short practice today?"

"Had to leave early. Got a chemistry midterm."

"How did practice go?"

"Fine," lied Willie Joe. "I'm in top shape."

"Gonna really show it to those Aggies?"

"You bet," said Willie Joe. Dead last against three of the "B" team. A humiliating defeat. He could feel the scholarship slipping through his wet fingers like a bar of soap.

As soon as Big Ray left the shower, Willie Joe turned the water down to a more comfortable level. He washed quickly so that he would be out of there before the rest of the team showed up.

Dripping water, Willie Joe grabbed a towel from the stack beside the lockers. He hated being wet more than anything in the world. That was unusual in a swimmer, but Willie Joe wasn't your usual swimmer. He was more like a fake swimmer.

When he had first embarked on his college career, it had seemed like a good idea. Being a fake swimmer was a lot easier than being a fake football player, for instance. On the other hand, it involved a lot of water. Willie Joe felt bloated all the time and imagined he sloshed when he walked. The more water managed to seep into his life, the more he hated it.

In the winter his wet hair froze, in the summer it was always plastered down against his head like a wet mop. He had a nasty fungus in his ears that he couldn't shake. It seemed as though his fingers and toes were constantly wrinkled, and he had the world's worst case of athlete's foot. His eyes were constantly bloodshot, and though his roommate blamed it on his dissipated life-style, Willie Joe knew it was from all that chlorine. He was in the water as little as possible—just enough to keep the coach off his back—but that was still way too much. He'd grown to dislike everything about the swim team except the scholarship. Even the bathing suits were the wrong color.

The only water Willie Joe had any interest in was carbonated and thoroughly mixed with a shot or two of whiskey.

His hair was still damp as he walked across campus to Whitehand Hall and took his seat in the crowded lecture room. Although chemistry had the reputation of being a bear of a course, he wasn't worried at all. He'd put a lot of effort into this exam. He was better prepared than he'd ever been before.

He'd scribbled the redox equations on the ledge over by the pencil sharpener. He had a periodic table stuffed inside his slide rule. The gas laws were written on the insteps of his tennis shoes, and a couple of complicated formulas were scratched on the bottom of his calculator. He was extremely well prepared and breezed through the exam without a hitch.

It never occurred to him that if he put half the time and energy into studying that he did into cheating, he'd get better grades with a lot less work. Things like that seldom occurred to Willie Joe. He was that kind of a person.

As he left the exam, he knew he really should go back to the pool and catch the afternoon practice session. Instead, he called the coach and told him his cousin had gotten sick again. Then he headed for the nearest bar.

Countless cold ones later, Willie Joe staggered back to the dorm in the dark. The evening had somehow slipped away from him. He was just climbing into the sack when his roommate, Frank Emerson, burst into the room, turning on all the lights.

Oh, no, not again, thought Willie Joe, pulling the pillow

over his head. Frank was a grad assistant down at the chemistry lab and was as strange as they came. Inorganic compounds got him all excited and the mere mention of carbon bonds would keep him babbling all night. The guy was loony. He was also straight as a rail, a real pain.

"I've done it," said Frank, pulling the pillow off Willie Joe's head. "This time I've really done it."

Willie Joe sighed and reached under the bed for the bottle of cheap white wine he kept there for occasions like this.

"Done what?" he asked, taking a slug and coughing. "Another perfect solvent?"

Frank blushed. He'd wasted a month's research looking for the perfect solvent, something that would dissolve anything it came into contact with. It had taken him that long to realize that even if he succeeded, no bottle in the world would be able to hold it. It was a lost cause.

"No, this one works," he said. Suddenly he frowned. "It's against the rules to drink in the dorms. You know that."

"So report me, test-tube face. I do what I want. What boring thing have you discovered this time?"

"It's not boring, and you should obey the rules. That's what rules are for, to be obeyed. They're for everyone's benefit." He set a small vial on the dresser. "This is it," he said with no small measure of pride.

"Great," said Willie Joe, taking another hit off the bottle. "No doubt you have something in that little jar that will change both the course of history and the face of the Earth. Now, how about turning off the lights so I can get a little shut-eye. I've got a meet in the morning."

"I call it a molecular sliding compound, and I'm going to give it to the U.S. Navy. Besides, it's a vial, not a jar. You should learn to be precise with your scientific terminology."

"Humph. I know a jar when I see one. What's the Navy want to slide for?"

"You don't understand. What this compound does is polarize the electrostatic charge between the hydrogen/oxygen bond, causing a great deal of molecular slippage and a subsequent near total decrease in the coefficient of friction."

Willie Joe squinted at his roommate through a haze of wine and stale beer. "Huh?" he said. "Put that in English."

"If you paid attention in your chemistry class, you would understand what I was saying."

"If I paid attention to everything I was supposed to, I'd never have any fun. What did you say?"

"The practical effect of this compound is that it effectively eliminates all friction from anything placed in water. Boats will be able to move across the sea with no resistance at all. The fuel savings will be astronomical. It will be possible for submarines to achieve incredible speed. Imagine, if you will, sailboats zipping along as fast as speedboats, battleships breaking the sound barrier in the Atlantic Ocean. Water will never be the same."

"It staggers the mind," said Willie Joe, pulling the pillow back over his head.

"I don't believe you grasp the full import of this discovery," said Frank. Willie Joe just snored, clutching the bottle to his chest like a glass teddy bear with a screw-tite cap.

The alarm went off at seven, and Willie Joe's mouth felt as though the football team had used it for a practice field. His head throbbed and his body ached all over. He staggered to the sink, tossed down some aspirin, and brushed the fuzz off his teeth. He felt terrible, and his brain just wouldn't get into gear.

This was it, the big day. It was likely to be his last day, too. He wouldn't be able to fake his marginal swimming skills any longer. So far he'd been able to get by with a batch of phony press clippings and a season-long case of the cramps. The coach had said if he didn't swim today against A&M, he'd be dropped from the squad. That meant he would lose his scholarship and his free ticket to the easy life at the University. He'd have to get a job, and that was unthinkable. He'd never had a job of any sort before and now was not the time to start.

As he put his hairbrush down, he saw that the vial was still on the dresser. The conversation with his roommate last night came back to him in blurred bits and pieces. Through the alcohol-induced fog he remembered something about moving effortlessly through water. If it worked for boats, why wouldn't it work for people? There were two ways to find out. Either he could wake up Frank and ask him, or he could bop his sleeping roommate on the head and steal the stuff.

Always the amoeba, Willie Joe bopped Frank on the head and stole the vial. It was clearly the path of least resistance.

The dressing room was full of steam and tension, as it was before every meet. Some of the athletes sat by themselves in silent contemplation, while others kidded each other with loud, nervous laughter. Willie Joe stood at his locker and stared at the vial like a drowning man might eyeball a life preserver or two. It was salvation. And to think that dummy of a roommate would have wasted it on the Navy. He started sloshing it on. It had a most unusual aroma, not unlike that of a dead armadillo after ten days on the side of the road. To put it politely, Willie Joe stank.

"Powerful after-shave you got there, W. J.," said Kevin Barker from the next locker. "Takes me right back to the farm."

Kevin was a butterfly man who sometimes did the crawl. He was so gung ho he shaved his head before every meet. Willie Joe hated people like that.

"Nobody asked you, chrome dome," snapped Willie Joe.

"Hey, take it easy," said Kevin. "I was only making a joke."

"Well, joke someplace else. I've got no sense of humor today." Willie Joe hid what was left of the vial behind his clothes and slammed his locker door shut. The coach was beginning to give his pep talk, urging all the men to go out and win this one for the Board of Regents. Willie Joe took the opportunity to slip into the showers and test the compound while no one was watching.

As he stood under the shower, the water ran off him like raindrops off the hood of a brand-new Cadillac. He grinned. This would be a piece of cake.

He went to the bench and sat down, hardly paying any attention at all to the preliminary races. The Aggies were ahead, but that didn't bother Willie Joe. He'd win this event, and that was all he cared about. It was in the bag.

"Glad to see you're suited up, W. J.," said the coach. "I hope your cousin is okay."

"She's much better. It was a miraculous recovery."

"Another one? Well, that's good. How're the cramps?"

"No problem, coach. I never felt better."

"Glad to hear that, son. You're on next. We need this one, and the hundred-meter freestyle may be our only chance."

"I'll do my best, coach."

"I know you will. Carry on." He wrinkled his nose. The boy smelled like he'd been rolling in bear grease.

Willie Joe took his place at the end of the pool. Unlike the others, he didn't jump into the water before the race to get used to the water. Instead he practiced looking cool and aloof. No sense in tipping his hand.

They lined up for the starting gun, taking their ready positions with care. The men on either side of Willie Joe were gagging, and someone went off to see if the ventilation system was broken. The gun went off, and so did the swimmers.

Willie Joe hit the water like a hot knife sliding through melted butter. His entry was so smooth he could hardly feel it when he broke the surface. He slid under the water like a human torpedo and was halfway across the pool, far ahead of everyone else, before he had to take his first stroke.

It proved to be his downfall.

He pushed his arms, and nothing happened. He kicked his feet, with no results. The compound was working, all right. It was working only too well. He was completely friction-free in the pool, but at the same time he couldn't push against the water. It was like pushing against air. Having lost the forward momentum from his dive, he sank to the bottom like a rock. The other swimmers passed over his head, leaving a trail of bubbles.

Willie Joe pushed against the bottom of the pool and shot straight up, leaping from the water like a dolphin at Marineland. He sank just as quickly. In the end, he had to walk across the bottom of the pool to the ladder at the shallow end.

Dead last again. Finished. All washed up. As he climbed out, he saw that the police were waiting for him. So was his roommate. Frank had a bandage wrapped around his head, and he looked pretty excited. He was yelling something about national security and the CIA. The coach looked as if he wanted to kill somebody. The water slid off Willie Joe like magic, collecting in small puddles at his feet.

It was all over. Willie Joe shook his head and groaned. The police came toward him with handcuffs. Jail would probably be better than having to face the coach. No telling what Frank would do if he got the chance. If he didn't go to jail, he'd have to get a job. Frank would probably make him work it off in the chem lab. He shuddered at the thought.

JACK C. HALDEMAN II lives on a forty-acre farm outside Archer, Florida, with his wife and daughter. He works part-time at the University of Florida in the field of artificial intelligence and expert systems, and in addition to the many

articles he has published on that subject, he is the author of eight science fiction novels and approximately 150 short stories. His most recent novel is The Fall of Winter, *published by Baen Books.*